In his famous Hugo Award Winning trilogy of
FOUNDATION novels, ISAAC ASIMOV has created an epic of nearly classic proportions. He
has conceived a whole new world for mankind,
set far in the future and spanning a period of
more than a thousand years.

In FOUNDATION AND EMPIRE, the second in
the series, he charts the struggles of the
Foundation as it battles an older community
of galactic civilization.

FOUNDATION and SECOND FOUNDATION are
the first and third novels in this series.

Isaac Asimov's remarkable FOUNDATION series:

Three classics of science fiction which cover more than a thousand years, producing an ideal universal ruling corporation.

FOUNDATION (N304) A portrait of the Foundation's rise to domination of the kingdoms of the Galaxy.

FOUNDATION AND EMPIRE (N305) Struggles between petty kingdoms and the Foundation's emergence as a state strong enough to defeat the First Empire.

SECOND FOUNDATION (N306) Galactic battles between the First and Second Foundation, bringing the epic to a close.

Isaac Asimov

FOUNDATION
AND EMPIRE

AVON
PUBLISHERS OF
DISCUS • CAMELOT • BARD

AVON BOOKS
A division of
The Hearst Corporation
959 Eighth Avenue
New York, New York 10019

First Printing, November, 1966
Eighth Printing, May, 1970

DEDICATION

TO MARY AND HENRY
For Patience and Endurance

Prologue

THE GALACTIC EMPIRE WAS FALLING.

It was a colossal Empire, stretching across millions of worlds from arm-end to arm-end of the mighty double-spiral that was the Milky Way. Its fall was colossal, too—and a long one, for it had a long way to go.

It had been falling for centuries before one man became really aware of that fall. That man was Hari Seldon, the man who represented the one spark of creative effort left among the gathering decay. He developed and brought to its highest pitch the science of psycho-history.

Psycho-history dealt not with man, but with man-masses. It was the science of mobs; mobs in their billions. It could forecast reactions to stimuli with something of the accuracy that a lesser science could bring to the forecast of a rebound of a billiard ball. The reaction of one man could be forecast by no known mathematics; the reaction of a billion is something else again.

Hari Seldon plotted the social and economic trends of the time, sighted along the curves and foresaw the continuing and accelerating fall of civilization and the gap of thirty thousand years that must elapse before a struggling new Empire could emerge from the ruins.

It was too late to stop that fall, but not too late to close the gap of barbarism. Seldon established two Foundations at "opposite ends of the Galaxy" and their location was so designed that in one short millennium events would knit and mesh so as to force out of them a stronger, more permanent, more quickly appearing Second Empire.

Foundation (Gnome Press, 1951) has told the story of one of those Foundations during the first two centuries of life.

It began as a settlement of physical scientists on Terminus, a planet at the extreme end of one of the spiral arms of the Galaxy. Separated from the turmoil of the Empire, they worked as compilers of a universal compendium of knowledge, the Encyclopedia Galactica, unaware of the deeper role planned for them by the already-dead Seldon.

As the Empire rotted, the outer regions fell into the hands of independent "kings." The Foundation was threatened by them. However, by playing one petty ruler against another, under the leadership of their first mayor, Salvor Hardin, they maintained a precarious independence. As sole possessors of atomic power among worlds which were losing their sciences and falling back on coal and oil, they even established an ascendancy. The Foundation became the "religious" center of the neighboring kingdoms.

Slowly, the Foundation developed a trading economy as the Encyclopedia receded into the background. Their Traders, dealing in atomic gadgets which not even the Empire in its heyday could have duplicated for compactness, penetrated hundreds of light-years through the Periphery.

Under Hober Mallow, the first of the Foundation's Merchant Princes, they developed the techniques of economic warfare to the point of defeating the Republic of Korell, even though that world was receiving support from one of the outer provinces of what was left of the Empire.

At the end of two hundred years, the Foundation was the most powerful state in the Galaxy, except for the remains of the Empire, which, concentrated in the central third of the Milky Way, still controlled three quarters of the population and wealth of the Universe.

It seemed inevitable that the next danger the Foundation would have to face was the final lash of the dying Empire.

The way must be cleared for the battle of Foundation and Empire.

CONTENTS

PROLOGUE

PART I THE GENERAL

PART II THE MULE

Part I   The General

1. Search for Magicians

BEL RIOSE . . . . *In his relatively short career, Riose earned the title of "The Last of the Imperials" and earned it well. A study of his campaigns reveals him to be the equal of Peurifoy in strategic ability and his superior perhaps in his ability to handle men. That he was born in the days of the decline of Empire made it all but impossible for him to equal Peurifoy's record as a conqueror. Yet he had his chance when, the first of the Empire's generals to do so, he faced the Foundation squarely. . . .**

—*Encyclopedia Galactica*

BEL RIOSE traveled without escort, which is not what court etiquette prescribes for the head of a fleet stationed in a yet-sullen stellar system on the Marches of the Galactic Empire.

But Bel Riose was young and energetic—energetic enough to be sent as near the end of the universe as possible by an unemotional and calculating court—and curious besides. Strange and improbable tales fancifully-repeated by hundreds and murkily-known to thousands intrigued the last faculty; the possibility of a military venture engaged the other two. The combination was overpowering.

He was out of the dowdy ground-car he had appropriated and at the door of the fading mansion that was his destina-

* All quotations from the Encyclopedia Galactica here reproduced are taken from the 116th Edition published in 1020 F.E. by the Encyclopedia Galactica Publishing Co., Terminus, with permission of the publishers.

11

tion. He waited. The photonic eye that spanned the doorway was alive, but when the door opened it was by hand.

Bel Riose smiled at the old man. "I am Riose—"

"I recognize you." The old man remained stiffly and unsurprised in his place. "Your business?"

Riose withdrew a step in a gesture of submission. "One of peace. If you are Ducem Barr, I ask the favor of conversation."

Ducem Barr stepped aside and in the interior of the house the walls glowed into life. The general entered into daylight.

He touched the wall of the study, then stared at his fingertips. "You have this on Siwenna?"

Barr smiled thinly. "Not elsewhere, I believe. I keep this in repair myself as well as I can. I must apologize for your wait at the door. The automatic device registers the presence of a visitor but will no longer open the door."

"Your repairs fall short?" The general's voice was faintly mocking.

"Parts are no longer available. If you will sit, sir. You drink tea?"

"On Siwenna? My good sir, it is socially impossible not to drink it here."

The old patrician retreated noiselessly with a slow bow that was part of the ceremonious legacy left by a *ci-devant* aristocracy of the last century's better days.

Riose looked after his host's departing figure, and his studied urbanity grew a bit uncertain at the edges. His education had been purely military; his experience likewise. He had, as the cliché has it, faced death many times; but always death of a very familiar and tangible nature. Consequently, there is no inconsistency in the fact that the idolized lion of the Twentieth Fleet felt chilled in the suddenly musty atmosphere of an ancient room.

The general recognized the small black-ivroid boxes that lined the shelves to be books. Their titles were unfamiliar. He guessed that the large structure at one end of the room was the receiver that transmuted the books into sight-and-sound on demand. He had never seen one in operation; but he had heard of them.

Once he had been told that long before, during the golden ages when the Empire had been co-extensive with the entire Galaxy, nine houses out of every ten had such receivers— and such rows of books.

12

But there were borders to watch now; books were for old men. And half the stories told about the old days were mythical anyway. More than half.

The tea arrived, and Riose seated himself. Ducem Barr lifted his cup. "To your honor."

"Thank you. To yours."

Ducem Barr said deliberately, "You are said to be young. Thirty-five?"

"Near enough. Thirty-four."

"In that case," said Barr, with soft emphasis, "I could not begin better than by informing you regretfully that I am not in the possession of love charms, potions, or philtres. Nor am I in the least capable of influencing the favors of any young lady as may appeal to you."

"I have no need of artificial aids in that respect, sir." The complacency undeniably present in the general's voice was stirred with amusement. "Do you receive many requests for such commodities?"

"Enough. Unfortunately, an uninformed public tends to confuse scholarship with magicianry, and love life seems to be that factor which requires the largest quantity of magical tinkering."

"And so would seem most natural. But I differ. I connect scholarship with nothing but the means of answering difficult questions."

The Siwennian considered somberly, "You may be as wrong as they!"

"That may turn out or not." The young general set down his cup in its flaring sheath and it refilled. He dropped the offered flavor-capsule into it with a small splash. "Tell me then, patrician, who are the magicians? The real ones."

Barr seemed startled at a title long-unused. He said, "There are no magicians."

"But people speak of them. Siwenna crawls with the tales of them. There are cults being built about them. There is some strange connection between it and those groups among your countrymen who dream and drivel of ancient days and what they call liberty and autonomy. Eventually the matter might become a danger to the State."

The old man shook his head. "Why ask me? Do you smell rebellion, with myself at the head?"

Riose shrugged, "Never. Never. Oh, it is not a thought completely ridiculous. Your father was an exile in his day;

13

you yourself a patriot and a chauvinist in yours. It is indelicate in me as a guest to mention it, but my business here requires it. And yet a conspiracy now? I doubt it. Siwenna has had the spirit beat out of it these three generations."

The old man replied with difficulty, "I shall be as indelicate a host as you a guest. I shall remind you that once a viceroy thought as you did of the spiritless Siwennians. By the orders of that viceroy my father became a fugitive pauper, my brothers martyrs, and my sister a suicide. Yet that viceroy died a death sufficiently horrible at the hands of these same slavish Siwennians."

"Ah, yes, and there you touch nearly on something I could wish to say. For three years the mysterious death of that viceroy has been no mystery to me. There was a young soldier of his personal guard whose actions were of interest. You were that soldier, but there is no need of details, I think."

Barr was quiet. "None. What do you propose?"

"That you answer my questions."

"Not under threats. I am old, but not yet so old that life means particularly overmuch."

"My good sir, these are hard times," said Riose, with meaning, "and you have children and friends. You have a country for which you have mouthed phrases of love and folly in the past. Come, if I should decide to use force, my aim would not be so poor as to strike you."

Barr said coldly, "What do you want?"

Riose held the empty cup as he spoke. "Patrician, listen to me. These are days when the most successful soldiers are those whose function is to lead the dress parades that wind through the imperial palace grounds on feast days and to escort the sparkling pleasure ships that carry His Imperial Splendor to the summer planets. I . . . I am a failure. I am a failure at thirty-four, and I shall stay a failure. Because, you see, I like to fight.

"That's why they sent me here. I'm too troublesome at court. I don't fit in with the etiquette. I offend the dandies and the lord admirals, but I'm too good a leader of ships and men to be disposed of shortly by being marooned in space. So Siwenna is the substitute. It's a frontier world; a rebellious and a barren province. It is far away, far enough away to satisfy all.

"And so I moulder. There are no rebellions to stamp

down, and the border viceroys do not revolt lately; at least, not since His Imperial Majesty's late father of glorious memory made an example of Mountel of Paramay."

"A strong Emperor," muttered Barr.

"Yes, and we need more of them. He is my master; remember that. These are his interests I guard."

Barr shrugged unconcernedly. "How does all this relate to the subject?"

"I'll show you in two words. The magicians I've mentioned come from beyond—out there beyond the frontier guards, where the stars are scattered thinly—"

" 'Where the stars are scattered thinly,' " quoted Barr, " 'And the cold of space seeps in'."

"Is that poetry?" Riose frowned. Verse seemed frivolous at the moment. "In any case, they're from the Periphery—from the only quarter where I am free to fight for the glory of the Emperor."

"And thus serve His Imperial Majesty's interests and satisfy your own love of a good fight."

"Exactly. But I must know what I fight; and there you can help."

"How do you know?"

Riose nibbled casually at a cakelet. "Because for three years I have traced every rumor, every myth, every breath concerning the magicians—and of all the library of information I have gathered, only two isolated facts are unanimously agreed upon, and are hence certainly true. The first is that the magicians come from the edge of the Galaxy opposite Siwenna; the second is that your father once met a magician, alive and actual, and spoke with him."

The aged Siwennian stared unblinkingly, and Riose continued, "You had better tell me what you know—"

Barr said thoughtfully, "It would be interesting to tell you certain things. It would be a psycho-historic experiment of my own."

"What kind of experiment?"

"Psycho-historic." The old man had an unpleasant edge to his smile. Then, crisply, "You'd better have more tea. I'm going to make a bit of a speech."

He leaned far back into the soft cushions of his chair. The wall-lights had softened to a pink-ivory glow, which mellowed even the soldier's hard profile.

Ducem Barr began, "My own knowledge is the result of

two accidents; the accidents of being born the son of my father, and of being born the native of my country. It begins over forty years ago, shortly after the great Massacre, when my father was a fugitive in the forests of the South, while I was a gunner in the viceroy's personal fleet. This same viceroy, by the way, who had ordered the Massacre, and who died such a cruel death thereafter."

Barr smiled grimly, and continued, "My father was a Patrician of the Empire and a Senator of Siwenna. His name was Onum B'arr."

Riose interrupted impatiently, "I know the circumstances of his exile very well. You needn't elaborate upon it."

The Siwennian ignored him and proceeded without deflection. "During his exile a wanderer came upon him; a merchant from the edge of the Galaxy; a young man who spoke a strange accent, knew nothing of recent Imperial history, and who was protected by an individual force-shield."

"An individual force-shield?" Riose glared. "You speak extravagance. What generator could be powerful enough to condense a shield to the size of a single man? By the Great Galaxy, did he carry five thousand myria-tons of atomic power-source about with him on a little wheeled gocart?"

Barr said quietly, "This is the magician of whom you hear whispers, stories and myths. The name 'magician' is not lightly earned. He carried no generator large enough to be seen, but not the heaviest weapon you can carry in your hand would have as much as creased the shield he bore."

"Is this all the story there is? Are the magicians born of maunderings of an old man broken by suffering and exile?"

"The story of the magicians antedated even my father, sir. And the proof is more concrete. After leaving my father, this merchant that men call a magician visited a Tech-man at the city to which my father had guided him, and there he left a shield-generator of the type he wore. That generator was retrieved by my father after his return from exile upon the execution of the bloody viceroy. It took a long time to find—

"The generator hangs on the wall behind you, sir. It does not work. It never worked but for the first two days; but if you'll look at it, you will see that no one in the Empire ever designed it."

Bel Riose reached for the belt of linked metal that clung to the curved wall. It came away with a little sucking noise as

16

the tiny adhesion-field broke at the touch of his hand. The ellipsoid at the apex of the belt held his attention. It was the size of a walnut.

"This—" he said.

"Was the generator," nodded Barr. "But it *was* the generator. The secret of its workings are beyond discovery now. Sub-electronic investigations have shown it to be fused into a single lump of metal and not all the most careful study of the diffraction patterns have sufficed to distinguish the discrete parts that had existed before fusion."

"Then your 'proof' still lingers on the frothy border of words backed by no concrete evidence."

Barr shrugged. "You have demanded my knowledge of me and threatened its extortion by force. If you choose to meet it with skepticism, what is that to me? Do you want me to stop?"

"Go on!" said the general, harshly.

"I continued my father's researches after he died, and then the second accident I mentioned came to help me, for Siwenna was well known to Hari Seldon."

"And who is Hari Seldon?"

"Hari Seldon was a scientist of the reign of the Emperor, Daluben IV. He was a psycho-historian; the last and greatest of them all. He once visited Siwenna, when Siwenna was a great commercial center, rich in the arts and sciences."

"Hmph," muttered Riose, sourly, "where is the stagnant planet that does not claim to have been a land of overflowing wealth in older days?"

"The days I speak of are the days of two centuries ago, when the Emperor yet ruled to the uttermost star; when Siwenna was a world of the interior and not a semi-barbarian border province. In those days, Hari Seldon foresaw the decline of Imperial power and the eventual barbarization of the entire Galaxy."

Riose laughed suddenly. "He foresaw that? Then he foresaw wrong, my good scientist. I suppose you call yourself that. Why, the Empire is more powerful now than it has been in a millennium. Your old eyes are blinded by the cold bleakness of the border. Come to the inner worlds some day; come to the warmth and the wealth of the center."

The old man shook his head somberly. "Circulation ceases first at the outer edges. It will take a while yet for the decay to reach the heart. That is, the apparent, obvious-to-all decay, as distinct from the inner decay that is an old story of some fifteen centuries."

"And so this Hari Seldon foresaw a Galaxy of uniform barbarism," said Riose, good-humoredly. "And what then, eh?"

"So he established two foundations at the extreme opposing ends of the Galaxy—Foundations of the best, and the youngest, and the strongest, there to breed, grow, and develop. The worlds on which they were placed were chosen carefully; as were the times and the surroundings. All was arranged in such a way that the future as foreseen by the unalterable mathematics of psycho-history would involve their early isolation from the main body of Imperial civilization and their gradual growth into the germs of the Second Galactic Empire—cutting an inevitable barbarian interregnum from thirty thousand years to scarcely a single thousand."

"And where did you find out all this? You seem to know it in detail."

"I don't and never did," said the patrician with composure. "It is the painful result of the piecing together of certain evidence discovered by my father and a little more found by myself. The basis is flimsy and the superstructure has been romanticized into existence to fill the huge gaps. But I am convinced that it is essentially true."

"You are easily convinced."

"Am I? It has taken forty years of research."

"Hmph. Forty years! I could settle the question in forty days. In fact, I believe I ought to. It would be—different."

"And how would you do that?"

"In the obvious way. I could become an explorer. I could find this Foundation you speak of and observe with my eyes. You say there are two?"

"The records speak of two. Supporting evidence has been found only for one, which is understandable, for the other is at the extreme end of the long axis of the Galaxy."

"Well, we'll visit the near one." The general was on his feet, adjusting his belt.

"You know where to go?" asked Barr.

"In a way. In the records of the last viceroy but one, he whom you murdered so effectively, there are suspicious tales of outer barbarians. In fact, one of his daughters was given in marriage to a barbarian prince. I'll find my way."

He held out a hand. "I thank you for your hospitality."

Ducem Barr touched the hand with his fingers and bowed formally. "Your visit was a great honor."

"As for the information you gave me," continued Bel Riose, "I'll know how to thank you for that when I return."

Ducem Barr followed his guest submissively to the outer door and said quietly to the disappearing ground car, "And *if* you return."

2. The Magicians

FOUNDATION ... *With forty years of expansion behind them, the Foundation faced the menace of Riose. The epic days of Hardin and Mallow had gone and with them a certain hard daring and resolution.* ...

THERE WERE four men in the room, and the room was set apart where none could approach. The four men looked at each other quickly, then lengthily at the table that separated them. There were four bottles on the table and as many full glasses, but no one had touched them.

And then the man nearest the door stretched out an arm and drummed a slow, padding rhythm on the table.

He said, "Are you going to sit and wonder forever? Does it matter who speaks first?"

"Speak you first, then," said the big man directly opposite. "You're the one who should be the most worried."

Sennett Forell chuckled with noiseless nonhumor. "Because you think I'm the richest. Well— Or is it that you expect me to continue as I have started. I don't suppose you forget that it was my own Trade Fleet that captured this scout ship of theirs."

"You had the largest fleet," said a third, "and the best pilots; which is another way of saying you are the richest. It was a fearful risk; and would have been greater for one of us."

Sennett Forell chuckled again. "There is a certain facility in risk-taking that I inherit from my father. After all, the essential point in running a risk is that the returns justify it. As to which, witness the fact that the enemy ship was isolated

20

and captured without loss to ourselves or warning to the others."

That Forell was a distant collateral relative of the late great Hober Mallow was recognized openly throughout the Foundation. That he was Mallow's illegitimate son was accepted quietly to just as wide an extent.

The fourth man blinked his little eyes stealthily. Words crept out from between thin lips. "It is nothing to sleep over in fat triumph, this grasping of little ships. Most likely, it will but anger that young man further."

"You think he needs motives?" questioned Forell, scornfully.

"I do, and this might, or will, save him the vexation of having to manufacture one." The fourth man spoke slowly, "Hober Mallow worked otherwise. And Salvor Hardin. They let others take the uncertain paths of force, while they maneuvered surely and quietly."

Forell shrugged. "This ship has proved its value. Motives are cheap and we have sold this one at a profit." There was the satisfaction of the born Trader in that. He continued, "The young man is of the old Empire."

"We knew that," said the second man, the big one, with rumbling discontent.

"We suspected that," corrected Forell, softly. "If a man comes with ships and wealth, with overtures of friendliness, and with offers of trade, it is only sensible to refrain from antagonizing him, until we are certain that the profitable mask is not a face after all. But now——"

There was a faint whining edge to the third man's voice as he spoke. "We might have been even more careful. We might have found out first. We might have found out before allowing him to leave. It would have been the truest wisdom."

"That has been discussed and disposed of," said Forell. He waved the subject aside with a flatly final gesture.

"The government is soft," complained the third man. "The mayor is an idiot."

The fourth man looked at the other three in turn and removed the stub of a cigar from his mouth. He dropped it casually into the slot at his right where it disappeared with a silent flash of disruption.

He said sarcastically, "I trust the gentleman who last

spoke is speaking through habit only. We can afford to re-member here that *we* are the government."

There was a murmur of agreement.

The fourth man's little eyes were on the table. "Then let us leave government policy alone. This young man . . . this stranger might have been a possible customer. There have been cases. All three of you tried to butter him into an ad-vance contract. We have an agreement—a gentleman's agree-ment—against it, but you tried."

"So did you," growled the second man.

"I know it," said the fourth, calmly.

"Then let's forget what we should have done earlier," in-terrupted Forell impatiently, "and continue with what we should do now. In any case, what if we had imprisoned him, or killed him, what then? We are not certain of his inten-tions even yet, and at the worst, we could not destroy an Empire by snipping short one man's life. There might be navies upon navies waiting just the other side of his nonre-turn."

"Exactly," approved the fourth man. "Now what did you get out of your captured ship? I'm too old for all this talk-ing."

"It can be told in a few enough words," said Forell, grimly. "He's an Imperial general or whatever rank corresponds to that over there. He's a young man who has proved his military brilliance—so I am told—and who is the idol of his men. Quite a romantic career. The stories they tell of him are no doubt half lies, but even so it makes him out to be a type of wonder man."

"Who are the 'they'?" demanded the second man.

"The crew of the captured ship. Look, I have all their statements recorded on micro-film, which I have in a secure place. Later on, if you wish, you can see them. You can talk to the men yourselves, if you think it necessary. I've told you the essentials."

"How did you get it out of them? How do you know they're telling the truth?"

Forell frowned. "I wasn't gentle, good sir. I knocked them about, drugged them crazy, and used the Probe unmercifully. They talked. You can believe them."

"In the old days," said the third man, with sudden irrele-vance, "they would have used pure psychology. Painless, you know, but very sure. No chance of deceit."

"Well, there is a good deal they had in the old days," said Forell, dryly. "These are the new days."

"But," said the fourth man, "what did he want here, this general, this romantic wonder-man?" There was a dogged, weary persistence about him.

Forell glanced at him sharply. "You think he confides the details of state policy to his crew? They didn't know. There was nothing to get out of them in that respect, and I tried, Galaxy knows."

"Which leaves us—"

"To draw our own conclusions, obviously." Forell's fingers were tapping quietly again. "The young man is a military leader of the Empire, yet he played the pretense of being a minor princeling of some scattered stars in an odd corner of the Periphery. That alone would assure us that his real motives are such as it would not benefit him to have us know. Combine the nature of his profession with the fact that the Empire has already subsidized one attack upon us in my father's time, and the possibilities become ominous. That first attack failed. I doubt that the Empire owes us love for that."

"There is nothing in your findings," questioned the fourth man guardedly, "which makes for certainty? You are withholding nothing?"

Forell answered levelly, "I can't withhold anything. From here on there can be no question of business rivalry. Unity is forced upon us."

"Patriotism?" There was a sneer in the third man's thin voice.

"Patriotism be damned," said Forell quietly. "Do you think I give two puffs of atomic emanation for the future Second Empire? Do you think I'd risk a single Trade mission to smooth its path? But—do you suppose Imperial conquest will help my business or yours? If the Empire wins, there will be a sufficient number of yearning carrion crows to crave the rewards of battle."

"And we're the rewards," added the fourth man, dryly.

The second man broke his silence suddenly, and shifted his bulk angrily, so that the chair creaked under him. "But why talk of that. The Empire can't win, can it? There is Seldon's assurance that we will form the Second Empire in the end. This is only another crisis. There have been three before this."

23

"Only another crisis, yes!" Forell brooded. "But in the case of the first two, we had Salvor Hardin to guide us; in the third, there was Hober Mallow. Whom have we now?"

He looked at the others somberly and continued, "Seldon's rules of psycho-history on which it is so comforting to rely probably have as one of the contributing variables, a certain normal initiative on the part of the people of the Foundation themselves. Seldon's laws help those who help themselves."

"The times make the man," said the third man. "There's another proverb for you."

"You can't count on that, not with absolute assurance," grunted Forell. "Now the way it seems to me is this. If this is the fourth crisis, then Seldon has foreseen it. If he has, then it can be beaten, and there should be a way of doing it.

"Now the Empire is stronger than we; it always has been. But this is the first time we are in danger of its direct attack, so that strength becomes terribly menacing. Then if it can be beaten, it must be once again as in all past crises by a method other than pure force. We must find the weak side of its enemy and attack it there."

"And what is that weak side?" asked the fourth man. "Do you intend advancing a theory?"

"No. That is the point I'm leading up to. Our great leaders of the past always saw the weak points of their enemies and aimed at that. But now——"

There was a helplessness in his voice, and for a moment none volunteered a comment.

Then the fourth man said, "We need spies."

Forell turned to him eagerly. "Right! I don't know when the Empire will attack. There may be time."

"Hober Mallow himself entered the Imperial dominions," suggested the second man.

But Forell shook his head. "Nothing so direct. None of us are precisely youthful; and all of us are rusty with red-tape and administrative detail. We need young men that are in the field now——"

"The independent traders?" asked the fourth man.

And Forell nodded his head and whispered, "If there is yet time——"

3. The Dead Hand

BEL ROISE interrupted his annoyed stridings to look up hopefully when his aide entered. "Any word of the *Starlet?*"

"None. The scouting party has quartered space, but the instruments have detected nothing. Commander Yume has reported that the Fleet is ready for an immediate attack in retaliation."

The general shook his head. "No, not for a patrol ship. Not yet. Tell him to double—Wait! I'll write out the message. Have it coded and transmitted by tight beam."

He wrote as he talked and thrust the paper at the waiting officer. "Has the Siwennian arrived yet?"

"Not yet."

"Well, see to it that he is brought in here as soon as he does arrive."

The aide saluted crisply and left. Riose resumed his caged stride.

When the door opened a second time, it was Ducem Barr that stood on the threshold. Slowly, in the footsteps of the ushering aide, he stepped into the garish room whose ceiling was an ornamented stereoscopic model of the Galaxy, and in the center of which Bel Riose stood in field uniform.

"Patrician, good day!" The general pushed forward a chair with his foot and gestured the aide away with a "That door is to stay closed till I open it."

He stood before the Siwennian, legs apart, hand grasping wrist behind his back, balancing himself slowly, thoughtfully, on the balls of his feet.

Then, harshly, "Patrician, are you a loyal subject of the Emperor?"

Barr, who had maintained an indifferent silence till then,

wrinkled a noncommittal brow. "I have no cause to love Imperial rule."

"Which is a long way from saying that you would be a traitor."

"True. But the mere act of not being a traitor is also a long way from agreeing to be an active helper."

"Ordinarily also true. But to refuse your help at this point," said Riose, deliberately, "will be considered treason and treated as such."

Barr's eyebrows drew together. "Save your verbal cudgels for your subordinates. A simple statement of your needs and wants will suffice me here."

Riose sat down and crossed his legs. "Barr, we had an earlier discussion half a year ago."

"About your magicians?"

"Yes. You remember what I said I would do."

Barr nodded. His arms rested limply in his lap. "You were going to visit them in their haunts, and you've been away these four months. Did you find them?"

"Find them? That I did," cried Riose. His lips were stiff as he spoke. It seemed to require effort to refrain from grinding molars. "Patrician, they are not magicians; they are devils. It is as far from belief as the outer nebulae from here. Conceive it! It is a world the size of a handkerchief, of a fingernail; with resources so petty, power so minute, a population so microscopic as would never suffice the most backward worlds of the dusty prefects of the Dark Stars. Yet with that, a people so proud and ambitious as to dream quietly and methodically of Galactic rule.

"Why, they are so sure of themselves that they do not even hurry. They move slowly, phlegmatically; they speak of necessary centuries. They swallow worlds at leisure; creep through systems with dawdling complacence.

"And they succeed. There is no one to stop them. They have built up a filthy trading community that curls its tentacles about the systems further than their toy ships dare reach. For parsecs, their Traders—which is what their agents call themselves—penetrate."

Ducem Barr interrupted the angry flow. "How much of this information is definite; and how much is simply fury?"

The soldier caught his breath and grew calmer. "My fury does not blind me. I tell you I was in worlds nearer to Siwenna than to the Foundation, where the Empire was a myth of the distance, and where Traders were living truths. We ourselves were mistaken for Traders."

"The Foundation itself told you they aimed at Galactic dominion?"

"Told me!" Riose was violent again. "It was not a matter of telling me. The officials said nothing. They spoke business exclusively. But I spoke to ordinary men. I absorbed the ideas of the common folk; their 'manifest destiny,' their calm acceptance of a great future. It is a thing that can't be hidden; a universal optimism they don't even try to hide."

The Siwennian openly displayed a certain quiet satisfaction. "You will notice that so far it would seem to bear out quite accurately my reconstruction of events from the paltry data on the subject that I had gathered."

"It is no doubt," replied Riose with vexed sarcasm, "a tribute to your analytical powers. It is also a hearty and bumptious commentary on the growing danger to the domains of His Imperial Majesty."

Barr shrugged his unconcern, and Riose leaned forward suddenly, to seize the old man's shoulders and stare with curious gentleness into his eyes.

He said, "Now, patrician, none of that. I have no desire to be barbaric. For my part, the legacy of Siwennian hostility to the Imperium is an odious burden, and one which I would do everything in my power to wipe out. But my province is the military and interference in civil affairs is impossible. It would bring about my recall and ruin my usefulness at once. You see that? I know you see that. Between yourself and myself then, let the atrocity of forty years ago be repaid by your vengeance upon its author and so forgotten. I need your help. I frankly admit it."

There was a world of urgency in the young man's voice, but Ducem Barr's head shook gently and deliberately in a negative gesture.

Riose said pleadingly, "You don't understand, patrician, and I doubt my ability to make you. I can't argue on your ground. You're the scholar, not I. But this I can tell you. Whatever you think of the Empire, you will admit its great services. Its armed forces have committed isolated crimes, but in the main they have been a force for peace and civilization. It was the Imperial navy that created the *Pax Imperium* that ruled over all the Galaxy for two thousand years. Contrast the two millennia of peace under the Sun-and-Spaceship of the Empire with the two millennia of interstellar anarchy that preceded it. Consider the wars and devastations of those old days and tell me if, with all its faults, the Empire is not worth preserving.

"Consider," he drove on forcefully, "to what the outer fringe of the Galaxy is reduced in these days of their break-away and independence, and ask yourself if for the sake of a petty revenge you would reduce Siwenna from its position as a province under the protection of a mighty Navy to a barbarian world in a barbarian Galaxy, all immersed in its fragmentary independence and its common degradation and misery."

"Is it so bad—so soon?" murmured the Siwennian.

"No," admitted Riose. "We would be safe ourselves no doubt, were our lifetimes quadrupled. But it is for the Empire I fight; that, and a military tradition which is something for myself alone, and which I can not transfer to you. It is a military tradition built on the Imperial institution which I serve."

"You are getting mystical, and I always find it difficult to penetrate another person's mysticism."

"No matter. You understand the danger of this Foundation."

"It was I who pointed out what you call the danger before ever you headed outward from Siwenna."

"Then you realize that it must be stopped in embryo or perhaps not at all. You have known of this Foundation before anyone had heard of it. You know more about it than anyone else in the Empire. You probably know how it might best be attacked; and you can probably forewarn me of its countermeasures. Come, let us be friends."

Ducem Barr rose. He said flatly, "Such help as I could give you means nothing. So I will make you free of it in the face of your strenuous demand."

"I will be the judge of its meaning."

"No, I am serious. Not all the might of the Empire could avail to crush this pygmy world."

"Why not?" Bel Riose's eyes glistened fiercely. "No, stay where you are. I'll tell you when you may leave. Why not? If you think I underestimate this enemy I have discovered, you are wrong. Patrician," he spoke reluctantly, "I lost a ship on my return. I have no proof that it fell into the hands of the Foundation; but it has not been

28

located since and were it merely an accident, its dead hulk should certainly have been found along the route we took. It is not an important loss—less than the tenth part of a fleabite, but it may mean that the Foundation has already opened hostilities. Such eagerness and such disregard for consequences might mean secret forces of which I know nothing. Can you help me then by answering a specific question? What is their military power?"

"I haven't any notion."

"Then explain yourself on your own terms. Why do you say the Empire can not defeat this small enemy?"

The Siwennian seated himself once more and looked away from Riose's fixed glare. He spoke heavily, "Because I have faith in the principles of psycho-history. It is a strange science. It reached mathematical maturity with one man, Hari Seldon, and died with him, for no man since has been capable of manipulating its intricacies. But in that short period, it proved itself the most powerful instrument ever invented for the study of humanity. Without pretending to predict the actions of individual humans, it formulated definite laws capable of mathematical analysis and extrapolation to govern and predict the mass action of human groups."

"So—"

"It was that psycho-history which Seldon and the group he worked with applied in full force to the establishment of the Foundation. The place, time, and conditions all conspire mathematically and so, inevitably, to the development of Universal Empire."

Riose's voice trembled with indignation. "You mean that this art of his predicts that I would attack the Foundation and lose such and such a battle for such and such a reason? You are trying to say that I am a silly robot following a predetermined course into destruction."

"No," replied the old patrician, sharply. "I have already said that the science had nothing to do with individual actions. It is the vaster background that has been foreseen."

"Then we stand clasped tightly in the forcing hand of the Goddess of Historical Necessity."

"Of *Psycho*-Historical Necessity, prompted Barr, softly.

"And if I exercise my prerogative of freewill? If I choose to attack next year, or not to attack at all? How pliable is the Goddess? How resourceful?"

Barr shrugged. "Attack now or never; with a single ship,

29

or all the force in the Empire; by military force or economic pressure; by candid declaration of war or by treacherous ambush. Do whatever you wish in your fullest exercise of freewill. You will still lose."

"Because of Hari Seldon's dead hand?"

"Because of the dead hand of the mathematics of human behavior that can neither be stopped, swerved, nor delayed."

The two faced each other in deadlock, until the general stepped back.

He said simply, "I'll take that challenge. It's a dead hand against a living will."

4. The Emperor

CLEON II *commonly called "The Great." The last strong Emperor of the First Empire, he is important for the political and artistic renaissance that took place during his long reign. He is best known to romance, however, for his connection with Bel Riose, and to the common man, he is simply "Riose's Emperor." It is important not to allow events of the last year of his reign to overshadow forty years of. . . .*

Encyclopedia Galactica

CLEON II was Lord of the Universe. Cleon II also suffered from a painful and undiagnosed ailment. By the queer twists of human affairs, the two statements are not mutually exclusive, nor even particularly incongruous. There have been a wearisomely large number of precedents in history.

But Cleon II cared nothing for such precedents. To meditate upon a long list of similar cases would not ameliorate personal suffering an electron's worth. It soothed him as little to think that where his great-grandfather had been the pirate ruler of a dust-speck planet, he himself slept in the pleasure palace of Ammenetik the Great, as heir of a line of Galactic rulers stretching backward into a tenuous past. It was at present no source of comfort to him that the efforts of his father had cleansed the realm of its leprous patches of rebellion and restored it to the peace and unity it had enjoyed under Stanel VI; that, as a consequence, in the twenty-five years of his reign, not one cloud of revolt had misted his burnished glory.

The Emperor of the Galaxy and the Lord of All whimpered as he lolled his head backward into the invigorating plane of force about his pillows. It yielded in a softness that

31

did not touch, and at the pleasant tingle, Cleon relaxed a bit. He sat up with difficulty and stared morosely at the distant walls of the grand chamber. It was a bad room to be alone in. It was too big. All the rooms were too big.

But better to be alone during these crippling bouts than to endure the prinking of the courtiers, their lavish sympathy, their soft, condescending dullness. Better to be alone than to watch those insipid masks behind which spun the tortuous speculations on the chances of death and the fortunes of the succession.

His thoughts hurried him. There were his three sons; three straight-backed youths full of promise and virtue. Where did they disappear on these bad days? Waiting, no doubt. Each watching the other; and all watching him.

He stirred uneasily. And now Brodrig craved audience. The low-born, faithful Brodrig; faithful because he was hated with a unanimous and cordial hatred that was the only point of agreement between the dozen cliques that divided his court.

Brodrig—the faithful favorite, who had to be faithful, since unless he owned the fastest speed-ship in the Galaxy and took to it the day of the Emperor's death, it would be the atom-chamber the day after.

Cleon II touched the smooth knob on the arm of his great divan, and the huge door at the end of the room dissolved to transparency.

Brodrig advanced along the crimson carpet, and knelt to kiss the Emperor's limp hand.

"Your health, sire?" asked the Privy Secretary in a low tone of becoming anxiety.

"I live," snapped the Emperor with exasperation, "if you can call it life where every scoundrel who can read a book of medicine uses me as a blank and receptive field for his feeble experiments. If there is a conceivable remedy, chemical, physical, or atomic, which has not yet been tried, why then, some learned babbler from the far corners of the realm will arrive tomorrow to try it. And still another newly-discovered book, or forgery more-like, will be used as authority.

"By my father's memory," he rumbled savagely, "it seems there is not a biped extant who can study a disease before his eyes with those same eyes. There is not one who can count a pulse-beat without a book of the ancients before him.

I'm sick and they call it 'unknown.' The fools! If in the course of millennia, human bodies learn new methods of falling askew, it remains uncovered by the studies of the ancients and uncurable forevermore. The ancients should be alive now, or I then."

The Emperor ran down to a low-breathed curse while Brodrig waited dutifully. Cleon II said peevishly, "How many are waiting outside?"

He jerked his head in the direction of the door.

Brodrig said patiently, "The Great Hall holds the usual number."

"Well, let them wait. State matters occupy me. Have the Captain of the Guard announce it. Or wait, forget the state matters. Just have it announced I hold no audience, and let the Captain of the Guard look doleful. The jackals among them may betray themselves." The Emperor sneered nastily.

"There is a rumor, sire," said Brodrig, smoothly, "that it is your heart that troubles you."

The Emperor's smile was little removed from the previous sneer. "It will hurt others more than myself if any act prematurely on that rumor. But what is it *you* want. Let's have this over."

Brodrig rose from his kneeling posture at a gesture of permission and said, "It concerns General Bel Riose, the Military Governor of Siwenna."

"Riose?" Cleon II frowned heavily. "I don't place him. Wait, is he the one who sent that quixotic message some months back? Yes, I remember. He panted for permission to enter a career of conquest for the glory of the Empire and Emperor."

"Exactly, sire."

The Emperor laughed shortly. "Did you think I had such generals left me, Brodrig? He seems to be a curious atavism. What was the answer? I believe you took care of it."

"I did, sire. He was instructed to forward additional information and to take no steps involving naval action without further orders from the Imperium."

"*Hmp*. Safe enough. Who is this Riose? Was he ever at court?"

Brodrig nodded and his mouth twisted ever so little. "He began his career as a cadet in the Guards ten years back. He had part in that affair off the Lemul Cluster."

"The Lemul Cluster? You know, my memory isn't quite—

33

Was that the time a young soldier saved two ships of the line from a head-on collision by . . . uh . . . something or other?" He waved a hand impatiently. "I don't remember the details. It was something heroic."

"Riose was that soldier. He received a promotion for it," Brodrig said dryly, "and an appointment to field duty as captain of a ship."

"And now Military Governor of a border system and still young. Capable man, Brodrig!"

"Unsafe, sire. He lives in the past. He is a dreamer of ancient times, or rather, of the myths of what ancient times used to be. Such men are harmless in themselves, but their queer lack of realism makes them fools for others." He added, "His men, I understand, are completely under his control. He is one of your *popular* generals."

"Is he?" the Emperor mused. "Well, come, Brodrig, I would not wish to be served entirely by incompetents. They certainly set no enviable standard for faithfulness themselves."

"An incompetent traitor is no danger. It is rather the capable men who must be watched."

"You among them, Brodrig?" Cleon II laughed and then grimaced with pain. "Well, then, you may forget the lecture for the while. What new development is there in the matter of this young conqueror? I hope you haven't come merely to reminisce."

"Another message, sire, has been received from General Riose."

"Oh? And to what effect?"

"He has spied out the land of these barbarians and advocates an expedition in force. His arguments are long and fairly tedious. It is not worth annoying Your Imperial Majesty with it at present, during your indisposition. Particularly since it will be discussed at length during the session of the Council of Lords." He glanced sidewise at the Emperor.

Cleon II frowned. "The Lords? Is it a question for them, Brodrig? It will mean further demands for a broader interpretation of the Charter. It always comes to that."

"It can't be avoided, sire. It might have been better if your august father could have beaten down the last rebellion without granting the Charter. But since it is here, we must endure it for the while."

"You're right, I suppose. Then the Lords it must be. But

why all this solemnity, man? It is, after all, a minor point. Success on a remote border with limited troops is scarcely a state affair."

Brodrig smiled narrowly. He said coolly, "It is an affair of a romantic idiot; but even a romantic idiot can be a deadly weapon when an unromantic rebel uses him as a tool. Sire, the man was popular here and is popular there. He is young. If he annexes a vagrant barbarian planet or two, he will become a conqueror. Now a young conqueror who has proven his ability to rouse the enthusiasm of pilots, miners, tradesmen and suchlike rabble is dangerous at any time. Even if he lacked the desire to do to you as your august father did to the usurper, Ricker, then one of our loyal Lords of the Domain may decide to use him as his weapon."

Cleon II moved an arm hastily and stiffened with pain. Slowly he relaxed, but his smile was weak, and his voice a whisper. "You are a valuable subject, Brodrig. You always suspect far more than is necessary, and I have but to take half your suggested precautions to be utterly safe. We'll put it up to the Lords. We shall see what they say and take our measures accordingly. The young man, I suppose, has made no hostile moves yet."

"He reports none. But already he asks for reinforcements."

"Reinforcements!" The Emperor's eyes narrowed with wonder. "What force has he?"

"Ten ships of the line, sire, with a full complement of auxiliary vessels. Two of the ships are equipped with motors salvaged from the old Grand Fleet, and one has a battery of power artillery from the same source. The other ships are new ones of the last fifty years, but are serviceable, nevertheless."

"Ten ships would seem adequate for any reasonable undertaking. Why, with less than ten ships my father won his first victories against the usurper. Who *are* these barbarians he's fighting?"

The Privy Secretary raised a pair of supercilious eyebrows. "He refers to them as 'the Foundation.' "

"The Foundation? What is it?"

"There is no record of it, sire. I have searched the archives carefully. The area of the Galaxy indicated falls within the ancient province of Anacreon, which two centuries since gave itself up to brigandage, barbarism, and anarchy. There is no planet known as Foundation in the province, however. There was a vague reference to a group of scientists sent to that province just before its separation from our protection. They were to prepare an Encyclopedia." He smiled thinly. "I believe they called it the Encyclopedia Foundation."

"Well," the Emperor considered it somberly, "that seems a tenuous connection to advance."

"I'm not advancing it, sire. No word was ever received from that expedition after the growth of anarchy in that region. If their descendants still live and retain their name, then they have reverted to barbarism most certainly."

"And so he wants reinforcements." The Emperor bent a fierce glance at his secretary. "This is most peculiar; to propose to fight savages with ten ships and to ask for more before a blow is struck. And yet I begin to remember this Riose; he was a handsome boy of loyal family. Brodrig, there are complications in this that I don't penetrate. There may be more importance in it than would seem."

His fingers played idly with the gleaming sheet that covered his stiffened legs. He said, "I need a man out there; one with eyes, brains and loyalty. Brodrig—"

The secretary bent a submissive head. "And the ships, sire?"

"Not yet." The Emperor moaned softly as he shifted his position in gentle stages. He pointed a feeble finger, "Not till we know more. Convene the Council of Lords for this day week. It will be a good opportunity for the new appropriation as well. I'll put *that* through or lives will end."

He leaned his aching head into the soothing tingle of the forcefield pillow, "Go now, Brodrig, and send in the doctor. He's the worst bumbler of the lot."

5. The War Begins

FROM the radiating point of Siwenna, the forces of the Empire reached out cautiously into the black unknown of the Periphery. Giant ships passed the vast distances that separated the vagrant stars at the Galaxy's rim, and felt their way around the outermost edge of Foundation influence.

Worlds isolated in their new barbarism of two centuries felt the sensation once again of Imperial overlords upon their soil. Allegiance was sworn in the face of the massive artillery covering capital cities.

Garrisons were left; garrisons of men in Imperial uniform with the Spaceship-and-Sun insignia upon their shoulders. The old men took notice and remembered once again the forgotten tales of their grandfathers' fathers of the times when the universe was big, and rich, and peaceful and that same Spaceship-and-Sun ruled all.

Then the great ships passed on to weave their line of forward bases further around the Foundation. And as each world was knotted into its proper place in the fabric, the report went back to Bel Riose at the General Headquarters he had established on the rocky barrenness of a wandering sunless planet.

Now Riose relaxed and smiled grimly at Ducem Barr. "Well, what do *you* think, patrician?"

"I? Of what value are my thoughts? I am not a military man." He took in with one wearily distasteful glance the crowded disorder of the rock-bound room which had been carved out of the wall of a cavern of artificial air, light, and heat which marked the single bubble of life in the vastness of a bleak world.

"For the help I could give you," he muttered, "or would

37

want to give you, you might return me to Siwenna."

"Not yet. Not yet." The general turned his chair to the corner which held the huge, brilliantly-transparent sphere that mapped the old Imperial prefect of Anacreon and its neighboring sectors. "Later, when this is over, you will go back to your books and to more. I'll see to it that the estates of your family are restored to you and to your children for the rest of time."

"Thank you," said Barr, with faint irony, "but I lack your faith in the happy outcome of all this."

Riose laughed harshly, "Don't start your prophetic croakings again. This map speaks louder than all your woeful theories." He caressed its curved invisible outline gently. "Can you read a map in radial projection? You can? Well, here, see for yourself. The stars in gold represent the Imperial territories. The red stars are those in subjection to the Foundation and the pink are those which are probably within the economic sphere of influence. Now watch—"

Riose's hand covered a rounded knob, and slowly an area of hard, white pinpoints changed into a deepening blue. Like an inverted cup they folded about the red and the pink.

"Those blue stars have been taken over by my forces," said Riose with quiet satisfaction, "and they still advance. No opposition has appeared anywhere. The barbarians are quiet. And particularly, no opposition has come from Foundation forces. They sleep peacefully and well."

"You spread your force thinly, don't you?" asked Barr.

"As a matter of fact," said Riose, "despite appearances, I don't. The key points which I garrison and fortify are relatively few, but they are carefully chosen. The result is that the force expended is small, but the strategic result great. There are many advantages, more than would ever appear to anyone who hasn't made a careful study of spatial tactics, but it is apparent to anyone, for instance, that I can base an attack from any point in an inclosing sphere, and that when I am finished it will be impossible for the Foundation to attack at flank or rear. I shall have no flank or rear with respect to them.

"This strategy of the Previous Inclosure has been tried before, notably in the campaigns of Loris VI, some two thousand years ago, but always imperfectly; always with the knowledge and attempted interference of the enemy. This is different."

38

"The ideal textbook case?" Barr's voice was languid and indifferent. Riose was impatient. "You still think my forces will fail?"

"They must."

"You understand that there is no case in military history where an inclosure has been completed that the attacking forces have not eventually won, except where an outside Navy exists in sufficient force to break the Inclosure."

"If you say so."

"And you still adhere to your faith."

"Yes."

Riose shrugged. "Then do so."

Barr allowed the angry silence to continue for a moment, then asked quietly, "Have you received an answer from the Emperor?"

Riose removed a cigarette from a wall container behind his head, placed a filter tip between his lips and puffed it aflame carefully. He said, "You mean my request for reinforcements? It came, but that's all. Just the answer."

"No ships."

"None. I half-expected that. Frankly, patrician, I should never have allowed myself to be stampeded by your theories into requesting them in the first place. It puts me in a false light."

"Does it?"

"Definitely. Ships are at a premium. The civil wars of the last two centuries have smashed up more than half of the Grand Fleet and what's left is in pretty shaky condition. You know it isn't as if the ships we build these days are worth anything. I don't think there's a man in the Galaxy today who can build a first-rate hyperatomic motor."

"I knew that," said the Siwennian. His eyes were thoughtful and introspective. "I didn't know that *you* knew it. So his Imperial Majesty can spare no ships. Psycho-history could have predicted that; in fact, it probably did. I should say that Hari Seldon's dead hand wins the opening round."

Riose answered sharply, "I have enough ships as it is. Your Seldon wins nothing. Should the situation turn more serious, then more ships *will* be available. As yet, the Emperor does not know all the story."

"Indeed? What haven't you told him?"

"Obviously—your theories." Riose looked sardonic. "The story is, with all respect to you, inherently improbable. If developments warrant; if events supply me with proof, then, but only then, would I make out the case of mortal danger.

"And in addition," Riose drove on, casually, "the story, unbolstered by fact, has a flavor of *lese majeste* that could scarcely be pleasant to His Imperial Majesty."

The old patrician smiled. "You mean that telling him his august throne is in danger of subversion by a parcel of ragged barbarians from the ends of the universe is not a warning to be believed or appreciated. Then you expect nothing from him."

"Unless you count a special envoy as something."

"And why a special envoy?"

"It's an old custom. A direct representative of the crown is present on every military campaign which is under government auspices."

"Really? Why?"

"It's a method of preserving the symbol of personal Imperial leadership in all campaigns. It's gained a secondary function of insuring the fidelity of generals. It doesn't always succeed in that respect."

"You'll find that inconvenient, general. Extraneous authority, I mean."

"I don't doubt that," Riose reddened faintly, "but it can't be helped—"

The receiver at the general's hand glowed warmly, and with an unobtrusive jar, the cylindered communication popped into its slot. Riose unrolled it, "Good! This is it!"

Ducem Barr raised a mildly questioning eyebrow.

Riose said, "You know we've captured one of these Trader people. Alive—and with his ship intact."

"I've heard talk of it."

"Well, they've just brought him in, and we'll have him here in a minute. You keep your seat, patrician. I want you here when I'm questioning him. It's why I asked you here today in the first place. You may understand him where I might miss important points."

The door signal sounded and a touch of the general's toe swung the door wide. The man who stood on the threshold was tall and bearded, wore a short coat of a soft, leathery plastic, with an attached hood shoved back on his neck. His hands were free, and if he noticed the men about him were armed, he did not trouble to indicate it.

He stepped in casually, and looked about with calculating

40

eyes. He favored the general with a rudimentary wave of the hand and a half nod.

"Your name?" demanded Riose, crisply.

"Lathan Devers." The trader hooked his thumbs into his wide and gaudy belt. "Are you the boss here?"

"You are a trader of the Foundation?"

"That's right. Listen, if you're the boss, you'd better tell your hired men here to lay off my cargo."

The general raised his head and regarded the prisoner coldly. "Answer questions. Do not volunteer orders."

"All right. I'm agreeable. But one of your boys blasted a two-foot hole in his chest already, by sticking his fingers where he wasn't supposed to."

Riose shifted his gaze to the lieutenant in charge. "Is this man telling the truth? Your report, Vrank, had it that no lives were lost."

"None were, sir," the lieutenant spoke stiffly, apprehensively, "at the time. There was later some disposition to search the ship, there having arisen a rumor that a woman was aboard. Instead, sir, many instruments of unknown nature were located, instruments which the prisoner claims to be his stock in trade. One of them flashed on handling, and the soldier holding it died."

The general turned back to the trader. "Does your ship carry atomic explosives?"

"Galaxy, no. What for? That fool grabbed an atomic puncher, wrong end forward and set at maximum dispersion. You're not supposed to do that. Might as well point a neut-gun at your head. I'd have stopped him, if five men weren't sitting on my chest."

Riose gestured at the waiting guard, "You go. The captured ship is to be sealed against all intrusion. Sit down, Devers."

The trader did so, in the spot indicated, and withstood stolidly the hard scrutiny of the Imperial general and the curious glance of the Siwennian patrician.

Riose said, "You're a sensible man, Devers."

"Thank you. Are you impressed by my face, or do you want something? Tell you what, though. I'm a good business man."

"It's about the same thing. You surrendered your ship when you might have decided to waste our ammunition and have yourself blown to electron-dust. It could result in good

41

treatment for you, if you continue that sort of outlook on life."

"Good treatment is what I mostly crave, boss."

"Good, and co-operation is what I mostly crave." Riose smiled, and said in a low aside to Ducem Barr, "I hope the word 'crave' means what I think it does. Did you ever hear such a barbarous jargon?"

Devers said blandly, "Right. I check you. But what kind of co-operation are you talking about, boss? To tell you straight, I don't know where I stand." He looked about him, "Where's this place, for instance, and what's the idea?"

"Ah, I've neglected the other half of the introductions. I apologize." Riose was in good humor. "That gentleman is Ducem Barr, Patrician of the Empire. I am Bel Riose, Peer of the Empire, and General of the Third Class in the armed forces of His Imperial Majesty."

The trader's jaw slackened. Then, "The Empire? I mean the old Empire they taught us about at school? Huh! Funny! I always had the sort of notion that it didn't exist any more."

"Look about you. It does," said Riose grimly.

"Might have known it though," and Lathan Devers pointed his beard at the ceiling. "That was a mightily polished-looking set of craft that took my tub. No kingdom of the Periphery could have turned them out." His brow furrowed. "So what's the game, boss? Or do I call you general?"

"The game is war."

"Empire versus Foundation, that it?"

"Right."

"Why?"

"I think you know why."

The trader stared sharply and shook his head.

Riose let the other deliberate, then said softly, "I'm sure you know why."

Lathan Devers muttered, "Warm here," and stood up to remove his hooded jacket. Then he sat down again and stretched his legs out before him.

"You know," he said, comfortably, "I figure you're thinking I ought to jump up with a whoop and lay about me. I can catch you before you could move if I choose my time, and this old fellow who sits there and doesn't say anything couldn't do much to stop me."

"But you won't," said Riose, confidently.

"I won't," agreed Devers, amiably. "First off, killing you
42

wouldn't stop the war, I suppose. There are more generals where you came from."

"Very accurately calculated."

"Besides which, I'd probably be slammed down about two seconds after I got you, and killed fast, or maybe slow, depending. But I'd be killed, and I never like to count on that when I'm making plans. It doesn't pay off."

"I said you were a sensible man."

"But there's one thing I would like, boss. I'd like you to tell me what you mean when you say I know why you're jumping us. I don't; and guessing games bother me no end."

"Yes? Ever hear of Hari Seldon?"

"No. I *said* I don't like guessing games."

Riose flicked a side glance at Ducem Barr who smiled with a narrow gentleness and resumed his inwardly-dreaming expression.

Riose said with a grimace, "Don't *you* play games, Devers. There is a tradition, or a fable, or sober history—I don't care what—upon your Foundation, that eventually you will found the Second Empire. I know quite a detailed version of Hari Seldon's psycho-historical claptrap, and your eventual plans of aggression against the Empire."

"That so?" Devers nodded thoughtfully. "And who told you all that?"

"Does that matter?" said Riose with dangerous smoothness. "You're here to question nothing. I want what you know about the Seldon Fable."

"But if it's a Fable—"

"Don't play with words, Devers."

"I'm not. In fact, I'll give it to you straight. You know all I know about it. It's silly stuff, half-baked. Every world has its yarns; you can't keep it away from them. Yes, I've heard that sort of talk; Seldon, Second Empire, and so on. They put kids to sleep at night with the stuff. The young squirts curl up in the spare rooms with their pocket projectors and suck up Seldon thrillers. But it's strictly non-adult. Non-intelligent adult, anyway." The trader shook his head.

The Imperial general's eyes were dark. "Is that really so? You waste your lies, man. I've been on the planet, Terminus. I know your Foundation. I've looked it in the face."

"And you ask me? Me, when I haven't kept foot on it for two months at a piece in ten years. You *are* wasting your time. But go ahead with your war, if it's fables you're after."

And Barr spoke for the first time, mildly, "You are so confident then that the Foundation will win?"

The trader turned. He flushed faintly and an old scar on one temple showed whitely, "Hm-m-m, the silent partner. How'd you squeeze *that* out of what I said, doc?"

Riose nodded very slightly at Barr, and the Siwennian continued in a low voice, "Because the notion *would* bother you if you thought your world might lose this war, and suffer the bitter reapings of defeat, I know. *My* world once did, and still does."

Lathan Devers fumbled his beard, looked from one of his opponents to the other, then laughed shortly. "Does he always talk like that, boss. Listen," he grew serious, "what's defeat? I've seen wars and I've seen defeats. What if the winner does take over? Who's bothered? Me? Guys like me?" He shook his head in derision.

"Get this," the trader spoke forcefully and earnestly, "there are five or six fat slobs who usually run an average planet. They get the rabbit punch, but I'm not losing peace of mind over them. See. The people? The ordinary run of guys? Sure, some get killed, and the rest pay extra taxes for a while. But it settles itself out; it runs itself down. And then it's the old situation again with a different five or six."

Ducem Barr's nostrils flared, and the tendons of his old right hand jerked; but he said nothing.

Lathan Devers' eyes were on him. They missed nothing. He said, "Look. I spend my life in space for my five-and-dime gadgets and my beer-and pretzel kickback from the Combines. There's fat fellows back there," his thumb jerked over his shoulder and back, "that sit home and collect my year's income every minute—out of skimmings from me and more like me. Suppose *you* run the Foundation. You'll still need us. You'll need us more than ever the Combines do—because you'd not know your way around, and we could bring in the hard cash. We'd make a better deal with the Empire. Yes, we would; and I'm a man of business. If it adds up to a plus mark, I'm for it."

And he stared at the two with sardonic belligerence.

The silence remained unbroken for minutes, and then a cylinder rattled into its slot. The general flipped it open, glanced at the neat printing and in-circuited the visuals with a sweep.

"Prepare plan indicating position of each ship in action. Await orders on full-armed defensive."

He reached for his cape. As he fastened it about his shoulders, he whispered in a stiff-lipped monotone to Barr, "I'm leaving this man to you. I'll expect results. This is war and I can be cruel to failures. Remember!" He left, with a salute to both.

Lathan Devers looked after him, "Well, something's hit him where it hurts. What goes on?"

"A battle, obviously," said Barr, gruffly. "The forces of the Foundation are coming out for their first battle. You'd better come along."

There were armed soldiers in the room. Their bearing was respectful and their faces were hard. Devers followed the proud old Siwennian patriarch out of the room.

The room to which they were led was smaller, barer. It contained two beds, a visi-screen, and shower and sanitary facilities. The soldiers marched out, and the thick door boomed hollowly shut.

"*Hmp?*" Devers stared disapprovingly about. "This looks permanent."

"It is," said Barr, shortly. The old Siwennian turned his back.

The trader said irritably, "What's your game, doc?"

"I have no game. You're in my charge, that's all."

The trader rose and advanced. His bulk towered over the unmoving patrician. "Yes? But you're in this cell with me and when you were marched here the guns were pointed just as hard at you as at me. Listen, you were all boiled up about my notions on the subject of war and peace."

He waited fruitlessly, "All right, let me ask you something. You said *your* country was licked once. By whom? Comet people from the outer nebulae?"

Barr looked up. "By the Empire."

"That so? Then what are you doing here?"

Barr maintained an eloquent silence.

The trader thrust out a lower lip and nodded his head slowly. He slipped off the flat-linked bracelet that hugged his right wrist and held it out. "What do you think of that?" He wore the mate to it on his left.

The Siwennian took the ornament. He responded slowly

45

to the trader's gesture and put it on. The odd tingling at the wrist passed away quickly.

Devers' voice changed at once. "Right, doc, you've got the action now. Just speak casually. If this room is wired, they won't get a thing. That's a Field Distorter you've got there; genuine Mallow design. Sells for twenty-five credits on any world from here to the outer rim. You get it free. Hold your lips still when you talk and take it easy. You've got to get the trick of it."

Ducem Barr was suddenly weary. The trader's boring eyes were luminous and urging. He felt unequal to their demands.

Barr said, "What do you want?" the words slurred from between unmoving lips.

"I've told you. You make mouth noises like what we call a patriot. Yet your own world has been mashed up by the Empire, and here you are playing ball with the Empire's fair-haired general. Doesn't make sense, does it?"

Barr said, "I have done my part. A conquering Imperial viceroy is dead because of me."

"That so? Recently?"

"Forty years ago."

"Forty . . . years . . . ago!" The words seemed to have meaning to the trader. He frowned, "That's a long time to live on memories. Does that young squirt in the general's uniform know about it?"

Barr nodded.

Devers' eyes were dark with thought. "You want the Empire to win?"

. And the old Siwennian patrician broke out in sudden deep anger, "May the Empire and all its works perish in universal catastrophe. All Siwenna prays that daily. I had brothers once, a sister, a father. But I have children now, grandchildren. The general knows where to find them."

Devers waited.

Barr continued in a whisper, "But that would not stop me if the results in view warranted the risk. They would know how to die."

The trader said gently, "You killed a viceroy once, huh? You know, I recognize a few things. We once had a mayor, Hober Mallow his name was. He visited Siwenna; that's your world, isn't it? He met a man named Barr."

Ducem Barr stared hard, suspiciously. "What do you know of this?"

"What every trader on the Foundation knows. You might be a smart old fellow put in here to get on my right side. Sure, they'd point guns at you, and you'd hate the Empire and be all-out for its smashing. Then I'd fall all over you and pour out my heart to you, and wouldn't the general be pleased. There's not much chance of that, doc.

"But just the same I'd like to see you prove that you're the son of Onum Barr of Siwenna—the sixth and youngest who escaped the massacre."

Ducem Barr's hand shook as he opened the flat metal box in a wall recess. The metal object he withdrew clanked softly as he thrust it into the trader's hands.

"Look at that," he said.

Devers stared. He held the swollen central link of the chain close to his eyes and swore softly. "That's Mallow's monogram, or I'm a space struck rookie, and the design is fifty years old if it's a day."

He looked up and smiled.

"Shake, doc. A man-sized atomic shield is all the proof I need," and he held out his large hand.

6. The Favorite

THE TINY SHIPS had appeared out of the vacant depths and darted into the midst of the Armada. Without a shot or a burst of energy, they weaved through the ship-swollen area, then blasted on and out, while the Imperial wagons turned after them like lumbering beasts. There were two noiseless flares that pinpointed space as two of the tiny gnats shriveled in atomic disintegration, and the rest were gone.

The great ships searched, then returned to their original task, and world by world, the great web of the Inclosure continued.

Brodrig's uniform was stately; carefully tailored and as carefully worn. His walk through the gardens of the obscure planet Wanda, now temporary Imperial headquarters, was leisurely; his expression was somber.

Bel Riose walked with him, his field uniform open at the collar, and doleful in its monotonous gray-black.

Riose indicated the smooth black bench under the fragrant tree-fern whose large spatulate leaves lifted flatly against the white sun. "See that, sir. It is a relic of the Imperium. The ornamented benches, built for lovers, linger on, fresh and useful, while the factories and the palaces collapse into unremembered ruin."

He seated himself, while Cleon II's Privy Secretary stood erect before him and clipped the leaves above neatly with precise swings of his ivory staff.

Riose crossed his legs and offered a cigarette to the other. He fingered one himself as he spoke, "It is what one would expect from the enlightened wisdom of His Imperial Majesty to send so competent an observer as yourself. It relieves any anxiety I might have felt that the press of more important and more immediate business might perhaps force into the shadows a small campaign on the Periphery."

"The eyes of the Emperor are everywhere," said Brodrig, mechanically. "We do not underestimate the importance of the campaign; yet still it would seem that too great an emphasis is being placed upon its difficulty. Surely their little ships are no such barrier that we must move through the intricate preliminary maneuver of an Inclosure."

Riose flushed, but he maintained his equilibrium. "I cannot risk the lives of my men, who are few enough, or the destruction of my ships which are irreplaceable, by a too-rash attack. The establishment of an Inclosure will quarter my casualties in the ultimate attack, howsoever difficult it be. The military reasons for that I took the liberty to explain yesterday."

"Well, well, I am not a military man. In this case, you assure me that what seems patently and obviously right is, in reality, wrong. We will allow that. Yet your caution shoots far beyond that. In your second communication, you requested re-inforcements. And these, against an enemy poor, small, and barbarous, with whom you had had not one skirmish at the time. To desire more forces under the circumstances would savor almost of incapacity or worse, had not your earlier career given sufficient proof of your boldness and imagination."

"I thank you," said the general, coldly, "but I would remind you that there is a difference between boldness and blindness. There is a place for a decisive gamble when you know your enemy and can calculate the risks at least roughly; but to move at all against an *unknown* enemy is boldness in itself. You might as well ask why the same man sprints safely across an obstacle course in the day, and falls over the furniture in his room at night."

Brodrig swept away the other's words with a neat flirt of the fingers. "Dramatic, but not satisfactory. You have been to this barbarian world yourself. You have in addition this enemy prisoner you coddle, this trader. Between yourself and the prisoner you are not in a night fog."

"No? I pray you to remember that a world which has developed in isolation for two centuries can not be interpreted to the point of intelligent attack by a month's visit. I am a soldier, not a cleft-chinned, barrel-chested hero of a sub-etheric trimensional thriller. Nor can a single prisoner, and one who is an obscure member of an economic group which has no close connection with the enemy world introduce me to all the inner secrets of enemy strategy."

"You have questioned him?"

"I have."

"Well?"

"It has been useful, but not vitally so. His ship is tiny, of no account. He sells little toys which are amusing if nothing else. I have a few of the cleverest which I intend sending to the Emperor as curiosities. Naturally, there is a good deal about the sh. and its workings which I do not understand, but then I am not a tech-man."

"But you have among you those who are," pointed out Brodrig.

"I, too, am aware of that," replied the general in faintly caustic tones. "But the fools have far to go before they could meet my needs. I have already sent for clever men who can understand the workings of the odd atomic field-circuits the ship contains. I have received no answer."

"Men of that type can not be spared, general. Surely, there must be one man of your vast province who understands atomics."

"Were there such a one, I would have him heal the limping, invalid motors that power two of my small fleet of ships. Two ships of my meager ten that can not fight a major battle for lack of sufficient power supply. One fifth of my force condemned to the carrion activity of consolidating positions behind the lines."

The secretary's fingers fluttered impatiently. "Your position is not unique in that respect, general. The Emperor has similar troubles."

The general threw away his shredded, never-lit cigarette, lit another, and shrugged. "Well, it is beside the immediate point, this lack of first-class tech-men. Except that I might have made more progress with my prisoner were my Psychic Probe in proper order."

The secretary's eyebrows lifted. "You have a Probe?"

"An old one. A superannuated one which fails me the one time I needed it. I set it up during the prisoner's sleep, and received nothing. So much for the Probe. I have tried it on my own men and the reaction is quite proper, but again there is not one among my staff of tech-men who can tell me why it fails upon the prisoner. Ducem Barr, who is a theoretician of parts, though no mechanic, says the psychic structure of the prisoner may be unaffected by the Probe since from childhood he has been subjected to alien environments and neural stimuli. I don't know. But he may yet be useful. I save him in that hope."

Brodrig leaned on his staff. "I shall see if a specialist is available in the capital. In the meanwhile, what of this other man you just mentioned, this Siwennian? You keep too many enemies in your good graces."

"He knows the enemy. He, too, I keep for future reference and the help he may afford me."

"But he is a Siwennian and the son of a proscribed rebel."

"He is old and powerless, and his family acts as hostage."

"I see. Yet I think that I should speak to this trader myself."

"Certainly."

"Alone," the secretary added coldly, making his point.

"Certainly," repeated Riose, blandly. "As a loyal subject of the Emperor, I accept his personal representative as my superior. However, since the trader is at the permanent base, you will have to leave the front areas at an interesting moment."

"Yes? Interesting in what way?"

"Interesting in that the Inclosure is complete today. Interesting in that within the week, the Twentieth Fleet of the Border advances inward towards the core of resistance." Riose smiled and turned away.

In a vague way, Brodrig felt punctured.

7. Bribery

SERGEANT MORI LUK made an ideal soldier of the ranks. He came from the huge agricultural planets of the Pleiades where only army life could break the bond to the soil and the unavailing life of drudgery; and he was typical of that background. Unimaginative enough to face danger without fear, he was strong and agile enough to face it successfully. He accepted orders instantly, drove the men under him unbendingly and adored his general unswervingly.

And yet with that, he was of a sunny nature. If he killed a man in the line of duty without a scrap of hesitation, it was also without a scrap of animosity.

That Sergeant Luk should signal at the door before entering was further a sign of tact, for he would have been perfectly within his rights to enter without signaling.

The two within looked up from their evening meal and one reached out with his foot to cut off the cracked voice which rattled out of the battered pocket-transmitter with bright liveliness.

"More books?" asked Lathan Devers.

The sergeant held out the tightly-wound cylinder of film and scratched his neck. "It belongs to Engineer Orre, but he'll have to have it back. He's going to send it to his kids, you know, like what you might call a souvenir, you know."

Ducem Barr turned the cylinder in his hands with interest. "And where did the engineer get it? He hasn't a transmitter also, has he?"

The sergeant shook his head emphatically. He pointed to the knocked-about remnant at the foot of the bed. "That's the only one in the place. This fellow, Orre, now, he got that book from one of these pig-pen worlds out here we

52

captured. They had it in a big building by itself and he had to kill a few of the natives that tried to stop him from taking it."

He looked at it appraisingly. "It makes a good souvenir —for kids."

He paused, then said stealthily, "There's big news floating about, by the way. It's only scuttlebutt, but even so, it's too good to keep. The general did it again." And he nodded slowly, gravely.

"That so?" said Devers. "And what did he do?"

"Finished the Inclosure, that's all." The sergeant chuckled with a fatherly pride. "Isn't he the corker, though? Didn't he work it fine? One of the fellows who's strong on fancy talk, say it went as smooth and even as the music of the spheres, whatever they are."

"The big offensive starts now?" asked Barr, mildly.

"Hope so," was the boisterous response. I want to get back on my ship now that my arm is in one piece again. I'm tired of sitting on my scupper out here."

"So am I," muttered Devers, suddenly and savagely. There was a bit of underlip caught in his teeth, and he worried it.

The sergeant looked at him doubtfully, and said, "I'd better go now. The captain's round is due and I'd just as soon he didn't catch me in here."

He paused at the door. "By the way, sir," he said with sudden, awkward shyness to the trader, "I heard from my wife. She says that little freezer you gave me to send her works fine. It doesn't cost her anything, and she just about keeps a month's supply of food froze up complete. I appreciate it."

"It's all right. Forget it."

The great door moved noiselessly shut behind the grinning sergeant.

Ducem Barr got out of his chair. "Well, he gives us a fair return for the freezer. Let's take a look at this new book. Ahh, the title is gone."

He unrolled a yard or so of the film and looked through at the light. Then he murmured, "Well, skewer me through the scupper, as the sergeant says. This is 'The Garden of Summa,' Devers."

"That so?" said the trader, without interest. He shoved aside what was left of his dinner. "Sit down, Barr. Listening

53

to this old-time literature isn't doing me any good. You heard what the sergeant said?"

"Yes, I did. What of it?"

"The offensive will start. And we sit here!"

"Where do you want to sit?"

"You know what I mean. There's no use just waiting."

"Isn't there?" Barr was carefully removing the old film from the transmitter and installing the new. "You told me a good deal of Foundation history in the last month, and it seems that the great leaders of past crises did precious little more than sit—and wait."

"Ah, Barr, but they knew where they were going."

"Did they? I suppose they said they did when it was over, and for all I know maybe they did. But there's no proof that things would not have worked out as well or better if they had not known where they were going. The deeper economic and sociological forces aren't directed by individual men."

Devers sneered. "No way of telling that things wouldn't have worked out worse, either. You're arguing tail-end backwards." His eyes were brooding. "You know, suppose I blasted him?"

"Whom? Riose?"

"Yes."

Barr sighed. His aging eyes were troubled with a reflection of the long past. "Assassination isn't the way out, Devers. I once tried it, under provocation, when I was twenty— but it solved nothing. I removed a villain from Siwenna, but not the Imperial yoke; and it was the Imperial yoke and not the villain that mattered."

"But Riose is not just a villain, doc. He's the whole blamed army. It would fall apart without him. They hang on him like babies. The sergeant out there slobbers every time he mentions him."

"Even so. There are other armies and other leaders. You must go deeper. There is this Brodrig, for instance—no one more than he has the ear of the Emperor. He could demand hundreds of ships where Riose must struggle with ten. I know him by reputation."

"That so? What about him?" The trader's eyes lost in frustration what they gained in sharp interest.

"You want a pocket outline? He's a low-born rascal who has by unfailing flattery tickled the whims of the Emperor.

54

He's well-hated by the court aristocracy, vermin themselves, because he can lay claim to neither family nor humility. He is the Emperor's adviser in all things, and the Emperor's tool in the worst things. He is faithless by choice but loyal by necessity. There is not a man in the Empire as subtle in villainy or as crude in his pleasures. And they say there is no way to the Emperor's favor but through him; and no way to his, but through infamy."

"Wow!" Devers pulled thoughtfully at his neatly trimmed beard. "And he's the old boy the Emperor sent out here to keep an eye on Riose. Do you know I have an idea?"

"I do now."

"Suppose this Brodrig takes a dislike to our young Army's Delight?"

"He probably has already. He's not noted for a capacity for liking."

"Suppose it gets really bad. The Emperor might hear about it, and Riose might be in trouble."

"Uh-huh. Quite likely. But how do you propose to get that to happen?"

"I don't know. I suppose he could be bribed?"

The patrician laughed gently. "Yes, in a way, but not in the manner you bribed the sergeant—not with a pocket freezer. And even if you reach his scale, it wouldn't be worth it. There's probably no one so easily bribed, but he lacks even the fundamental honesty of honorable corruption. He doesn't *stay* bribed; not for any sum. Think of something else."

Devers swung a leg over his knee and his toe nodded quickly and restlessly. "It's the first hint, though—"

He stopped; the door signal was flashing once again, and the sergeant was on the threshold once more. He was excited, and his broad face was red and unsmiling.

"Sir," he began, in an agitated attempt at deference, "I am very thankful for the freezer, and you have always spoken to me very fine, although I am only the son of a farmer and you are great lords."

His Pleiade accent had grown thick, almost too much so for easy comprehension; and with excitement, his lumpish peasant derivation wiped out completely the soldierly bearing so long and so painfully cultivated.

Barr said softly, "What is it, sergeant?"

"Lord Brodrig is coming to see you. Tomorrow! I know,
55

because the captain told me to have my men ready for dress review tomorrow for . . . for him. I thought—I might warn you."

Barr said, "Thank you, sergeant, we appreciate that. But it's all right, man; no need for—."

But the look on Sergeant Luk's face was now unmistakably one of fear. He spoke in a rough whisper, "You don't hear the stories the men tell about him. He has sold himself to the space fiend. No, don't laugh. There are most terrible tales told about him. They say he has men with blast-guns who follow him everywhere, and when he wants pleasure, he just tells them to blast down anyone they meet. And they do—and he laughs. They say even the Emperor is in terror of him, and that he forces the Emperor to raise taxes and won't let him listen to the complaints of the people.

"And he hates the general, that's what they say. They say he would like to kill the general, because the general is so great and wise. But he can't because our general is a match for anyone and he knows Lord Brodrig is a bad 'un."

The sergeant blinked; smiled in a sudden incongruous shyness at his own outburst; and backed toward the door. He nodded his head, jerkily. "You mind my words. Watch him."

He ducked out.

And Devers looked up, hard-eyed. "This breaks things our way, doesn't it, doc?"

"It depends," said Barr, dryly, "on Brodrig, doesn't it?"

But Devers was thinking, not listening.

He was thinking hard.

Lord Brodrig ducked his head as he stepped into the cramped living quarters of the trading ship, and his two armed guards followed quickly, with bared guns and the professionally hard scowls of the hired bravos.

The Privy Secretary had little of the look of the lost soul about him just then. If the space fiend had bought him, he had left no visible mark of possession. Rather might Brodrig have been considered a breath of court-fashion come to enliven the hard, bare ugliness of an army base.

The stiff, tight lines of his sheened and immaculate costume gave him the illusion of height, from the very top of which his cold, emotionless eyes stared down the declivity of a long nose at the trader. The mother-of-pearl ruches

56

at his wrists fluttered filmly as he brought his ivory stick to the ground before him and leaned upon it daintily.

"No," he said, with a little gesture, "you remain here. Forget your toys; I am not interested in them."

He drew forth a chair, dusted it carefully with the irridescent square of fabric attached to the top of his white stick, and seated himself. Devers glanced towards the mate to the chair, but Brodrig said lazily, "You will stand in the presence of a Peer of the Realm."

He smiled.

Devers shrugged. "If you're not interested in my stock in trade, what am I here for?"

The Privy Secretary waited coldly, and Devers added a slow, "Sir."

"For privacy," said the secretary. "Now is it likely that I would come two hundred parsecs through space to inspect trinkets? It's *you* I want to see." He extracted a small pink tablet from an engraved box and placed it delicately between his teeth. He sucked it slowly and appreciatively.

"For instance," he said, "who are you? Are you really a citizen of this barbarian world that is creating all this fury of military frenzy?"

Devers nodded gravely.

"And you were really captured by him *after* the beginning of this squabble he calls a war. I am referring to our young general."

Devers nodded again.

"So! Very well, my worthy Outlander. I see your fluency of speech is at a minimum. I shall smooth the way for you. It seems that our general here is fighting an apparently meaningless war with frightful transports of energy— and this over a forsaken fleabite of a world at the end of nowhere, which to a logical man would not seem worth a single blast of a single gun. Yet the general is not illogical. On the contrary, I would say he was extremely intelligent. Do you follow me?"

"Can't say I do, sir."

The secretary inspected his fingernails and said, "Listen further, then. The general would not waste his men and ships on a sterile feat of glory. I know he *talks* of glory and of Imperial honor, but it is quite obvious that the affectation of being one of the insufferable old demigods of the Heroic Age won't wash. There is something more than glory here—

57

and he does take queer, unnecessary care of you. Now if you were *my* prisoner and told *me* as little of use as you have our general, I would slit open your abdomen and strangle you with your own intestines."

Devers remained wooden. His eyes moved slightly, first to one of the secretary's bully-boys, and then to the other. They were ready; eagerly ready.

The secretary smiled. "Well, now, you're a silent devil. According to the general, even a Psychic Probe made no impression, and that was a mistake on his part, by the way, for it convinced me that our young military whizz-bang was lying." He seemed in high humor.

"My honest tradesman," he said, "I have a Psychic Probe of my own, one that ought to suit you peculiarly well. You see this—"

And between thumb and forefinger, held negligently, were intricately designed, pink-and-yellow rectangles which were most definitely obvious in identity.

Devers said so. "It looks like cash," he said.

"Cash it is—and the best cash of the Empire, for it is backed by my estates, which are more extensive than the Emperor's own. A hundred thousand credits. All here! Between two fingers! Yours!"

"For what, sir? I am a good trader, but all trades go in both directions."

"For what? For the truth! What is the general after? Why is he fighting this war?"

Lathan Devers sighed, and smoothed his beard thoughtfully.

"What he's after?" His eyes were following the motions of the secretary's hands as he counted the money slowly, bill by bill. "In a word, the Empire."

"*Hmp.* How ordinary! It always comes to that in the end. But how? What is the road that leads from the Galaxy's edge to the peak of Empire so broadly and invitingly?"

"The Foundation," said Devers, bitterly, "has secrets. They have books, old books—so old that the language they are in is only known to a few of the top men. But the secrets are shrouded in ritual and religion, and none may use them. I tried and now I am here—and there is a death sentence waiting for me, there."

"I see. And these old secrets? Come, for one hundred thousand I deserve the intimate details."

"The transmutation of elements," said Devers, shortly.

The secretary's eyes narrowed and lost some of their detachment. "I have been told that practical transmutation is impossible by the laws of atomics."

"So it is, if atomic forces are used. But the ancients were smart boys. There are sources of power greater than the atoms. If the Foundation used those sources as I suggested—"

Devers felt a soft, creeping sensation in his stomach. The bait was dangling; the fish was nosing it.

The secretary said suddenly, "Continue. The general, I am sure, is aware of all this. But what does he intend doing once he finishes this opera-bouffe affair?"

Devers kept his voice rock-steady. "With transmutation he controls the economy of the whole set-up of your Empire. Mineral holdings won't be worth a sneeze when Riose can make tungsten out of aluminum and iridium out of iron. An entire production system based on the scarcity of certain elements and the abundance of others is thrown completely out of whack. There'll be the greatest disjointment the Empire has ever seen, and only Riose will be able to stop it. *And* there is the question of this new power I mentioned, the use of which won't give Riose religious heebies.

"There's nothing that can stop him now. He's got the Foundation by the back of the neck, and once he's finished with it, he'll be Emperor in two years."

"So." Brodrig laughed lightly. "Iridium out of iron, that's what you said, isn't it? Come, I'll tell you a state secret. Do you know that the Foundation has already been in communication with the general?"

Devers' back stiffened.

"You look surprised. Why not? It seems logical now. They offered him a hundred tons of iridium a year to make peace. A hundred tons of *iron* converted to iridium in violation of their religious principles to save their necks. Fair enough, but no wonder our rigidly incorruptible general, refused—when he can have the iridium and the Empire as well. And poor Cleon called him his one honest general. My bewhiskered merchant, you have earned your money."

He tossed it, and Devers scrambled after the flying bills.

Lord Brodrig stopped at the door and turned. "One reminder, trader. My playmates with the guns here have neither middle ears, tongues, education, nor intelligence. They can neither hear, speak, write, nor even make sense to a

Psychic Probe. But they are very expert at interesting executions. I have bought you, man, at one hundred thousand credits. You will be good and worthy merchandise. Should you forget that you are bought at any time and attempt to . . . say . . . repeat our conversation to Riose, you will be executed. But executed my way."

And in that delicate face there were sudden hard lines of eager cruelty that changed the studied smile into a red-lipped snarl. For one fleeting second, Devers saw that space fiend who had bought his buyer, look out of his buyer's eyes.

Silently, he preceded the two thrusting blast-guns of Brodrig's "playmates" to his quarters.

And to Ducem Barrs' question, he said with brooding satisfaction, "No, that's the queerest part of it. *He* bribed *me.*"

Two months of difficult war had left their mark on Bel Riose. There was heavy-handed gravity about him; and he was short-tempered.

It was with impatience that he addressed the worshipping Sergeant Luk. "Wait outside, soldier, and conduct these men back to their quarters when I am through. No one is to enter until I call. No one at all, you understand."

The sergeant saluted himself stiffly out of the room, and Riose with muttered disgust scooped up the waiting papers on his desk, threw them into the top drawer and slammed it shut.

"Take seats," he said shortly, to the waiting two. "I haven't much time. Strictly speaking, I shouldn't be here at all, but it is necessary to see you."

He turned to Ducem Barr, whose long fingers were caressing with interest the crystal cube in which was set the simulacrum of the lined, austere face of His Imperial Majesty, Cleon II.

"In the first place, patrician," said the general, "your Seldon is losing. To be sure, he battles well, for these men of the Foundation swarm like senseless bees and fight like madmen. Every planet is defended viciously, and once taken, every planet heaves so with rebellion it is as much trouble to hold as to conquer. But they are taken, and they are held. Your Seldon is losing."

"But he has not yet lost," murmured Barr politely.

"The Foundation itself retains less optimism. They offer

me millions in order that I may not put this Seldon to the final test."

"So rumor goes."

"Ah, is rumor preceding me? Does it prate also of the latest?"

"What is the latest?"

"Why, that Lord Brodrig, the darling of the Emperor, is now second in command at his own request."

Devers spoke for the first time. "At his own request, boss? How come? Or are you growing to like the fellow?" He chuckled.

Riose said, calmly, "No, can't say I do. It's just that he bought the office at what I considered a fair and adequate price."

"Such as?"

"Such as a request to the Emperor for reinforcements."

Devers' contemptuous smile broadened. "He has communicated with the Emperor, huh? And I take it, boss, you're just waiting for these reinforcements, but they'll come any day. Right?"

"Wrong! They have already come. Five ships of the line; smooth and strong, with a personal message of congratulations from the Emperor, and more ships on the way. What's wrong, trader?" he asked, sardonically.

Devers spoke through suddenly frozen lips. "Nothing!"

Riose strode out from behind his desk and faced the trader, hand on the butt of his blast-gun.

"I say, what's wrong, trader? The news would seem to disturb you. Surely, you have no sudden birth of interest in the Foundation."

"I haven't."

"Yes—there are queer points about you."

"That so, boss?" Devers smiled tightly, and balled the fists in his pockets. "Just you line them up and I'll knock them down for you."

"Here they are. You were caught easily. You surrendered at first blow with a burnt-out shield. You're quite ready to desert your world, and that without a price. Interesting, all this, isn't it?"

"I crave to be on the winning side, boss. I'm a sensible man; you called me that yourself."

Riose said with tight throatiness, "Granted! Yet no trader since has been captured. No trade ship but has had the speed

61

to escape at choice. No trade ship but has had a screen that could take all the beating a light cruiser could give it, should it choose to fight. And no trader but has fought to death when occasion warranted. Traders have been traced as the leaders and instigators of the guerilla warfare on occupied planets and of the flying raids in occupied space.

"Are you the *only* sensible man then? You neither fight nor flee, but turn traitor without urging. You are unique, amazingly unique—in fact, suspiciously unique."

Devers said softly, "I take your meaning, but you have nothing on me. I've been here now six months, and I've been a good boy."

"So you have, and I have repaid you by good treatment. I have left your ship undisturbed and treated you with every consideration. Yet you fall short. Freely offered information, for instance, on your gadgets might have been helpful. The atomic principles on which they are built would seem to be used in some of the Foundation's nastiest weapons. Right?"

"I am only a trader," said Devers, "and not one of these bigwig technicians. I sell the stuff; I don't make it."

"Well, that will be seen shortly. It is what I came here for. For instance, your ship will be searched for a personal force-shield. You have never worn one; yet all soldiers of the Foundation do. It will be significant evidence that there is information you do not choose to give me. Right?"

There was no answer. He continued, "And there will be more direct evidence. I have brought with me the Psychic Probe. It failed once before, but contact with the enemy is a liberal education."

His voice was smoothly threatening and Devers felt the gun thrust hard in his midriff—the general's gun, hitherto in its holster.

The general said quietly, "You will remove your wristband and any other metal ornament you wear and give them to me. Slowly! Atomic fields can be distorted, you see, and Psychic Probes might probe only into static. That's right. I'll take it."

The receiver on the general's desk was glowing and a message capsule clicked into the slot, near which Barr stood and still held the trimensional Imperial bust.

Riose stepped behind his desk, with his blast-gun held ready. He said to Barr, "You too, patrician. Your wristband condemns you. You have been helpful earlier, however, and

I am not vindictive, but I shall judge the fate of your be-hostaged family by the results of the Psychic Probe."

And as Riose leaned over to take out the message capsule, Barr lifted the crystal-enveloped bust of Cleon and quietly and methodically brought it down upon the general's head.

It happened too suddenly for Devers to grasp. It was as if a sudden demon had grown into the old man.

"Out!" said Barr, in a tooth-clenched whisper. "Quickly!" He seized Riose's dropped blaster and buried it in his blouse.

Sergeant Luk turned as they emerged from the narrowest possible crack of the door.

Barr said easily, "Lead on, sergeant!"

Devers closed the door behind him.

Sergeant Luk led in silence to their quarters, and then, with the briefest pause, continued onward, for there was the nudge of a blast-gun muzzle in his ribs, and a hard voice in his ears which said. "To the trade ship."

Devers stepped forward to open the air lock, and Barr said, "Stand where you are, Luk. You've been a decent man, and we're not going to kill you."

But the sergeant recognized the monogram on the gun. He cried in choked fury, "You've killed the general."

With a wild, incoherent yell, he charged blindly upon the blasting fury of the gun and collapsed in blasted ruin.

The trade ship was rising above a dead planet before the signal lights began their eerie blink and against the creamy cobweb of the great Lens in the sky which was the Galaxy, other black forms rose.

Devers said grimly, "Hold tight, Barr—and let's see if they've got a ship that can match my speed."

He knew they hadn't!

And once in open space, the trader's voice seemed lost and dead as he said, "The line I fed Brodrig was a little too good. It seems as if he's thrown in with the general."

Swiftly they raced into the depths of the star-mass that was the Galaxy.

8. To Trantor

DEVERS bent over the little dead globe, watching for a tiny sign of life. The directional control was slowly and thoroughly sieving space with its jabbing tight sheaf of signals.

Barr watched patiently from his seat on the low cot in the corner. He asked, "No more signs of them?"

"The Empire boys? No." The trader growled the words with evident impatience. "We lost the scuppers long ago. Space! With the blind jumps we took through hyperspace, it's lucky we didn't land up in a sun's belly. They couldn't have followed us even is they outranged us, which they didn't."

He sat back and loosened his collar with a jerk. "I don't know what those Empire boys have done here. I think some of the gaps are out of alignment."

"I take it, then, you're trying to get to the Foundation."

"I'm calling the Association—or trying to."

"The Association? Who are they?"

"Association of Independent Traders. Never heard of it, huh? Well, you're not alone. We haven't made our splash yet!"

For a while there was a silence that centered about the unresponsive Reception Indicator, and Barr said, "Are you within range?"

"I don't know. I haven't but a small notion where we are, going by dead reckoning. That's why I have to use directional control. It could take years, you know."

"Might it?"

Barr pointed; and Devers jumped and adjusted his earphones. Within the little murky sphere there was a tiny glowing whiteness.

For half an hour, Devers nursed the fragile, groping thread of communication that reached through hyperspace to connect two points that laggard light would take five hundred years to bind together.

Then he sat back, hopelessly. He looked up, and shoved the earphones back.

"Let's eat, doc. There's a needle-shower you can use if you want to, but go easy on the hot water."

He squatted before one of the cabinets that lined one wall and felt through the contents. "You're not a vegetarian, I hope?"

Barr said, "I'm omnivorous. But what about the Association. Have you lost them?"

"Looks so. It was extreme range, a little too extreme. Doesn't matter, though. I got all that counted."

He straightened, and placed the two metal containers upon the table. "Just give it five minutes, doc, then slit it open by pushing the contact. It'll be plate, food, and fork—sort of handy for when you're in a hurry, if you're not interested in such incidentals as napkins. I suppose you want to know what I got out of the Association."

"If it isn't a secret."

Devers shook his head. "Not to you. What Riose said was true."

"About the offer of tribute?"

"Uh-huh. They offered it, *and* had it refused. Things are bad. There's fighting in the outer suns of Loris."

"Loris is close to the Foundation?"

"Huh? Oh, you wouldn't know. It's one of the original Four Kingdoms. You might call it part of the inner line of defense. That's not the worst. They've been fighting large ships previously never encountered. Which means Riose wasn't giving us the works. He *has* received more ships. Brodrig *has* switched sides, and I *have* messed things up."

His eyes were bleak as he joined the food-container contact-points and watched it fall open neatly. The stewlike dish steamed its aroma through the room. Ducem Barr was already eating.

"So much," said Barr, "for improvisations, then. We can do nothing here; we can not cut through the Imperial lines to return to the Foundation; we can do nothing but that which is most sensible—to wait patiently. However, if Riose has reached the inner line I trust the wait will not be too long."

And Devers put down his fork. "Wait, is it?" he snarled, glowering. "That's all right for *you*. You've got nothing at stake."

"Haven't I?" Barr smiled thinly.

"No. In fact, I'll tell you." Devers' irritation skimmed the surface. "I'm tired of looking at this whole business as if it were an interesting something-or-other on a microscope slide. I've got friends somewhere out there, dying; and a whole world out there, my home, dying also. You're an outsider. You don't know."

"I have seen friends die." The old man's hands were limp in his lap and his eyes were closed. "Are you married?"

Devers said, "Traders don't marry."

"Well, I have two sons and a nephew. They have been warned, but—for reasons—they could take no action. Our escape means their death. My daughter and my two grand-children have, I hope, left the planet safely before this, but even excluding them, I have already risked and lost more than you."

Devers was morosely savage. "I know. But that was a matter of choice. You might have played ball with Riose. I never asked you to—"

Barr shook his head. "It was not a matter of choice, Devers. Make your conscience free; I didn't risk my sons for you. I cooperated with Riose as long as I dared. But there was the Psychic Probe."

The Siwennian patrician opened his eyes and they were sharp with pain. "Riose came to me once; it was over a year ago. He spoke of a cult centering about the magicians, but missed the truth. It is not quite a cult. You see, it is forty years now that Siwenna has been gripped in the same unbearable vise that threatens your world. Five revolts have been ground out. Then I discovered the ancient records of Hari Seldon—and now this 'cult' waits.

"It waits for the coming of the 'magicians' and for that day it is ready. My sons are leaders of those who wait. It is *that* secret which is in my mind and which the Probe must never touch. And so they must die as hostages; for the alternative is their death as rebels and half of Siwenna with them. You see, I had no choice! And I am no outsider."

Devers' eyes fell, and Barr continued softly, "It is on a Foundation victory that Siwenna's hopes depend. It is for a Foundation victory that my sons are sacrificed. And Hari

66

Seldon does not pre-calculate the inevitable salvation of Siwenna as he does that of the Foundation. I have no certainty for *my* people—only hope."

"But you are still satisfied to wait. Even with the Imperial Navy at Loris."

"I would wait, in perfect confidence," said Barr, simply, "if they had landed on the planet, Terminus, itself."

The trader frowned hopelessly. "I don't know. It can't really work like that; not just like magic. Psycho-history or not, they're terribly strong, and we're weak. What can Seldon do about it?"

"There's nothing to *do*. It's all already *done*. It's proceeding now. Because you don't hear the wheels turning and the gongs beating doesn't mean it's any the less certain."

"Maybe; but I wish you had cracked Riose's skull for keeps. He's more the enemy than all his army."

"Cracked his skull? With Brodrig his second in command?" Barr's face sharpened with hate. "All Siwenna would have been my hostage. Brodrig has proven his worth long since. There exists a world which five years ago lost one male in every ten—and simply for failure to meet outstanding taxes. This same Brodrig was the tax-collector. No, Riose may live. His punishments are mercy in comparison."

"But six months, *six months,* in the enemy Base, with nothing to show for it." Devers' strong hands clasped each other tautly, so that his knuckles cracked "Nothing to show for it!"

"Well, now, wait. You remind me—" Barr fumbled in his pouch. "You might want to count this." And he tossed the small sphere of metal on the table.

Devers snatched it. "What is it?"

"The message capsule. The one that Riose received just before I jacked him. Does that count as something?"

"I don't know. Depends on what's in it!" Devers sat down and turned it over carefully in his hand.

When Barr stepped from his cold shower and, gratefully, into the mild warm current of the air dryer, he found Devers silent and absorbed at the workbench.

The Siwennian slapped his body with a sharp rhythm and spoke above the punctuating sounds. "What are you doing?"

Devers looked up. Droplets of perspiration glittered in his beard. "I'm going to open this capsule."

"*Can* you open it without Riose's personal characteristic?"

There was mild surprise in the Siwennian's voice.

"If I can't, I'll resign from the Association and never skipper a ship for what's left of my life. I've got a three-way electronic analysis of the interior now, and I've got little jiggers that the Empire never heard of, especially made for jimmying capsules. I've been a burgler before this, y'know. A trader has to be something of everything."

He bent low over the little sphere, and a small flat instrument probed delicately and sparked redly at each fleeting contact.

He said, "This capsule is a crude job, anyway. These Imperial boys are no shakes at this small work. I can see that. Ever see a Foundation capsule? It's half the size and impervious to electronic analysis in the first place."

And then he was rigid, the shoulder muscles beneath his tunic tautening visibly. His tiny probe pressed slowly—

It was noiseless when it came, but Devers relaxed and sighed. In his hand was the shining sphere with its message unrolled like a parchment tongue.

"It's from Brodrig," he said. Then, with contempt, "The message medium is permanent. In a Foundation capsule, the message would be oxidized to gas within the minute."

But Ducem Barr waved him silent. He read the message quickly.

FROM: AMMEL BRODRIG, ENVOY EXTRAORDINARY OF HIS IMPERIAL MAJESTY, PRIVY SECRETARY OF THE COUNCIL, AND PEER OF THE REALM.
TO: BEL RIOSE, MILITARY GOVERNOR OF SIWENNA, GENERAL OF THE IMPERIAL FORCES, AND PEER OF THE REALM, I GREET YOU.
PLANET #1120 NO LONGER RESISTS. THE PLANS OF OFFENSE AS OUTLINED CONTINUE SMOOTHLY. THE ENEMY WEAKENS VISIBLY AND THE ULTIMATE ENDS IN VIEW WILL SURELY BE GAINED.

Barr raised his head from the almost microscopic print and cried bitterly, "The fool! The forsaken blasted fop! *That* a message?"

"Huh?" said Devers. He was vaguely disappointed.

"It says nothing," ground out Barr. "Our lick-spittle courtier is playing at general now. With Riose away, he is the field commander and must soothe his paltry spirit by

68

spewing out his pompous reports concerning military affairs he has nothing to do with. 'So-and-so planet no longer resists.' 'The offensive moves on.' 'The enemy weakens.' The vacuum-headed peacock."

"Well, now, wait a minute. Hold on—"

"Throw it away." The old man turned away in mortification. "The Galaxy knows I never expected it to be world-shakingly important, but in wartime it is reasonable to assume that even the most routine order left undelivered might hamper military movements and lead to complications later. It's why I snatched it. But this! Better to have left it. It would have wasted a minute of Riose's time that will now be put to more constructive use."

But Devers had arisen. "Will you hold on and stop throwing your weight around? For Seldon's sake—"

He held out the sliver of message before Barr's nose, "Now read that again. What does he mean by 'ultimate ends in view'?"

"The conquest of the Foundation. Well?"

"Yes? And maybe he means the conquest of the Empire. You know he *believes* that to be the ultimate end."

"And if he does?"

"If he does!" Devers' one-sided smile was lost in his beard. "Why, watch them, and I'll show you."

With one finger the lavishly monogrammed sheet of message-parchment was thrust back into its slot. With a soft twang, it disappeared and the globe was a smooth, unbroken whole again. Somewhere inside was the tiny oiled whir of the controls as they lost their setting by random movements.

"Now there is no known way of opening this capsule without knowledge of Riose's personal characteristic, is there?"

"To the Empire, no," said Barr.

"Then the evidence it contains is unknown to us and absolutely authentic."

"To the Empire, yes," said Barr.

"And the Emperor can open it, can't he? Personal Characteristics of Government officials must be on file. They are at the Foundation."

"At the Imperial capital as well," agreed Barr.

"Then when you, a Siwennian patrician and Peer of the Realm, tell this Cleon, this Emperor, that his favorite tame-parrot and his shiniest general are getting together to knock

69

him over, and hand him the capsule as evidence, what will *he* think Brodrig's 'ultimate ends' are?"

Barr sat down weakly. "Wait, I don't follow you." He stroked one thin cheek, and said, "You're not really serious, are you?"

"I am." Devers was angrily excited. "Listen, nine out of the last ten Emperors got their throats cut, or their gizzards blasted out by one or another of their generals with big-time notions in their heads. You told me that yourself more than once. Old man Emperor would believe us so fast it would make Riose's head swim."

Barr muttered feebly, "He *is* serious. For the Galaxy's sake, man, you can't beat a Seldon crisis by a far-fetched, impractical, storybook scheme like that. Suppose you had never got hold of the capsule. Suppose Brodrig hadn't used the word 'ultimate.' Seldon doesn't depend on wild luck."

"If wild luck comes our way, there's no law says Seldon can't take advantage of it."

"Certainly. But . . . but," Barr stopped, then spoke calmly but with visible retraint. "Look, in the first place, how will you get to the planet Trantor? You don't know its location in space, and I certainly don't remember the co-ordinates, to say nothing of the ephemerae. You don't even know your own position in space."

"You can't get lost in space," grinned Devers. He was at the controls already. "Down we go to the nearest planet, and back we come with complete bearings and the best navigation charts Brodrig's hundred thousand smackers can buy."

"*And* a blaster in our belly. Our descriptions are probably in every planet in this quarter of the Empire."

"Doc," said Devers, patiently, "don't be a hick from the sticks. Riose said my ship surrendered too easily and, brother, he wasn't kidding. This ship has enough fire-power and enough juice in its shield to hold off anything we're likely to meet this deep inside the frontier. And we have personal shields, too. The Empire boys never found them, you know, but they weren't meant to be found."

"All right," said Barr, "all right. Suppose yourself on Trantor. How do you see the Emperor then? You think he keeps office hours?"

"Suppose we worry about that on Trantor," said Devers.

And Barr muttered helplessly, "All right again. I've wanted

to see Trantor before I die for half a century now. Have your way."

The hyperatomic motor was cut in. The lights flickered and there was the slight internal wrench that marked the shift into hyperspace.

9. On Trantor

THE STARS were as thick as weeds in an unkempt field, and for the first time, Lathan Devers found the figures to the right of the decimal point of prime importance in calculating the cuts through the hyper-regions. There was a claustrophobic sensation about the necessity for leaps of not more than a light-year. There was a frightening harshness about the sky which glittered unbrokenly in every direction. It was being lost in a sea of radiation.

And in the center of a cluster of ten thousand stars, whose light tore to shreds the feebly encircling darkness, there circled the huge Imperial planet, Trantor.

But it was more than a planet; it was the living pulse beat of an Empire of twenty million stellar systems. It had only one function, administration; one purpose, government; and one manufactured product, law.

The entire world was one functional distortion. There was no living object on its surface but man, his pets, and his parasites. No blade of grass or fragment of uncovered soil could be found outside the hundred square miles of the Imperial Palace. No water outside the Palace grounds existed but in the vast underground cisterns that held the water supply of a world.

The lustrous, indestructible, incorruptible metal that was the unbroken surface of the planet was the foundation of the huge, metal structures that mazed the planet. They were structures connected by causeways; laced by corridors; cubbyholed by offices; basemented by the huge retail centers that covered square miles; penthoused by the glittering amusement world that sparkled into life each night.

One could walk around the world of Trantor and never

leave that one conglomerate building, nor see the city.

A fleet of ships greater in number than all the war fleets the Empire had ever supported landed their cargoes on Trantor each day to feed the forty billions of humans who gave nothing in exchange but the fulfillment of the necessity of untangling the myriads of threads that spiraled into the central administration of the most complex government Humanity had ever known.

Twenty agricultural worlds were the granary of Trantor. A universe was its servant—

Tightly held by the huge metal arms on either side, the trade ship was gently lowered down the huge ramp that led to the hangar. Already Devers had fumed his way through the manifold complications of a world conceived in paper work and dedicated to the principle of the form-in-quadruplicate.

There had been the preliminary halt in space, where the first of what had grown into a hundred questionnaires had been filled out. There were the hundred cross-examinations, the routine administration of a simple Probe, the photographing of the ship, the Characteristic-Analysis of the two men, and the subsequent recording of the same, the search for contraband, the payment of the entry tax—and finally the question of the identity cards and visitor's visa.

Ducem Barr was a Siwennian and subject of the Emperor, but Lathan Devers was an unknown without the requisite documents. The official in charge at the moment was devastated with sorrow, but Devers could not enter. In fact, he would have to be held for official investigation.

From somewhere a hundred credits in crisp, new bills backed by the estates of Lord Brodrig made their appearance, and changed hands quietly. The official hemmed importantly and the devastation of his sorrow was assuaged. A new form made its appearance from the appropriate pigeonhole. It was filled out rapidly and efficiently, with the Devers characteristic thereto formally and properly attached.

The two men, trader and patrician, entered Siwenna.

In the hangar, the trade ship was another vessel to be cached, photographed, recorded, contents noted, identity cards of passengers facsimiled, and for which a suitable fee was paid, recorded, and receipted.

And then Devers was on a huge terrace under the bright

white sun, along which women chattered, children shrieked, and men sipped drinks languidly and listened to the huge televisors blaring out the news of the Empire.

Barr paid a requisite number of iridium coins and appropriated the uppermost member of a pile of newspapers. It was the Trantor *Imperial News*, official organ of the government. In the back of the news room, there was the soft clicking noise of additional editions being printed in long-distance sympathy with the busy machines at the *Imperial News* offices ten thousand miles away by corridor—six thousand by air-machine—just as ten million sets of copies were being likewise printed at that moment in ten million other news rooms all over the planet.

Barr glanced at the headlines and said softly, "What shall we do first?"

Devers tried to shake himself out of his depression. He was in a universe far removed from his own, on a world that weighed him down with its intricacy, among people whose doings were incomprehensible and whose language was nearly so. The gleaming metallic towers that surrounded him and continued onwards in never-ending multiplicity to beyond the horizon oppressed him; the whole busy, unheeding life of a world-metropolis cast him into the horrible gloom of isolation and pygmyish unimportance.

He said, "I better leave it to you, doc."

Barr was calm, low-voiced. "I tried to tell you, but it's hard to believe without seeing for yourself, I know that. Do you know how many people want to see the Emperor every day? About one million. Do you know how many he sees? About ten. We'll have to work through the civil service, and that makes it harder. But we can't afford the aristocracy."

"We have almost one hundred thousand."

"A single Peer of the Realm would cost us that, and it would take at least three or four to form an adequate bridge to the Emperor. It may take fifty chief commissioners and senior supervisors to do the same, but they would cost us only a hundred apiece perhaps. I'll do the talking. In the first place, they wouldn't understand your accent, and in the second, you don't know the etiquette of Imperial bribery. It's an art, I assure you. Ah!"

The third page of the *Imperial News* had what he wanted and he passed the paper to Devers.

Devers read slowly. The vocabulary was strange, but he understood. He looked up, and his eyes were dark with concern. He slapped the news sheet angrily with the back of his hand. "You think this can be trusted?"

"Within limits," replied Barr, calmly. "It's highly improbable that the Foundation fleet was wiped out. They've probably reported *that* several times already, if they've gone by the usual war-reporting technique of a world capital far from the actual scene of fighting. What it means, though, is that Riose has won another battle, which would be none-too-unexpected. It says he's captured Loris. Is that the capital planet of the Kingdom of Loris?"

"Yes," brooded Devers, "or of what used to be the Kingdom of Loris. And it's not twenty parsecs from the Foundation. Doc, we've got to work fast."

Barr shrugged. "You can't go fast on Trantor. If you try, you'll end up at the point of an atom-blaster, most likely."

"How long will it take?"

"A month, if we're lucky. A month, and our hundred thousand credits—if even that will suffice. And that is providing the Emperor does not take it into his head in the meantime to travel to the Summer Planets, where he sees no petitioners at all."

"But the Foundation—"

"—Will take care of itself, as heretofore. Come, there's the question of dinner. I'm hungry. And afterwards, the evening is ours and we may as well use it. We shall never see Trantor or any world like it again, you know."

The Home Commissioner of the Outer Provinces spread his pudgy hands helplessly and peered at the petitioners with owlish nearsightedness. "But the Emperor is indisposed, gentlemen. It is really useless to take the matter to my superior. His Imperial Majesty has seen no one in a week."

"He will see us," said Barr, with an affectation of confidence. "It is but a question of seeing a member of the staff of the Privy Secretary."

"Impossible," said the commissioner emphatically. "It would be the worth of my job to attempt that. Now if you could but be more explicit concerning the nature of your business. I'm willing to help you, understand, but naturally I want something less vague, something I can present to my superior as reason for taking the matter further."

"If my business were such that it could be told to any but the highest," suggested Barr, smoothly, "it would

75

scarcely be important enough to rate audience with His Imperial Majesty. I propose that you take a chance. I might remind you that if His Imperial Majesty attaches the importance to our business which we guarantee that he will, you will stand certain to receive the honors you will deserve for helping us now."

"Yes, but—" and the commissioner shrugged, wordlessly.

"It's a chance," agreed Barr. "Naturally, a risk should have its compensation. It is a rather great favor to ask you, but we have already been greatly obliged with your kindness in offering us this opportunity to explain our problem. But if you would *allow* us to express our gratitude just slightly by—"

Devers scowled. He had heard this speech with its slight variations twenty times in the past month. It ended, as always, in a quick shift of the half-hidden bills. But the epilogue differed here. Usually the bills vanished immediately; here they remained in plain view, while slowly the commissioner counted them, inspecting them front and back as he did so.

There was a subtle change in his voice. "Backed by the Privy Secretary, hey? Good money!"

"To get back to the subject—" urged Barr.

"No, but wait," interrupted the commissioner, "let us go back by easy stages. I really do wish to know what your business can be. This money, it is fresh and new, and you must have a good deal, for it strikes me that you have seen other officials before me. Come, now, what about it?"

Barr said, "I don't see what you are driving at."

"Why, see here, it might be proven that you are upon the planet illegally, since the Identification and Entry Cards of your silent friend are certainly inadequate. He is not a subject of the Emperor."

"I deny that."

"It doesn't matter that you do," said the commissioner, with sudden bluntness. "The official who signed his Cards for the sum of a hundred credits has confessed—under pressure —and we know more of you than you think."

"If you are hinting, sire, that the sum we have asked you to accept is inadequate in view of the risks—"

The commissioner smiled. "On the contrary, it is more than adequate." He tossed the bills aside. "To return to what I was saying, it is the Emperor himself who has become interested in your case. Is it not true, sirs, that you have recently been guests of General Riose? Is it not true that you have escaped from the midst of his army with, to put it mildly, astonishing ease? Is it not true that you possess a small fortune in bills backed by Lord Brodrig's estates? In short, is it not true that you are a pair of spies and assassins sent here to— Well, you shall tell us yourself who paid you and for what!"

"Do you know," said Barr, with silky anger, "I deny the right of a petty commissioner to accuse us of crimes. We will leave."

"You will not leave." The commissioner arose, and his eyes no longer seemed near-sighted. "You need answer no question now; that will be reserved for a later—and more forceful—time. Nor am I a commissioner; I am a Lieutenant of the Imperial Police. You are under arrest."

There was a glitteringly efficient blast-gun in his fist as he smiled. "There are greater men than you under arrest this day. It is a hornet's nest we are cleaning up."

Devers snarled and reached slowly for his own gun. The lieutenant of police smiled more broadly and squeezed the contacts. The blasting line of force struck Devers' chest in an accurate blaze of destruction—that bounced harmlessly off his personal shield in sparkling spicules of light.

Devers shot in turn, and the lieutenant's head fell from off an upper torso that had disappeared. It was still smiling as it lay in the jag of sunshine which entered through the new-made hole in the wall.

It was through the back entrance that they left.

Devers said huskily, "Quickly to the ship. They'll have the alarm out in no time." He cursed in a ferocious whisper. "It's another plan that's backfired. I could swear the space fiend himself is against me."

It was in the open that they became aware of the jabbering crowds that surrounded the huge televisors. They had no time to wait; the disconnected roaring words that reached them, they disregarded. But Barr snatched a copy of the *Imperial News* before diving into the huge barn of the hangar, where the ship lifted hastily through a giant cavity burnt fiercely into the roof.

"Can you get away from them?" asked Barr.

Ten ships of the traffic-police wildly followed the runaway craft that had burst out of the lawful, radio-beamed Path of

77

Leaving, and then broken every speed law in creation. Further behind still, sleek vessels of the Secret Service were lifting in pursuit of a carefully described ship manned by two thoroughly identified murderers.

"Watch me," said Devers, and savagely shifted into hyperspace two thousand miles above the surface of the Trantor. The shift, so near a planetary mass, meant unconsciousness for Barr and a fearful haze of pain for Devers, but light-years further, space about them was clear.

Devers' somber pride in his ship burst to the surface. He said, "There's not an Imperial ship that could follow me anywhere."

And then, bitterly, "But there is nowhere left to run to for us, and we can't fight their weight. What's there to do? What can anyone do?"

Barr moved feebly on his cot. The effect of the hypershift had not yet worn off, and each of his muscles ached. He said, "No one has to do anything. It's all over. Here!"

He passed the copy of the *Imperial News* that he still clutched, and the headlines were enough for the trader.

"Recalled and arrested—Riose and Brodrig," Devers muttered. He stared blankly at Barr. "Why?"

"The story doesn't say, but what does it matter? The war with the Foundation is over, and at this moment, Siwenna is revolting. Read the story and see." His voice was drifting off. "We'll stop in some of the provinces and find out the details later. If you don't mind, I'll go to sleep now."

And he did.

In grasshopper jumps of increasing magnitude, the trade ship was spanning the Galaxy in its return to the Foundation.

10. The War Ends

LATHAN DEVERS felt definitely uncomfortable, and vaguely resentful. He had received his own decoration and withstood with mute stoicism the turgid oratory of the mayor which accompanied the slip of crimson ribbon. That had ended his share of the ceremonies, but, naturally, formality forced him to remain. And it was formality, chiefly—the type that couldn't allow him to yawn noisily or to swing a foot comfortably onto a chair seat—that made him long to be in space, where he belonged.

The Siwennese delegation, with Ducem Barr a lionized member, signed the Convention, and Siwenna became the first province to pass directly from the Empire's political rule to the Foundation's economic one.

Five Imperial Ships of the Line—captured when Siwenna rebelled behind the lines of the Empire's Border Fleet—flashed overhead, huge and massive, detonating a roaring salute as they passed over the city.

Nothing but drinking, etiquette, and small talk now—

A voice called him. It was Forell; the man who, Devers realized coldly, could buy twenty of him with a morning's profits—but a Forell who now crooked a finger at him with genial condescension.

He stepped out upon the balcony into the cool night wind, and bowed properly, while scowling into his bristling beard. Barr was there, too; smiling. He said, "Devers, you'll have to come to my rescue. I'm being accused of modesty, a horrible and thoroughly unnatural crime."

"Devers," Forell removed the fat cigar from the side of his mouth when he spoke, "Lord Barr claims that your trip to Cleon's capital had nothing to do with the recall of Riose."

"Nothing at all, sir." Devers was curt. "We never saw the Emperor. The reports we picked up on our way back concerning the trial, showed it up to be the purest frame-up. There was a mess of rigmarole about the general being tied up with subversive interests at the court."

"And he was innocent?"

"Riose?" interposed Barr. "Yes! By the Galaxy, yes. Brodrig was a traitor on general principles but was never guilty of the specific accusations brought against him. It was a judicial farce; but a necessary one, a predictable one, an inevitable one."

"By psycho-historical necessity, I presume." Forell rolled the phrase sonorously with the humorous ease of long familiarity.

"Exactly." Barr grew serious. "It never penetrated earlier, but once it was over and I could . . . well . . . look at the answers in the back of the book, the problem became simple. We can see, *now*, that the social background of the Empire makes wars of conquest impossible for it. Under weak Emperors, it is torn apart by generals competing for a worthless and surely death-bringing throne. Under strong Emperors, the Empire is frozen into a paralytic rigor in which disintegration apparently ceases for the moment, but only at the sacrifice of all possible growth."

Forell growled bluntly through strong puffs, "You're not clear, Lord Barr."

Barr smiled slowly. "Mm, I suppose so. It's the difficulty of not being trained in psycho-history. Words are a pretty fuzzy substitute for mathematical equations. But let's see now—"

Barr considered, while Forell relaxed, back to railing, and Devers looked into the velvet sky and thought wonderingly of Trantor.

Then Barr said, "You see, sir, you—and Devers—and everyone no doubt, had the idea that beating the Empire meant first prying apart the Emperor and his general. You, and Devers, and everyone else were right—right all the time, as far as the principle of internal disunion was concerned.

"You were wrong, however, in thinking that this internal split was something to be brought about by individual acts, by inspirations of the moment. You tried bribery and lies. You appealed to ambition and to fear. But you got nothing for all your pains. In fact, appearances were worse after each attempt.

80

"And through all this wild threshing up of tiny ripples, the Seldon tidal wave continued onward, quietly—but quite irresistibly."

Ducem Barr turned away, and looked over the railing at the lights of a rejoicing city. He said, "There was a dead hand pushing all of us; the mighty general and the great Emperor; my world and your world—the dead hand of Hari Seldon. He knew that a man like Riose would have to fail, since it was his success that brought failure; and the greater the success, the surer the failure."

Forell said dryly, "I can't say you're getting clearer."

"A moment," continued Barr earnestly. "Look at the situation. A weak general could never have endangered us, obviously. A strong general during the time of a weak Emperor would never have endangered us, either; for he would have turned his arms towards a much more fruitful target. Events have shown that three-fourths of the Emperors of the last two centuries were rebel generals and rebel viceroys before they were Emperors.

"So it is only the combination of strong Emperor *and* strong general that can harm the Foundation; for a strong Emperor can not be dethroned easily, and a strong general is forced to turn outwards, past the frontiers.

"*But*, what keeps the Emperor strong? What kept Cleon strong? It's obvious. He is strong, because he permits no strong subjects. A courtier who becomes too rich, or a general who becomes too popular is dangerous. All the recent history of the Empire proves that to any Emperor intelligent enough to be strong.

"Riose won victories, so the Emperor grew suspicious. All the atmosphere of the times forced him to be suspicious. Did Riose refuse a bribe? Very suspicious; ulterior motives. Did his most trusted courtier suddenly favor Riose? Very suspicious; ulterior motives. It wasn't the individual acts that were suspicious. Anything else would have done—which is why our individual plots were unnecessary and rather futile. It was the *success* of Riose that was suspicious. So he was recalled, and accused, condemned, murdered. The Foundation wins again.

"Why, look, there is not a conceivable combination of events that does not result in the Foundation winning. It was inevitable; whatever Riose did, whatever we did."

The Foundation magnate nodded ponderously. "So! But

what if the Emperor and the general had been the same person. Hey? What then? That's a case you didn't cover, so you haven't proved your point yet."

Barr shrugged. "I can't *prove* anything; I haven't the mathematics. But I appeal to your reason. With an Empire in which every aristocrat, every strong man, every pirate can aspire to the Throne—and, as history shows, often successfully—what would happen to even a strong Emperor who preoccupied himself with foreign wars at the extreme end of the Galaxy? How long would he have to remain away from the capital before somebody raised the standards of civil war and forced him home. The social environment of the Empire would make that time short.

"I once told Riose that not all the Empire's strength could swerve the dead hand of Hari Seldon."

"Good! Good!" Forell was expansively pleased. "Then you imply the Empire can never threaten us again."

"It seems to me so," agreed Barr. "Frankly, Cleon may not live out the year, and there's going to be a disputed succession almost as a matter of course, which might mean the *last* civil war for the Empire."

"Then," said Forell, "there are no more enemies."

Barr was thoughtful. "There's a Second Foundation."

"At the other end of the Galaxy? Not for centuries."

Devers turned suddenly at this, and his face was dark as he faced Forell. "There are internal enemies, perhaps."

"Are there?" asked Forell, coolly. "Who, for instance?"

"People, for instance, who might like to spread the wealth a bit, and keep it from concentrating too much *out* of the hands that work for it. See what I mean?"

Slowly, Forell's gaze lost its contempt and grew one with the anger of Devers' own.

Part II   The Mule

11. Bride and Groom

THE MULE. Less is known of "The Mule" than of any character of comparable significance to Galactic history. His real name is unknown; his early life mere conjecture. Even the period of his greatest renown is known to us chiefly through the eyes of his antagonists and, principally, through those of a young bride. . . .

—Encyclopedia Galactica

BAYTA'S first sight of Haven was entirely the contrary of spectacular. Her husband pointed it out—a dull star lost in the emptiness of the Galaxy's edge. It was past the last sparse clusters, to where straggling points of light gleamed lonely. And even among these it was poor and inconspicuous.

Toran was quite aware that as the earliest prelude to married life, the Red Dwarf lacked impressiveness and his lips curled self-consciously. "I know, Bay— It isn't exactly a proper change, is it? I mean from the Foundation to this."

"A horrible change, Toran. I should never have married you."

And when his face looked momentarily hurt, before he caught himself, she said with her special "cozy" tone, "All right, silly. Now let your lower lip droop and give me that special dying-duck look—the one just before you're supposed to bury your head on my shoulder, while I stroke your hair full of static electricity. You were fishing for some drivel, weren't you? You were expecting me to say 'I'd be happy anywhere with you, Toran!' or 'The interstellar depths themselves would be home, my sweet, were you but with me!' Now you admit it."

She pointed a finger at him and snatched it away an instant before his teeth closed upon it.

He said, "If I surrender, and admit you're right, will you prepare dinner?"

She nodded contentedly. He smiled, and just looked at her.

She wasn't beautiful on the grand scale to others—he admitted that—even if everybody did look twice. Her hair was dark and glossy, though straight, her mouth a bit wide— but her meticulous, close-textured eyebrows separated a white, unlined forehead from the warmest mahogany eyes ever filled with smiles.

And behind a very sturdily-built and staunchly-defended facade of practical, unromantic, hard-headedness towards life, there was just that little pool of softness that would never show if you poked for it, but could be reached if you knew just how—and never let on that you were looking for it.

Toran adjusted the controls unnecessarily and decided to relax. He was one interstellar jump, and then several milli-microparasecs "on the straight" before manipulation by hand was necessary. He leaned over backwards to look into the storeroom, where Bayta was juggling appropriate containers.

There was quite a bit of smugness about his attitude towards Bayta—the satisfied awe that marks the triumph of someone who has been hovering at the edge of an inferiority complex for three years.

After all he was a provincial—and not merely a provincial, but the son of a renegade Trader. And she was of the Foundation itself—and not merely that, but she could trace her ancestry back to Mallow.

And with all that, a tiny quiver underneath. To take her back to Haven, with its rock-world and cave-cities was bad enough. To have her face the traditional hostility of Trader for Foundation—nomad for city dweller—was worse.

Still— After supper, the last jump!

Haven was an angry crimson blaze, and the second planet was a ruddy patch of light with atmosphere-blurred rim and a half-sphere of darkness. Bayta leaned over the large view-table with its spidering of crisscross lines that centered Haven II neatly.

She said gravely, "I wish I had met your father first. If he takes a dislike to me—"

"Then," said Toran matter-of-factly, "you would be the first pretty girl to inspire *that* in him. Before he lost his arm and stopped roving around the Galaxy, he— Well, if you ask him about it, he'll talk to you about it till your ears wear down to a nubbin. After a while I got to thinking that he was embroidering; because he never told the same story twice the same way—"

Haven II was rushing up at them now. The landlocked sea wheeled ponderously below them, slate-gray in the lowering dimness and lost to sight, here and there, among the wispy clouds. Mountains jutted raggedly along the coast.

The sea became wrinkled with nearness and, as it veered off past the horizon just at the end, there was one vanishing glimpse of shore-hugging ice fields.

Toran grunted under the fierce deceleration, "Is your suit locked?"

Bayta's plump face was round and ruddy in the incasing sponge-foam of the internally-heated, skin-clinging costume.

The ship lowered crunchingly on the open field just short of the lifting of the plateau.

They climbed out awkwardly into the solid darkness of the outer-galactic night, and Bayta gasped as the sudden cold bit, and the thin wind swirled emptily. Toran seized her elbow and nudged her into an awkward run over the smooth, packed ground towards the sparking of artificial light in the distance.

The advancing guards met them halfway, and after a whispered exchange of words, they were taken onward. The wind and the cold disappeared when the gate of rock opened and then closed behind them. The warm interior, white with wall-light, was filled with an incongruous humming bustle. Men looked up from their desks, and Toran produced documents.

They were waved onward after a short glance and Toran whispered to his wife, "Dad must have fixed up the preliminaries. The usual lapse here is about five hours."

They burst into the open and Bayta said suddenly, "Oh, *my*—"

The cave city was in daylight—the white daylight of a young sun. Not that there was a sun, of course. What should have been the sky was lost in the unfocused glow of an over-all brilliance. And the warm air was properly thick and fragrant with greenery.

Bayta said, "Why, Toran, it's beautiful."

Toran grinned with anxious delight. "Well, now, Bay, it isn't like anything on the Foundation, of course, but it's the biggest city on Haven II—twenty thousand people, you know—and you'll get to like it. No amusement palaces, I'm afraid, but no secret police either."

"Oh, Torie, it's just like a toy city. It's all white and pink—and so clean."

"Well—" Toran looked at the city with her. The houses were two stories high for the most part, and of the smooth vein rock indigenous to the region. The spires of the Foundation were missing, and the colossal community houses of the Old Kingdoms—but the smallness was there and the individuality; a relic of personal initiative in a Galaxy of mass life.

He snapped to sudden attention. "Bay— There's Dad! Right there—where I'm pointing, silly. Don't you see him?"

She did. It was just the impression of a large man, waving frantically, fingers spread wide as though groping wildly in air. The deep thunder of a drawn-out shout reached them. Bayta trailed her husband, rushing downwards over the close-cropped lawn. She caught sight of a smaller man, white-haired, almost lost to view behind the robust One-arm, who still waved and still shouted.

Toran cried over his shoulder, "It's my father's half brother. The one who's been to the Foundation. You know."

They met in the grass, laughing and incoherent, and Toran's father let out a final whoop for sheer joy. He hitched at his short jacket and adjusted the metal-chased belt that was his one concession to luxury.

His eyes shifted from one of the youngsters to the other, and then he said, a little out of breath, "You picked a rotten day to return home, boy!"

"What? Oh, it *is* Seldon's birthday, isn't it?"

"It is. I had to rent a car to make the trip here, and dragoon Randu to drive it. Not a public vehicle to be had at gun's point."

His eyes were on Bayta now, and didn't leave. He spoke to her more softly, "I have the crystal of you right here—and it's good, but I can see the fellow who took it was an amateur."

86

He had the small cube of transparency out of his jacket pocket and in the light the laughing little face within sprang to vivid colored life as a miniature Bayta.

"That one!" said Bayta. "Now I wonder why Toran should send that caricature. I'm surprised you let me come near you, sir."

"Are you now? Call me Fran. I'll have none of this fancy mess. For that, I think you can take my arm, and we'll go on to the car. Till now I never did think my boy knew what he was ever up to. I think I'll change that opinion. I think I'll *have* to change that opinion."

Toran said to his half uncle softly, "How is the old man these days? Does he still hound the women?"

Randu puckered up all over his face when he smiled. "When he can, Toran, when he can. There are times when he remembers that his next birthday will be his sixtieth, and that disheartens him. But he shouts it down, this evil thought, and then he is himself. He is a Trader of the ancient type. But you, Toran. Where did you find such a pretty wife?"

The young man chuckled and linked arms. "Do you want a three years' history at a gasp, uncle?"

It was in the small living room of the home that Bayta struggled out of her traveling cloak and hood and shook her hair loose. She sat down, crossing her knees, and returned the appreciative stare of this large, ruddy man.

She said, "I know what you're trying to estimate, and I'll help you; Age, twenty-four, height, five-four, weight, one-ten, educational specialty, history." She noticed that he always crooked his stand so as to hide the missing arm.

But now Fran leaned close and said, "Since you mention it—weight, one-twenty."

He laughed loudly at her flush. Then he said to the company in general, "You can always tell a woman's weight by her upper arm—with due experience, of course. Do you want a drink, Bay?"

"Among other things," she said, and they left together, while Toran busied himself at the book shelves to check for new additions.

Fran returned alone and said, "She'll be down later."

He lowered himself heavily into the large corner chair and placed his stiff-jointed left leg on the stool before it. The laughter had left his red face, and Toran turned to face him.

87

Fran said, "Well, you're home, boy, and I'm glad you are. I like your woman. She's no whining ninny."

"I married her," said Toran simply.

"Well, that's another thing altogether, boy." His eyes darkened. "It's a foolish way to tie up the future. In my longer life, and more experienced, I never did such a thing."

Randu interrupted from the corner where he stood quietly. "Now Franssart, what comparisons are you making? Till your crash landing six years ago you were never in one spot long enough to establish residence requirements for marriage. And since then, who would have you?"

The one-armed man jerked erect in his seat and replied hotly, "Many, you snowy dotard—"

Toran said with hasty tact, "It's largely a legal formality, Dad. The situation has its conveniences."

"Mostly for the woman," grumbled Fran.

"And even if so," argued Randu, "it's up to the boy to decide. Marriage is an old custom among the Foundationers."

"The Foundationers are not fit models for an honest Trader," smoldered Fran.

Toran broke in again, "My wife is a Foundationer." He looked from one to the other, and then said quietly, "She's coming."

The conversation took a general turn after the evening meal, which Fran had spiced with three tales of reminiscence composed of equal parts of blood, women, profits, and embroidery. The small televisor was on, and some classic drama was playing itself out in an unregarded whisper. Randu had hitched himself into a more comfortable position on the low couch and gazed past the slow smoke of his long pipe to where Bayta had knelt down upon the softness of the white fur mat brought back once long ago from a trade mission and now spread out only upon the most ceremonious occasions.

"You have studied history, my girl?" he asked, pleasantly.

Bayta nodded. "I was the despair of my teachers, but I learned a bit, eventually."

"A citation for scholarship," put in Toran, smugly, "that's all!"

"And what did you learn?" proceeded Randu, smoothly.

"Everything? Now?" laughed the girl.

The old man smiled gently. "Well then, what do you think of the Galactic situation?"

"I think," said Bayta, concisely, "that a Seldon crisis is pending—and that if it isn't then away with the Seldon plan altogether. It is a failure."

(*"Whew,"* muttered Fran, from his corner. "What a way to speak of Seldon." But he said nothing aloud.)

Randu sucked at his pipe speculatively. "Indeed? Why do you say that? I was to the Foundation, you know, in my younger days, and I, too, once thought great dramatic thoughts. But, now, why do you say that?"

"Well," Bayta's eyes misted with thought as she curled her bare toes into the white softness of the rug and nestled her little chin in one plump hand, "it seems to me that the whole essence of Seldon's plan was to create a world better than the ancient one of the Galactic Empire. It was falling apart, that world, three centuries ago, when Seldon first established the Foundation—and if history speaks truly, it was falling apart of the triple disease of inertia, despotism, and maldistribution of the goods of the universe."

Randu nodded slowly, while Toran gazed with proud, luminous eyes at his wife, and Fran in the corner clucked his tongue and carefully refilled his glass.

Bayta said, "If the story of Seldon is true, he foresaw the complete collapse of the Empire through his laws of psycho-history, and was able to predict the necessary thirty thousand years of barbarism before the establishment of a new Second Empire to restore civilization and culture to humanity. It was the whole aim of his life-work to set up such conditions as would insure a speedier rejuvenation."

The deep voice of Fran burst out, "And that's why he established the two Foundations, honor be to his name."

"And that's why he established the two Foundations," assented Bayta. "Our Foundation was a gathering of the scientists of the dying Empire intended to carry on the science and learning of man to new heights. And the Foundation was so situated in space and the historical environment was such that through the careful calculations of his genius, Seldon foresaw that in one thousand years, it would become a newer, greater Empire."

There was a reverent silence.

The girl said softly, "It's an old story. You all know it. For almost three centuries every human being of the Foundation has known it. But I thought it would be appropriate to go through it—just quickly. Today *is* Seldon's birthday, you know, and even if I *am* of the Foundation, and you are of Haven, we have that in common—"

She lit a cigarette slowly, and watched the glowing tip absently. "The laws of history are as absolute as the laws of physics, and if the probabilities of error are greater, it is only because history does not deal with as many humans as physics does atoms, so that individual variations count for more. Seldon predicted a series of crises through the thousand years of growth, each of which would force a new turning of our history into a pre-calculated path. It is those crises which direct us—and therefore a crisis must come now.

"Now!" she repeated, forcefully. "It's almost a century since the last one, and in that century, every vice of the Empire has been repeated in the Foundation. Inertia! Our ruling class knows one law; no change. Despotism! They know one rule; force. Maldistribution! They know one desire; to hold what is theirs."

"While others starve!" roared Fran suddenly with a mighty blow of his fist upon the arm of his chair. "Girl, your words are pearls. The fat guts on their moneybags ruin the Foundation, while the brave Traders hide their poverty on dregs of worlds like Haven. It's a disgrace to Seldon, a casting of dirt in his face, a spewing in his beard." He raised his arm high, and then his face lengthened. "If I had my other arm! If—once—they had listened to me!"

"Dad," said Toran, "take it easy."

"Take it easy. Take it easy," his father mimicked savagely. "We'll live here and die here forever—and you say, take it easy."

"That's our modern Lathan Devers," said Randu, gesturing with his pipe, "this Fran of ours. Devers died in the slave mines eighty years ago with your husband's great-grandfather, because he lacked wisdom and didn't lack heart—"

"Yes, by the Galaxy, I'd do the same if I were he," swore Fran. "Devers was the greatest Trader in history—greater than the overblown windbag, Mallow, the Foundationers worship. If the cutthroats who lord the Foundation killed him because he loved justice, the greater the blood-debt owed them."

"Go on, girl," said Randu. "Go on, or, surely, he'll talk all the night and rave all the next day."

"There's nothing to go on about," she said, with a sudden

gloom. "There must be a crisis, but I don't know how to make one. The progressive forces on the Foundation are oppressed fearfully. You Traders may have the will, but you are hunted and disunited. If all the forces of good will in and out of the Foundation could combine—"

Fran's laugh was a raucous jeer, "Listen to her, Randu, listen to her. In and out of the Foundation, she says. Girl, girl, there's no hope in the flab-sides of the Foundation. Among them some hold the whip and the rest are whipped —dead whipped. Not enough spunk left in the whole rotten world to outface one good Trader."

Bayta's attempted interruptions broke feebly against the overwhelming wind.

Toran leaned over and put a hand over her mouth. "Dad," he said, coldly, "you've never been on the Foundation. You know nothing about it. I tell you that the underground there is brave and daring enough. I could tell you that Bayta was one of them—"

"All right, boy, no offense. Now, where's the cause for anger?" He was genuinely perturbed.

Toran drove on fervently, "The trouble with you, Dad, is that you've got a provincial outlook. You think because some hundred thousand Traders scurry into holes on an unwanted planet at the end of nowhere, that they're a great people. Of course, any tax collector from the Foundation that gets here never leaves again, but that's cheap heroism. What would you do if the Foundation sent a fleet?"

"We'd blast them," said Fran, sharply.

"And get blasted—with the balance in their favor. You're outnumbered, outarmed, outorganized—and as soon as the Foundation thinks it worth its while, you'll realize that. So you had better seek your allies—on the Foundation itself, if you can."

"Randu," said Fran, looking at his brother like a great, helpless bull.

Randu took his pipe away from his lips, "The boy's right, Fran. When you listen to the little thoughts deep inside you, you know he is. But they're uncomfortable thoughts, so you drown them out with that roar of yours. But they're still there. Toran, I'll tell you why I brought all this up."

He puffed thoughtfully awhile, then dipped his pipe into the neck of the tray, waited for the silent flash, and withdrew

91

it clean. Slowly, he filled it again with precise tamps of his little finger.

He said, "Your little suggestion of Foundation's interest in us, Toran, is to the point. There have been two recent visits lately—for tax purposes. The disturbing point is that the second visitor was accompanied by a light patrol ship. They landed in Gleiar City—giving us the miss for a change —and they never lifted off again, naturally. But now they'll surely be back. Your father is aware of all this, Toran, he really is.

"Look at the stubborn rakehell. He knows Haven is in trouble, and he knows we're helpless, but he repeats his formulas. It warms and protects him. But once he's had his say, and roared his defiance, and feels he's discharged his duty as a man and a Bull Trader, why he's as reasonable as any of us."

"Any of who?" asked Bayta.

He smiled at her. "We've formed a little group, Bayta—just in our city. We haven't done anything, yet. We haven't even managed to contact the other cities yet, but it's a start."

"But towards what?"

Randu shook his head. "We don't know—yet. We hope for a miracle. We have decided that, as you say, a Seldon crisis must be at hand." He gestured widely upwards. "The Galaxy is full of the chips and splinters of the broken Empire. The generals swarm. Do you suppose the time may come when one will grow bold?"

Bayta considered, and shook her head decisively, so that the long straight hair with the single inward curl at the end swirled about her ears. "No, not a chance. There's not one of those generals who doesn't know that an attack on the Foundation is suicide. Bel Riose of the old Empire was a better man than any of them, and he attacked with the resources of a galaxy, and couldn't win against the Seldon Plan. Is there one general that doesn't know that?"

"But what if we spur them on?"

"Into where? Into an atomic furnace? With what could you possibly spur them?"

"Well, there is one—a new one. In this past year or two, there has come word of a strange man whom they call the Mule."

"The Mule?" She considered. "Ever hear of him, Torie?" Toran shook his head. She said, "What about him?"

"I don't know. But he wins victories at, they say, impossible odds. The rumors may be exaggerated, but it would be interesting, in any case, to become acquainted with him. Not every man with sufficient ability and sufficient ambition would believe in Hari Seldon and his laws of psycho-history. We could encourage that disbelief. He might attack."

"And the Foundation would win."

"Yes—but not necessarily easily. It might be a crisis, and we could take advantage of such a crisis to force a compromise with the despots of the Foundation. At the worst, they would forget us long enough to enable us to plan farther."

"What do you think, Torie?"

Toran smiled feebly and pulled at a loose brown curl that fell over one eye. "The way he describes it, it can't hurt; but who is the Mule? What do you know of him, Randu?"

"Nothing yet. For that, we could use you, Toran. And your wife, if she's willing. We've talked of this, your father and I. We've talked of this thoroughly."

"In what way, Randu? What do you want of us?" The young man cast a quick inquisitive look at his wife.

"Have you had a honeymoon?"

"Well . . . yes . . . if you call the trip from the Foundation a honeymoon."

"How about a better one on Kalgan? It's semitropical—beaches—water sports—bird hunting—quite the vacation spot. It's about seven thousand parsecs in—not too far."

"What's on Kalgan?"

"The Mule! His men, at least. He took it last month, and without a battle, though Kalgan's warlord broadcast a threat to blow the planet to ionic dust before giving it up."

"Where's the warlord now?"

"He isn't," said Randu, with a shrug. "What do you say?"

"But what are we to do?"

"I don't know. Fran and I are old; we're provincial. The Traders of Haven are all essentially provincial. Even you say so. Our trading is of a very restricted sort, and we're not the Galaxy roamers our ancestors were. Shut up, Fran! But you two know the Galaxy. Bayta, especially, speaks with a nice Foundation accent. We merely wish whatever you can find out. If you can make contact . . . but we wouldn't expect that. Suppose you two think it over. You can meet our entire group if you wish . . . oh, not before next

93

week. You ought to have some time to catch your breath."

There was a pause and then Fran roared, "Who wants another drink? I mean, besides me?"

12. Captain and Mayor

CAPTAIN HAN PRITCHER was unused to the luxury of his surroundings and by no means impressed. As a general thing, he discouraged self-analysis and all forms of philosophy and metaphysics not directly connected with his work.

It helped.

His work consisted largely of what the War Department called "intelligence," the sophisticates, "espionage," and the romanticists, "spy stuff." And, unfortunately, despite the frothy shrillness of the televisors, "intelligence," "espionage," and "spy stuff" are at best a sordid business of routine betrayed and bad faith. It is excused by society since it is in the "interest of the State," but since philosophy seemed always to lead Captain Pritcher to the conclusion that even in that holy interest, society is much more easily soothed than one's own conscience—he discouraged philosophy.

And now, in the luxury of the mayor's anteroom, his thoughts turned inward despite himself.

Men had been promoted over his head continuously, though of lesser ability—that much was admitted. He had withstood an eternal rain of black marks and official reprimands, and survived it. And stubbornly he had held to his own way in the firm belief that insubordination in that same holy "interest of the State" would yet be recognized for the service it was.

So here he was in the anteroom of the mayor—with five soldiers as a respectful guard, and probably a court-martial awaiting him.

The heavy, marble doors rolled apart smoothly, silently, revealing satiny walls, a red plastic carpeting, and two more marble doors, metal-inlaid, within. Two officials in the straight-lined costume of three centuries back, stepped out, and called:

"An audience to Captain Han Pritcher of Information."

They stepped back with a ceremonious bow as the captain started forward. His escort stopped at the outer door, and he entered the inner alone.

On the other side of the doors, in a large room strangely simple, behind a large desk strangely angular, sat a small man, almost lost in the immensity.

Mayor Indbur—successively the third of that name—was the grandson of the first Indbur, who had been brutal and capable; and who had exhibited the first quality in spectacular fashion by his manner of seizing power, and the latter by the skill with which he put an end to the last farcical remnants of free election and the even greater skill with which he maintained a relatively peaceful rule.

Mayor Indbur was also the son of the second Indbur, who was the first Mayor of the Foundation to succeed to his post by right of birth—and who was only half his father, for he was merely brutal.

So Mayor Indbur was the third of the name and the second to succeed by right of birth, and he was the least of the three, for he was neither brutal nor capable—but merely an excellent bookkeeper born wrong.

Indbur the Third was a peculiar combination of ersatz characteristics to all but himself.

To him, a stilted geometric love of arrangement was "system," an indefatigable and feverish interest in the pettiest facets of day-to-day bureaucracy was "industry," indecision when right was "caution," and blind stubbornness when wrong, "determination."

And withal he wasted no money, killed no man needlessly, and meant extremely well.

If Captain Pritcher's gloomy thoughts ran along these lines as he remained respectfully in place before the large desk, the wooden arrangement of his features yielded no insight into the fact. He neither coughed, shifted weight, nor shuffled his feet until the thin face of the mayor lifted slowly as the busy stylus ceased in its task of marginal notations, and a sheet of close-printed paper was lifted from one neat stack and placed upon another neat stack.

Mayor Indbur clasped his hands carefully before him, deliberately refraining from disturbing the careful arrangement of desk accessories.

He said, in acknowledgment, "Captain Han Pritcher of Information."

And Captain Pritcher in strict obedience to protocol bent one knee nearly to the ground and bowed his head until he heard the words of release.

"Arise, Captain Pritcher!"

The mayor said with an air of warm sympathy, "You are here, Captain Pritcher, because of certain disciplinary action taken against yourself by your superior officer. The papers concerning such action have come, in the ordinary course of events, to my notice, and since no event in the Foundation is of disinterest to me, I took the trouble to ask for further information on your case. You are not, I hope, surprised."

Captain Pritcher said unemotionally, "Excellence, no. Your justice is proverbial."

"Is it? Is it?" His tone was pleased, and the tinted contact lenses he wore caught the light in a manner that imparted a hard, dry gleam to his eyes. Meticulously, he fanned out a series of metal-bound folders before him. The parchment sheets within crackled sharply as he turned them, his long finger following down the line as he spoke.

"I have your record here, captain—complete. You are forty-three and have been an Officer of the Armed Forces for seventeen years. You were born in Loris, of Anacreonian parents, no serious childhood diseases, an attack of myo . . . well, that's of no importance . . . education, pre-military, at the Academy of Sciences, major, hyper-engines, academic standing . . . hm-m-m, very good, you are to be congratulated . . . entered the Army as Under-Officer on the one hundred second day of the 293rd year of the Foundation Era."

He lifted his eyes momentarily as he shifted the first folder, and opened the second.

"You see," he said, "in my administration, nothing is left to chance. Order! System!"

He lifted a pink, scented jelly-globule to his lips. It was his one vice, and but dolingly indulged in. Witness the fact that the mayor's desk lacked that almost-inevitable atom-

97

flash for the disposal of dead tobacco. For the mayor did not smoke.

Nor, as a matter of course, did his visitors.

The mayor's voice droned on, methodically, slurringly, mumblingly—now and then interspersed with whispered comments of equally mild and equally ineffectual commendation or reproof.

Slowly, he replaced the folders as originally, in a single neat pile.

"Well, captain," he said, briskly, "your record is unusual. Your ability is outstanding, it would seem, and your services valuable beyond question. I note that you have been wounded in the line of duty twice, and that you have been awarded the Order of Merit for bravery beyond the call of duty. Those are facts not lightly to be minimized."

Captain Pritcher's expressionless face did not soften. He remained stiffly erect. Protocol required that a subject honored by an audience with the mayor may not sit down—a point perhaps needlessly reinforced by the fact that only one chair existed in the room, the one underneath the mayor. Protocol further required no statements other than those needed to answer a direct question.

The mayor's eyes bore down hard upon the soldier and his voice grew pointed and heavy. "However, you have not been promoted in ten years, and your superiors report, over and over again, of the unbending stubbornness of your character. You are reported to be chronically insubordinate, incapable of maintaining a correct attitude towards superior officers, apparently uninterested in maintaining frictionless relationships with your colleagues, and an incurable troublemaker, besides. How do you explain that, captain?"

"Excellence, I do what seems right to me. My deeds on behalf of the State, and my wounds in that cause bear witness that what seems right to me is also in the interest of the State."

"A soldierly statement, captain, but a dangerous doctrine. More of that, later. Specifically, you are charged with refusing an assignment three times in the face of orders signed by my legal delegates. What have you to say to that?"

"Excellence, the assignment lacks significance in a critical time, where matters of first importance are being ignored."

"Ah, and who tells you these matters you speak of are of

98

the first importance at all, and if they are, who tells you further that they are ignored?"

"Excellence, these things are quite evident to me. My experience and my knowledge of events—the value of neither of which my superiors deny—make it plain."

"But, my good captain, are you blind that you do not see that by arrogating to yourself the right to determine Intelligence policy, you usurp the duties of your superior?"

"Excellence, my duty is primarily to the state, and not to my superior."

"Fallacious, for your superior has his superior, and that superior is myself, and I am the State. But come, you shall have no cause to complain of this justice of mine that you say is proverbial. State in your own words the nature of the breach in discipline that has brought all this on."

"Excellence, in the last year and a half I have been engaged in living the life of a retired merchant mariner upon the world of Kalgan. My instructions were to direct Foundation activity upon the planet, perfect an organization to act as check upon the warlord of Kalgan, particularly as regards his foreign policy."

"This is known to me. Continue!"

"Excellence, my reports have continually stressed the strategic positions of Kalgan and the systems it controls. I have reported on the ambition of the warlord, his resources, his determination to extend his domain and his essential friendliness—or, perhaps, neutrality—towards the Foundation."

"I have read your reports thoroughly. Continue!"

"Excellence, I returned two months ago. At that time, there was no sign of impending war; no sign of anything but an almost superfluity of ability to repel any conceivable attack. One month ago, an unknown soldier of fortune, took Kalgan without a fight. The man who was once warlord of Kalgan is apparently no longer alive. Men do not speak of treason—they speak only of the power and genius of this strange condottiere—this Mule."

"This who?" the mayor leaned forward, and looked offended.

"Excellence, he is known as the Mule. He is spoken of little, in a factual sense, but I have gathered the scraps and fragments of knowledge and winnowed out the most probable of them. He is apparently a man of neither birth nor standing. His father, unknown. His mother, dead in childbirth.

His upbringing, that of a vagabond. His education, that of the tramp worlds, and the backwash alleys of space. He has no name other than that of the Mule, a name reportedly applied by himself to himself, and signifying, by popular explanation, his immense physical strength, and stubbornness of purpose."

"What is his military strength, captain? Never mind his physique."

"Excellence, men speak of huge fleets, but in this they may be influenced by the strange fall of Kalgan. The territory he controls is not large, though its exact limits are not capable of definite determination. Nevertheless, this man must be investigated."

"Hm-m-m. So! So!" The mayor fell into a reverie, and slowly with twenty-four strokes of his stylus drew six squares in hexagonal arrangements upon the blank top sheet of a pad, which he tore off, folded neatly in three parts and slipped into the waste-paper slot at his right hand. It slid towards a clean and silent atomic disintegration.

"Now then, tell me, captain, what is the alternative? You have told me what 'must' be investigated. What have you been *ordered* to investigate?"

"Excellence, there is a rat hole in space that, it seems does not pay its taxes."

"Ah, and is that all? You are not aware, and have not been told that these men who do not pay their taxes, are descendants of the wild Traders of our early days—anarchists, rebels, social maniacs who claim Foundation ancestry and deride Foundation culture. You are not aware, and have not been told, that this rat hole in space, is not one, but many; that these rat holes are in greater number than we know; that these rat holes conspire together, one with the other, and all with the criminal elements that still exist throughout Foundation territory. Even here, captain, even here!"

The mayor's momentary fire subsided quickly. "You are not aware, captain?"

"Excellence, I have been told all this. But as servant of the State, I must serve faithfully—and he serves most faithfully who serves Truth. Whatever the political implications of these dregs of the ancient Traders—the warlords who have inherited the splinters of the old Empire have the power. The Traders have neither arms nor resources. They have not even unity. I am not a tax collector to be sent on a child's errand."

"Captain Pritcher, you are a soldier, and count guns. It is a failing to be allowed you up to the point where it involves disobedience to myself. Take care. My justice is not simply weakness. Captain, it has already been proven that the generals of the Imperial Age and the warlords of the present age are equally impotent against us. Seldon's science which predicts the course of the Foundation is based, not on individual heroism, as you seem to believe, but on the social and economic trends of history. We have passed successfully through four crises already, have we not?"

"Excellence, we have. Yet Seldon's science is known—only to Seldon. We ourselves have but faith. In the first three crises, as I have been carefully taught, the Foundation was led by wise leaders who foresaw the nature of the crises and took the proper precautions. Otherwise—who can say?"

"Yes, captain, but you omit the fourth crisis. Come, captain, we had no leadership worthy of the name then, and we faced the cleverest opponent, the heaviest armor, the strongest force of all. Yet we won by the inevitability of history."

"Excellence, that is true. But this history you mention became inevitable only after we had fought desperately for over a year. The inevitable victory we won cost us half a thousand ships and half a million men. Excellence, Seldon's plan helps those who help themselves."

Mayor Indbur frowned and grew suddenly tired of his patient exposition. It occurred to him that there was a fallacy in condescension, since it was mistaken for permission to argue eternally; to grow contentious; to wallow in dialectic.

He said, stiffly, "Nevertheless, captain, Seldon guarantees victory over the warlords, and I can not, in these busy times, indulge in a dispersal of effort. These Traders you dismiss are Foundation-derived. A war with them would be a civil war. Seldon's plan makes no guarantee there for us—since they *and* we are Foundation. So they must be brought to heel. You have your orders."

"Excellence—"

"You have been asked no question, captain. You have your orders. You will obey those orders. Further argument of any sort with myself or those representing myself will be considered treason. You are excused."

101

Captain Han Pritcher knelt once more, then left with slow, backward steps.

Mayor Indbur, third of his name, and second mayor of Foundation history to be so by right of birth, recovered his equilibrium, and lifted another sheet of paper from the neat stack at his left. It was a report on the saving of funds due to the reduction of the quantity of metal-foam edging on the uniforms of the police force. Mayor Indbur crossed out a superfluous comma, corrected a misspelling, made three marginal notations, and placed it upon the neat stack at his right. He lifted another sheet of paper from the neat stack at his left—

Captain Han Pritcher of Information found a Personal Capsule waiting for him when he returned to barracks. It contained orders, terse and redly underlined with a stamped "URGENT" across it, and the whole initialed with a precise, capital "I".

Captain Han Pritcher was ordered to the "rebel world called Haven" in the strongest terms.

Captain Han Pritcher, alone in his light one-man speedster, set his course quietly and calmly for Kalgan. He slept that night the sleep of a successfully stubborn man.

13. Lieutenant and Clown

IF, from a distance of seven thousand parsecs, the fall of Kalgan to the armies of the Mule had produced reverberations that had excited the curiosity of an old Trader, the apprehension of a dogged captain, and the annoyance of a meticulous mayor—to those on Kalgan itself, it produced nothing and excited no one. It is the invariable lesson to humanity that distance in time, and in space as well, lends focus. It is not recorded, incidentally, that the lesson has ever been permanently learned.

Kalgan was—Kalgan. It alone of all that quadrant of the Galaxy seemed not to know that the Empire had fallen, that the Stannells no longer ruled, that greatness had departed, and peace had disappeared.

Kalgan was the luxury world. With the edifice of mankind crumbling, it maintained its integrity as a producer of pleasure, a buyer of gold and a seller of leisure.

It escaped the harsher vicissitudes of history, for what conqueror would destroy or even seriously damage a world so full of the ready cash that would buy immunity.

Yet even Kalgan had finally become the headquarters of a warlord and its softness had been tempered to the exigencies of war.

Its tamed jungles, its mildly modeled shores, and its garishly glamorous cities echoed to the march of imported mercenaries and impressed citizens. The worlds of its province had been armed and its money invested in battleships rather than bribes for the first time in its history. Its ruler proved beyond doubt that he was determined to defend what was his and eager to seize what was others.

He was a great one of the Galaxy, a war and peace

maker, a builder of Empire, an establisher of dynasty.

And an unknown with a ridiculous nickname had taken him—and his arms—and his budding Empire—and had not even fought a battle.

So Kalgan was as before, and its uniformed citizens hurried back to their older life, while the foreign professionals of war merged easily into the newer bands that descended.

Again as always, there were the elaborate luxury hunts for the cultivated animal life of the jungles that never took human life; and the speedster bird-chases in the air above, that was fatal only to the Great Birds.

In the cities, the escapers of the Galaxy could take their varieties of pleasure to suit their purse, from the ethereal sky-palaces of spectacle and fantasy that opened their doors to the masses at the jingle of half a credit, to the unmarked, unnoted haunts to which only those of great wealth were of the cognoscenti.

To the vast flood, Toran and Bayta added not even a trickle. They registered their ship in the huge common hangar on the East Peninsula, and gravitated to that compromise of the middle-classes, the Inland Sea—where the pleasures were yet legal, and even respectable, and the crowds not yet beyond endurance.

Bayta wore dark glasses against the light, and a thin, white robe against the heat. Warm-tinted arms, scarcely the goldener for the sun, clasped her knees to her, and she stared with firm, abstracted gaze at the length of her husband's outstretched body—almost shimmering in the brilliance of white sun-splendor.

"Don't overdo it," she had said at first, but Toran was of a dying-red star. Despite three years of the Foundation, sunlight was a luxury, and for four days now his skin, treated beforehand for ray resistance, had not felt the harshness of clothing, except for the brief shorts.

Bayta huddled close to him on the sand and they spoke in whispers.

Toran's voice was gloomy, as it drifted upwards from a relaxed face, "No, I admit we're nowhere. But where is he? Who is he? This mad world says nothing of him. Perhaps he doesn't exist."

"He exists," replied Bayta, with lips that didn't move.

"He's clever, that's all. And your uncle is right. He's a man we could use—if there's time."

A short pause. Toran whispered, "Know what I've been doing, Bay? I'm just daydreaming myself into a sun-stupor. Things figure themselves out so neatly—so sweetly." His voice nearly trailed off, then returned, "Remember the way Dr. Amann talked back at college, Bay. The Foundation can never lose, but that does not mean the *rulers* of the Foundation can't. Didn't the real history of the Foundation begin when Salvor Hardin kicked out the Encyclopedists and took over the planet Terminus as the first mayor? And then in the next century, didn't Hober Mallow gain power by methods almost as drastic? That's *twice* the rulers were defeated, so it can be done. So why not by us?"

"It's the oldest argument in the books, Torie. What a waste of good reverie."

"Is it? Follow it out. What's Haven? Isn't it part of the Foundation? It's simply part of the external proletariat, so to speak. If we become top dog, it's still the Foundation winning, and only the current rulers losing."

"Lots of difference between 'we can' and 'we will.' You're just jabbering."

Toran squirmed. "Nuts, Bay, you're just in one of your sour, green moods. What do you want to spoil my fun for? I'll just go to sleep if you don't mind."

But Bayta was craning her head, and suddenly—quite a *non sequitur*—she giggled, and removed her glasses to look down the beach with only her palm shading her eyes.

Toran looked up, then lifted and twisted his shoulders to follow her glance.

Apparently, she was watching a spindly figure, feet in air, who teetered on his hands for the amusement of a haphazard crowd. It was one of the swarming acrobatic beggars of the shore, whose supple joints bent and snapped for the sake of the thrown coins.

A beach guard was motioning him on his way and with a surprising one-handed balance, the clown brought a thumb to his nose in an upside-down gesture. The guard advanced threateningly and reeled backward with a foot in his stomach. The clown righted himself without interrupting the motion of the initial kick and was away, while the frothing guard was held off by a thoroughly unsympathetic crowd.

The clown made his way raggedly down the beach. He

105

brushed past many, hesitated often, stopped nowhere. The original crowd had dispersed. The guard had departed.

"He's a queer fellow," said Bayta, with amusement, and Toran agreed indifferently. The clown was close enough now to be seen clearly. His thin face drew together in front into a nose of generous planes and fleshy tip that seemed all but prehensile. His long, lean limbs and spidery body, accentuated by his costume, moved easily and with grace, but with just a suggestion of having been thrown together at random.

To look was to smile.

The clown seemed suddenly aware of their regard, for he stopped after he had passed, and, with a sharp turn, approached. His large, brown eyes fastened upon Bayta.

She found herself disconcerted.

The clown smiled, but it only saddened his beaked face, and when he spoke it was with the soft, elaborate phrasing of the Central Sectors.

"Were I to use the wits the good Spirits gave me," he said, "then I would say this lady can not exist—for what sane man would hold a dream to be reality. Yet rather would I not be sane and lend belief to charmed, enchanted eyes."

Bayta's own eyes opened wide. She said, "Wow!"

Toran laughed, "Oh, you enchantress. Go ahead, Bay, that deserves a five-credit piece. Let him have it."

But the clown was forward with a jump. "No, my lady, mistake me not. I spoke for money not at all, but for bright eyes and sweet face."

"Well, *thanks*," then, to Toran, "Golly, you think the sun's in his eyes?"

"Yet not alone for eyes and face," babbled the clown, as his words hurled past each other in heightened frenzy, "but also for a mind, clear and sturdy—and kind as well."

Toran rose to his feet, reached for the white robe he had crooked his arm about for four days, and slipped into it. "Now, bud," he said, "suppose you tell me what you want, and stop annoying the lady."

The clown fell back a frightened step, his meager body cringing. "Now, sure I meant no harm. I am a stranger here, and it's been said I am of addled wits; yet there is something in a face that I can read. Behind this lady's fairness, there is a heart that's kind, and that would help me in my trouble for all I speak so boldly."

106

"Will five credits cure your trouble?" said Toran, dryly, and held out the coin.

But the clown did not move to take it, and Bayta said, "Let me talk to him, Torie." She added swiftly, and in an undertone, "There's no use being annoyed at his silly way of talking. That's just his dialect; and our speech is probably as strange to him."

She said, "What is your trouble? You're not worried about the guard, are you? He won't bother you."

"Oh, no, not he. He's but a windlet that blows the dust about my ankles. There is another that I flee, and he is a storm that sweeps the worlds aside and throws them plunging at each other. A week ago, I ran away, have slept in city streets, and hid in city crowds. I've looked in many faces for help in need. I find it here." He repeated the last phrase in softer, anxious tones, and his large eyes were troubled, "I find it here."

"Now," said Bayta, reasonably, "I would like to help, but really, friend, I'm no protection against a world-sweeping storm. To be truthful about it, I could use—"

There was an uplifted, powerful voice that bore down upon them.

"Now, then, you mud-spawned rascal—"

It was the beach guard, with a fire-red face, and snarling mouth, that approached at a run. He pointed with his low-power stun pistol.

"Hold him, you two. Don't let him get away." His heavy hand fell upon the clown's thin shoulder, so that a whimper was squeezed out of him.

Toran said, "What's he done?"

"What's he done? What's he done? Well, now, that's good!" The guard reached inside the dangling pocket attached to his belt, and removed a purple handkerchief, with which he mopped his bare neck. He said with relish, "I'll tell you what he's done. He's run away. The word's all over Kalgan and I would have recognized him before this if he had been on his feet instead of on his hawkface top." And he rattled his prey in a fierce good humor.

Bayta said with a smile, "Now where did he escape from, sir?"

The guard raised his voice. A crowd was gathering, pop-eyed and jabbering, and with the increase of audience, the guard's sense of importance increased in direct ratio.

"Where did he escape from?" he declaimed in high sarcasm. "Why, I suppose you've heard of the Mule, now."

All jabbering stopped, and Bayta felt a sudden iciness trickle down into her stomach. The clown had eyes only for her—he still quivered in the guard's brawny grasp.

"And who," continued the guard heavily, "would this infernal ragged piece be, but his lordship's own court fool who's run away." He jarred his captive with a massive shake, "Do you admit it, fool?"

There was only white fear for answer, and the soundless sibilance of Bayta's voice close to Toran's ear.

Toran stepped forward to the guard in friendly fashion, "Now, my man, suppose you take your hand away for just a while. This entertainer you hold has been dancing for us and has not yet danced out his fee."

"Here!" The guard's voice rose in sudden concern. "There's a reward—"

"You'll have it, if you can prove he's the man you want. Suppose you withdraw till then. You know that you're interfering with a guest, which could be serious for you."

"But you're interfering with his lordship and that *will* be serious for you." He shook the clown once again, "Return the man's fee, carrion."

Toran's hand moved quickly and the guard's stun pistol was wrenched away with half a finger nearly following it. The guard howled his pain and rage. Toran shoved him violently aside, and the clown, unhanded, scuttled behind him.

The crowd, whose fringes were now lost to the eye, paid little attention to the latest development. There was among them a craning of necks, and a centrifugal motion as if many had decided to increase their distance from the center of activity.

Then there was a bustle, and a rough order in the distance. A corridor formed itself and two men strode through, electric whips in careless readiness. Upon each purple blouse was designed an angular shaft of lightning with a splitting planet underneath.

A dark giant, in lieutenant's uniform, followed them; dark of skin, and hair, and scowl.

The dark man spoke with the dangerous softness that meant he had little need of shouting to enforce his whims. He said, "Are you the man who notified us?"

108

The guard was still holding his wrenched hand, and with a pain-distorted face mumbled, "I claim the reward, your mightiness, and I accuse that man—"

"You'll get your reward," said the lieutenant, without looking at him. He motioned curtly to his men, "Take him."

Toran felt the clown tearing at his robe with a maddened grip.

He raised his voice and kept it from shaking, "I'm sorry, lieutenant; this man is mine."

The soldiers took the statement without blinking. One raised his whip casually, but the lieutenant's snapped order brought it down.

His dark mightiness swung forward and planted his square body before Toran, "Who are you?"

And the answer rang out, "A citizen of the Foundation."

It worked—with the crowd, at any rate. The pent-up silence broke into an intense hum. The Mule's name might excite fear, but, it was, after all, a new name and scarcely stuck as deeply in the vitals as the old one of the Foundation—that had destroyed the Empire—and the fear of which ruled a quadrant of the Galaxy with ruthless despotism.

The lieutenant kept face. He said, "Are you aware of the identity of the man behind you?"

"I have been told he's a runaway from the court of your leader, but my only sure knowledge is that he is a friend of mine. You'll need firm proof of his identity to take him."

There were high-pitched sighs from the crowd, but the lieutenant let it pass. "Have you your papers of Foundation citizenship with you?"

"At my ship."

"You realize that your actions are illegal? I can have you shot."

"Undoubtedly. But then you would have shot a Foundation citizen and it is quite likely that your body would be sent to the Foundation—quartered—as part compensation. It's been done by other warlords."

The lieutenant wet his lips. The statement was true. He said, "Your name?"

Toran followed up his advantage, "I will answer further questions at my ship. You can get the cell number at the Hangar; it is registered under the name 'Bayta'."

"You won't give up the runaway?"

"To the Mule, perhaps. Send your master!"

The conversation had degenerated to a whisper and the lieutenant turned sharply away.

"Disperse the crowd!" he said to his men, with suppressed ferocity.

The electric whips rose and fell. There were shrieks and a vast surge of separation and flight.

Toran interrupted his reverie only once on their way back to the Hangar. He said, almost to himself, "Galaxy, Bay, what a time I had! I was so scared——"

"Yes," she said, with a voice that still shook, and eyes that still showed something akin to worship, "it was quite out of character."

"Well, I still don't know what happened. I just got up there with a stun pistol that I wasn't even sure I knew how to use, and talked back to him. I don't know why I did it."

He looked across the aisle of the short-run air vessel that was carrying them out of the beach area, to the seat on which the Mule's clown scrunched up in sleep, and added distastefully, "It was the hardest thing I've ever done."

The lieutenant stood respectfully before the colonel of the garrison, and the colonel looked at him and said, "Well done. Your part's over now."

But the lieutenant did not retire immediately. He said darkly, "The Mule has lost face before a mob, sir. It will be necessary to undertake disciplinary action to restore proper atmosphere of respect."

"Those measures have already been taken."

The lieutenant half turned, then, almost with resentment, "I'm willing to agree, sir, that orders are orders, but standing before that man with his stun pistol and swallowing his insolence whole, was the hardest thing I've ever done."

14. The Mutant

THE "HANGAR" on Kalgan is an institution peculiar unto itself, born of the need for the disposition of the vast number of ships brought in by the visitors from abroad, and the simultaneous and consequent vast need for living accommodations for the same. The original bright one who had thought of the obvious solution had quickly become a millionaire. His heirs—by birth or finance—were easily among the richest on Kalgan.

The "hangar" spreads fatly over square miles of territory, and "hangar" does not describe it at all sufficiently. It is essentially a hotel—for ships. The traveler pays in advance and his ship is awarded a berth from which it can take off into space at any desired moment. The visitor then lives in his ship as always. The ordinary hotel services such as the replacement of food and medical supplies at special rates, simple servicing of the ship itself, special intra-Kalgan transportation for a nominal sum are to be had, of course.

As a result, the visitor combines hangar space and hotel bill into one, at a saving. The owners sell temporary use of ground space at ample profits. The government collects huge taxes. Everyone has fun. Nobody loses. Simple!

The man who made his way down the shadow-borders of the wide corridors that connected the multitudinous wings of the "hangar" had in the past speculated on the novelty and usefulness of the system described above, but these were reflections for idle moments—distinctly unsuitable at present.

The ships hulked in their height and breadth down the long lines of carefully aligned cells, and the man discarded line after line. He was an expert at what he was doing now—and if his preliminary study of the hangar registry had failed

111

to give specific information beyond the doubtful indication of a specific wing—one containing hundreds of ships—his specialized knowledge could winnow those hundreds into one.

There was the ghost of a sigh in the silence, as the man stopped and faded down one of the lines; a crawling insect beneath the notice of the arrogant metal monsters that rested there.

Here and there the sparkling of light from a porthole would indicate the presence of an early returner from the organized pleasures to simpler—or more private—pleasures of his own.

The man halted, and would have smiled if he ever smiled. Certainly the convolutions of his brain performed the mental equivalent of a smile.

The ship he stopped at was sleek and obviously fast. The peculiarity of its design was what he wanted. It was not a usual model—and these days most of the ships of this quadrant of the Galaxy either imitated Foundation design or were built by Foundation technicians. But this was special. This was a Foundation ship—if only because of the tiny bulges in the skin that were the nodes of the protective screen that only a Foundation ship could possess. There were other indications, too.

The man felt no hesitation.

The electronic barrier strung across the line of the ships as a concession to privacy on the part of the management was not at all important to him. It parted easily, and without activating the alarm, at the use of the very special neutralizing force he had at his disposal.

So the first knowledge within the ship of the intruder without was the casual and almost friendly signal of the muted buzzer in the ship's living room that was the result of a palm placed over the little photocell just one side of the main air lock.

And while that successful search went on, Toran and Bayta felt only the most precarious security within the steel walls of the *Bayta*. The Mule's clown who had reported that within his narrow compass of body he held the lordly name of Magnifico Giganticus, sat hunched over the table and gobbled at the food set before him.

His sad, brown eyes lifted from his meal only to follow Bayta's movements in the combined kitchen and larder where he ate.

"The thanks of a weak one are of but little value," he muttered, "but you have them, for truly, in this past week, little but scraps have come my way—and for all my body is small, yet is my appetite unseemly great."

"Well, then, eat!" said Bayta, with a smile. "Don't waste your time on thanks. Isn't there a Central Galaxy proverb about gratitude that I once heard?"

"Truly there is, my lady. For a wise man, I have been told, once said, 'Gratitude is best and most effective when it does not evaporate itself in empty phrases.' But alas, my lady, I am but a mass of empty phrases, it would seem. When my empty phrases pleased the Mule, it brought me a court dress, and a grand name—for, see you, it was originally simply Bobo, one that pleases him not—and then when my empty phrases pleased him not, it would bring upon my poor bones beatings and whippings."

Toran entered from the pilot room, "Nothing to do now but wait, Bay. I hope the Mule is capable of understanding that a Foundation ship is Foundation territory."

Magnifico Giganticus, once Bobo, opened his eyes wide and exclaimed, "How great is the Foundation before which even the cruel servants of the Mule tremble."

"Have you heard of the Foundation, too?" asked Bayta, with a little smile.

"And who has not?" Magnifico's voice was a mysterious whisper. "There are those who say it is a world of great magic, of fires that can consume planets, and secrets of mighty strength. They say that not the highest nobility of the Galaxy could achieve the honor and deference considered only the natural due of a simple man who could say 'I am a citizen of the Foundation,'—were he only a salvage miner of space, or a nothing like myself."

Bayta said, "Now, Magnifico, you'll never finish if you make speeches. Here, I'll get you a little flavored milk. It's good."

She placed a pitcher of it upon the table and motioned Toran out of the room.

"Torie, what are we going to do now—about him?" and she motioned towards the kitchen.

"How do you mean?"

"If the Mule comes, are we going to give him up?"

"Well, what else, Bay?" He sounded harassed, and the

113

gesture with which he shoved back the moist curl upon his forehead testified to that.

He continued impatiently, "Before I came here I had a sort of vague idea that all we had to do was to ask for the Mule, and then get down to business—just business, you know, nothing definite."

"I know what you mean, Torie. I wasn't much hoping to see the Mule myself, but I did think we could pick up *some* firsthand knowledge of the mess, and then pass it over to people who know a little know more about this interstellar intrigue. I'm no storybook spy."

"You're not behind me, Bay." He folded his arms and frowned. "What a situation! You'd never know there *was* a person like the Mule, except for this last queer break. Do you suppose he'll come for his clown?"

Bayta looked up at him, "I don't know that I want him to. I don't know what to say or do. Do you?"

The inner buzzer sounded with its intermittent burring noise. Bayta's lips moved wordlessly, "The Mule!"

Magnifico was in the doorway, eyes wide, his voice a whimper, "The Mule?"

Toran murmured, "I've got to let them in."

A contact opened the air lock and the outer door closed behind the newcomer. The scanner showed only a single shadowed figure.

"It's only one person," said Toran, with open relief, and his voice was almost shaky as he bent toward the signal tube, "Who are you?"

"You'd better let me in and find out, hadn't you?" The words came thinly out the receiver.

"I'll inform you that this is a Foundation ship and consequently Foundation territory by international treaty."

"I know that."

"Come with your arms free, or I'll shoot. I'm well-armed."

"Done!"

Toran opened the inner door and closed contact on his blast pistol, thumb hovering over the pressure point. There was the sound of footsteps and then the door swung open, and Magnifico cried out, "It's not the Mule. It's but a man."

The "man" bowed to the clown somberly, "Very accurate. I'm not the Mule." He held his hands apart, "I'm not armed, and I come on a peaceful errand. You might relax

114

and put the blast pistol away. Your hand isn't steady enough for my peace of mind."

"Who are you?" asked Toran, brusquely.

"I might ask *you* that," said the stranger, coolly, "since you're the one under false pretenses, not I."

"How so?"

"You're the one who claims to be a Foundation citizen when there's not an authorized Trader on the planet."

"That's not so. How would you know?"

"Because I *am* a Foundation citizen, and have my papers to prove it. Where are yours?"

"I think you'd better get out."

"I think not. If you know anything about Foundation methods, and despite your imposture you might, you'd know that if I don't return alive to my ship at a specified time, there'll be a signal at the nearest Foundation headquarters —so I doubt if your weapons will have much effect, practically speaking."

There was an irresolute silence and then Bayta said, calmly, "Put the blaster away, Toran, and take him at face value. He sounds like the real thing."

"Thank you," said the stranger.

Toran put his gun on the chair beside him, "Suppose you explain all this now."

The stranger remained standing. He was long of bone and large of limb. His face consisted of hard flat planes and it was somehow evident that he never smiled. But his eyes lacked hardness.

He said, "News travels quickly, especially when it is apparently beyond belief. I don't suppose there's a person on Kalgan who doesn't know that the Mule's men were kicked in the teeth today by two tourists from the Foundation. I knew of the important details before evening, and, as I said, there are no Foundation tourists aside from myself on the planet. We know about those things."

"Who are the 'we'?"

"'We' are—'we'! Myself for one! I knew you were at the Hangar—you had been overheard to say so. I had my ways of checking the registry, and my ways of finding the ship."

He turned to Bayta suddenly, "You're from the Foundation—by birth, aren't you?"

"Am I?"

"You're a member of the democratic opposition—they call

115

it 'the underground.' I don't remember your name, but I do the face. You got out only recently—and wouldn't have if you were more important."

Bayta shrugged, "You know a lot."

"I do. You escaped with a man. That one?"

"Does it matter what I say?"

"No. I merely want a thorough mutual understanding. I believe that the password during the week you left so hastily was 'Seldon, Hardin, and Freedom.' Porfirat Hart was your section leader."

"Where'd you get that?" Bayta was suddenly fierce. "Did the police get him?" Toran held her back, but she shook herself loose and advanced.

The man from the Foundation said quietly, "Nobody has him. It's just that the underground spreads widely and in queer places. I'm Captain Han Pritcher of Information, and I'm a section leader myself—never mind under what name."

He waited, then said, "No, you don't have to believe me. In our business it is better to overdo suspicion than the opposite. But I'd better get past the preliminaries."

"Yes," said Toran, "suppose you do."

"May I sit down? Thanks." Captain Pritcher swung a long leg across his knee and let an arm swing loose over the back of the chair. "I'll start out by saying that I don't know what all this is about—from your angle. You two aren't from the Foundation, but it's not a hard guess that you're from one of the independent Trading worlds. That doesn't bother me overmuch. But out of curiosity, what do you want with that fellow, that clown you snatched to safety? You're risking your life to hold on to him."

"I can't tell you that."

"Hm-m-m. Well, I didn't think you would. But if you're waiting for the Mule himself to come behind a fanfarade of horns, drums, and electric organs—relax! The Mule doesn't work that way."

"What?" It came from both Toran and Bayta, and in the corner where Magnifico lurked with ears almost visibly expanded, there was a sudden joyful start.

"That's right. I've been trying to contact him myself, and doing a rather more thorough job of it than you two amateurs can. It won't work. The man makes no personal appearance, does not allow himself to be photographed or simulated, and is seen only by his most intimate associates."

"Is that supposed to explain your interest in us, captain?" questioned Toran.

"No. That clown is the key. That clown is one of the very few that *have* seen him. I want him. He may be the proof I need—and I need something. Galaxy knows—to awaken the Foundation."

"It needs awakening?" broke in Bayta with sudden sharpness. "Against what? And in what role do you act as alarm, that of rebel democrat or of secret police and provocateur?"

The captain's face set in its hard lines. "When the entire Foundation is threatened, Madame Revolutionary, both democrats and tyrants perish. Let us save the tyrants from a greater, that we may overthrow them in their turn."

"Who's the greater tyrant you speak of?" flared Bayta.

"The Mule! I know a bit about him, enough to have been my death several times over already, if I had moved less nimbly. Send the clown out of the room. This will require privacy."

"Magnifico," said Bayta, with a gesture, and the clown left without a sound.

The captain's voice was grave and intense, and low enough so that Toran and Bayta drew close.

He said, "The Mule is a shrewd operator—far too shrewd not to realize the advantage of the magnetism and glamour of personal leadership. If he gives that up, it's for a reason. That reason must be the fact that personal contact would reveal something that is of overwhelming importance *not* to reveal."

He waved aside questions, and continued more quickly, "I went back to his birthplace for this, and questioned people who for their knowledge will not live long. Few enough are still alive. They remember the baby born thirty years before —the death of his mother—his strange youth. *The Mule is not a human being!*"

And his two listeners drew back in horror at the misty implications. Neither understood, fully or clearly, but the menace of the phrase was definite.

The captain continued, "He is a mutant, and obviously from his subsequent career, a highly successful one. I don't know his powers or the exact extent to which he is what our thrillers would call a 'superman,' but the rise from nothing to the conqueror of Kalgan's warlord in two years is revealing. You see, don't you, the danger? Can a genetic accident of unpredictable biological properties be taken into account in the Seldon plan?"

Slowly, Bayta spoke, "I don't believe it. This is some sort of complicated trickery. Why didn't the Mule's men kill us when they could have, if he's a superman?"

"I told you that I don't know the extent of his mutation. He may not be ready, yet, for the Foundation, and it would be a sign of the greatest wisdom to resist provocation until ready. Suppose you let me speak to the clown."

The captain faced the trembling Magnifico, who obviously distrusted this huge, hard man who faced him.

The captain began slowly, "Have you seen the Mule with your own eyes?"

"I have but too well, respected sir. And felt the weight of his arm with my own body as well."

"I have no doubt of that. Can you describe him?"

"It is frightening to recall him, respected sir. He is a man of mighty frame. Against him, even you would be but a spindling. His hair is of a burning crimson, and with all my strength and weight I could not pull down his arm, once extended—not a hair's thickness." Magnifico's thinness seemed to collapse upon itself in a huddle of arms and legs. "Often, to amuse his general or to amuse only himself, he would suspend me by one finger in my belt from a fearful height, while I chattered poetry. It was only after the twentieth verse that I was withdrawn, and each improvised and each a perfect rhyme, or else start over. He is a man of overpowering might, respected sir, and cruel in the use of his power—and his eyes, respected sir, no one sees."

"What? What's that last?"

"He wears spectacles, respected sir, of a curious nature. It is said that they are opaque and that he sees by a powerful magic that far transcends human powers. I have heard," and his voice was small and mysterious, "that to see his eyes is to see death; that he kills with his eyes, respected sir."

Magnifico's eyes wheeled quickly from one watching face to another. He quavered, "It is true. As I live, it is true."

Bayta drew a long breath, "Sounds like you're right, captain. Do you want to take over?"

"Well, let's look at the situation. You don't owe anything here? The hangar's barrier above is free?"

"I can leave any time."

"Then leave. The Mule may not wish to antagonize the Foundation, but he runs a frightful risk in letting Magnifico get away. It probably accounts for the hue and cry after the poor devil in the first place. So there may be ships waiting for you upstairs. If you're lost in space, who's to pin the crime?"

"You're right," agreed Toran, bleakly.

"However, you've got a shield and you're probably speedier than anything they've got, so as soon as you're clear of the atmosphere make the circle in neutral to the other hemisphere, then just cut a track outwards at top acceleration."

"Yes," said Bayta coldly, "and when we are back on the Foundation, what then, captain?"

"Why, you are then co-operative citizens of Kalgan, are you not? I know nothing to the contrary, do I?"

Nothing was said. Toran turned to the controls. There was an imperceptible lurch.

It was when Toran had left Kalgan sufficiently far in the rear to attempt his first interstellar jump, that Captain Pritcher's face first creased slightly—for no ship of the Mule had in any way attempted to bar their leaving.

"Looks like he's letting us carry off Magnifico," said Toran. "Not so good for your story."

"Unless," corrected the captain, "he wants us to carry him off, in which case it's not so good for the Foundation."

It was after the last jump, when within neutral-flight distance of the Foundation, that the first ultra-wave news broadcast reached the ship.

And there was one news item barely mentioned. It seemed that a warlord—unidentified by the bored speaker—had made representations to the Foundation concerning the forceful abduction of a member of his court. The announcer went on to the sports news.

Captain Pritcher said icily, "He's one step ahead of us after all." Thoughtfully, he added, "He's ready for the Foundation, and he uses this as an excuse for action. It makes things more difficult for us. We will have to act before we are really ready."

15. The Psychologist

THERE WAS REASON to the fact that the element known as "pure science" was the freest form of life on the Foundation. In a Galaxy where the predominance—and even survival—of the Foundation still rested upon the superiority of its technology—even despite its large access of physical power in the last century and a half—a certain immunity adhered to The Scientist. He was needed, and he knew it.

Likewise, there was reason to the fact that Ebling Mis—only those who did not know him added his titles to his name—was the freest form of life in the "pure science" of the Foundation. In a world where science was respected, he was The Scientist—with capital letters and no smile. He was needed, and he knew it.

And so it happened, that when others bent their knee, he refused and added loudly that his ancestors in their time bowed no knee to any stinking mayor. And in his ancestors' time the mayor was elected anyhow, and kicked out at will, and that the only people that inherited anything by right of birth were the congenital idiots.

So it also happened, that when Ebling Mis decided to allow Indbur to honor him with an audience, he did not wait for the usual rigid line of command to pass his request up and the favored reply down, but, having thrown the less disreputable of his two formal jackets over his shoulders and pounded an odd hat of impossible design on one side of his head, and lit a forbidden cigar into the bargain, he barged past two ineffectually bleating guards and into the mayor's palace.

The first notice his excellence received of the intrusion was when from his garden he heard the gradually nearing uproar of expostulation and the answering bull-roar of inarticulate swearing.

Slowly, Indbur lay down his trowel; slowly, he stood up; and slowly, he frowned. For Indbur allowed himself a daily vacation from work, and for two hours in the early afternoon, weather permitting, he was in his garden. There in his garden, the blooms grew in squares and triangles, interlaced in a severe order of red and yellow, with little dashes of violet at the apices, and greenery bordering the whole in rigid lines. There in his garden no one disturbed him—*no one!*

Indbur peeled off his soil-stained gloves as he advanced toward the little garden door.

Inevitably, he said, "What is the meaning of this?"

It is the precise question and the precise wording thereof that has been put to the atmosphere on such occasions by an incredible variety of men since humanity was invented. It is not recorded that it has ever been asked for any purpose other than dignified effect.

But the answer was literal this time, for Mis's body came plunging through with a bellow, and a shake of a fist at the ones who were still holding tatters of his cloak.

Indbur motioned them away with a solemn, displeased frown, and Mis bent to pick up his ruin of a hat, shake about a quarter of the gathered dirt off it, thrust it under his armpit and say:

"Look here, Indbur, those unprintable minions of yours will be charged for one good cloak. Lots of good wear left in this cloak." He puffed and wiped his forehead with just a trace of theatricality.

The mayor stood stiff with displeasure, and said haughtily from the peak of his five-foot-two, "It has not been brought to my attention, Mis, that you have requested an audience. You have certainly not been assigned one."

Ebling Mis looked down at his mayor with what was apparently shocked disbelief, "Ga-LAX-y, Indbur, didn't you get my note yesterday? I handed it to a flunky in purple uniform day before. I would have handed it to you direct, but I know how you like formality."

"Formality!" Indbur turned up exasperated eyes. Then, strenuously, "Have you ever heard of proper organization? At all future times you are to submit your request for an audience, properly made out in triplicate, at the government office intended for the purpose. You are then to wait until the ordinary course of events brings you notification of the time of audience to be granted. You are then to appear, properly clothed—properly clothed, do you understand—and with proper respect, too. You may leave."

"What's wrong with my clothes?" demanded Mis, hotly. "Best cloak I had till those unprintable fiends got their claws on it. I'll leave just as soon as I deliver what I came to deliver. Ga-LAX-y, if it didn't involve a Seldon Crisis, I would leave right now."

"Seldon crisis!" Indbur exhibited first interest. Mis *was* a great psychologist—a democrat, boor, and rebel certainly, but a psychologist, too. In his uncertainty, the mayor even failed to put into words the inner pang that stabbed suddenly when Mis plucked a casual bloom, held it to his nostrils expectantly, then flipped it away with a wrinkled nose.

Indbur said coldly, "Would you follow me? This garden wasn't made for serious conversation."

He felt better in his built-up chair behind his large desk from which he could look down on the few hairs that quite ineffectually hid Mis's pink scalp-skin. He felt much better when Mis cast a series of automatic glances about him for a non-existent chair and then remained standing in uneasy shifting fashion. He felt best of all when in response to a careful pressure of the correct contact, a liveried underling scurried in, bowed his way to the desk, and laid thereon a bulky, metal-bound volume.

"Now, in order," said Indbur, once more master of the situation, "to make this unauthorized interview as short as possible, make your statement in the fewest possible words."

Ebling Mis said unhurriedly, "You know what I'm doing these days?"

"I have your reports here," replied the mayor, with satisfaction, "together with authorized summaries of them. As I understand it, your investigations into the mathematics of psycho-history have been intended to duplicate Hari Seldon's work and, eventually, trace the projected course of future history, for the use of the Foundation."

"Exactly," said Mis, dryly. "When Seldon first established the Foundation, he was wise enough to include no psychologists among the scientists placed here—so that the

122

Foundation has always worked blindly along the course of historical necessity. In the course of my researches, I have based a good deal upon hints found at the Time Vault."

"I am aware of that, Mis. It is a waste of time to repeat."

"I'm not repeating," blared Mis, "because what I'm going to tell you isn't in any of those reports."

"How do you mean, not in the reports?" said Indbur, stupidly. "How could—"

"Ga-LAX-y! Let me tell this my own way, you offensive little creature. Stop putting words into my mouth and questioning my every statement or I'll tramp out of here and let everything crumble around you. Remember, you unprintable fool, the Foundation will come through because it must, but if I walk out of here now—*you* won't."

Dashing his hat on the floor, so that clods of earth scattered, he sprang up the stairs of the dais on which the wide desk stood and shoving papers violently, sat down upon a corner of it.

Indbur thought frantically of summoning the guard, or using the built-in blasters of his desk. But Mis's face was glaring down upon him and there was nothing to do but cringe the best face upon it.

"Dr. Mis," he began, with weak formality, "you must—"

"Shut up," said Mis, ferociously, "and listen. If this thing here," and his palm came down heavily on the metal of the bound data, "is a mess of my reports—throw it out. Any report I write goes up through some twenty-odd officials, gets to you, and then sort of winds down through twenty more. That's fine if there's nothing you don't want kept secret. Well, I've got something confidential here. It's so confidential, even the boys working for me haven't got wind of it. They did the work, of course, but each just a little unconnected piece —and I put it together. You know what the Time Vault is?"

Indbur nodded his head, but Mis went on with loud enjoyment of the situation, "Well, I'll tell you anyhow because I've been sort of imagining this unprintable situation for a Ga-LAX-y of a long time; I can read your mind, you puny fraud. You've got your hand right near a little knob that'll call in about five hundred or so armed men to finish me off, but you're afraid of what I know—you're afraid of a Seldon Crisis. Besides which, if you touch anything on your desk, I'll knock your unprintable head off before anyone gets here. You and your bandit father and pirate grandfather have been blood-sucking the Foundation long enough anyway."

"This is treason," gabbled Indbur.

"It certainly is," gloated Mis, "but what are you going to do about it? Let me tell you about the Time Vault. That Time Vault is what Hari Seldon placed here at the beginning to help us over the rough spots. For every crisis, Seldon has prepared a personal simulacrum to help—and explain. Four crises so far—four appearances. The first time he appeared at the height of the first crisis. The second time, he appeared at a moment just after the successful evolution of the second crisis. Our ancestors were there to listen to him both times. At the third and fourth crises, he was ignored—probably because he was not needed, but recent investigations —*not* included in those reports you have—indicate that he appeared anyway, and at the proper times. Get it?"

He did not wait for any answer. His cigar, a tattered, dead ruin was finally disposed of, a new cigar groped for, and lit. The smoke puffed out violently.

He said, "Officially I've been trying to rebuild the science of psycho-history. Well, no one man is going to do *that*, and it won't get done in any one century, either. But I've made advances in the more simple elements and I've been able to use it as an excuse to meddle with the Time Vault. What I *have* done, involves the determination, to a pretty fair kind of certainty, of the exact date of the next appearance of Hari Seldon. I can give you the exact day, in other words, that the coming Seldon Crisis, the fifth, will reach its climax."

"How far off?" demanded Indbur, tensely.

And Mis exploded his bomb with cheerful nonchalance, "Four months," he said. "Four unprintable months, less two days."

"Four months," said Indbur, with uncharacteristic vehemence. "Impossible."

"Impossible, my unprintable eye."

"Four months? Do you understand what that means? For a crisis to come to a head in four months would mean that it has been preparing for years."

"And why not? Is there a law of Nature that requires the process to mature in the full light of day?"

"But nothing impends. Nothing hangs over us." Indbur almost wrung his hands for anxiety. With a sudden spasmodic

124

recrudescence of ferocity, he screamed, "*Will* you get off my desk and let me put it in order? How do you expect me to *think*?"

Mis, startled, lifted heavily and moved aside.

Indbur replaced objects in their appropriate niches with a feverish motion. He was speaking quickly, "You have no right to come here like this. If you had presented your theory——"

"It is not a *theory*."

"I say it *is* a theory. If you had presented it together with your evidence and arguments, in appropriate fashion, it would have gone to the Bureau of Historical Sciences. There it could have been properly treated, the resulting analyses submitted to me, and then, of course, proper action would have been taken. As it is, you've vexed me to no purpose. Ah, here it is."

He had a sheet of transparent, silvery paper in his hand which he shook at the bulbous psychologist beside him.

"This is a short summary I prepare myself—weekly—of foreign matters in progress. Listen—we have completed negotiations for a commercial treaty with Mores, continue negotiations for one with Lyonesse, sent a delegation to some celebration or other on Bonde, received some complaint or other from Kalgan and we've promised to look into it, protested some sharp trade practices in Asperta and they've promised to look into it—and so on and so on." The mayor's eyes swarmed down the list of coded notations, and then he carefully placed the sheet in its proper place in the proper folder in the proper pigeonhole.

"I tell you, Mis, there's not a thing there that breathes anything but order and peace——"

The door at the far, long end opened, and, in far too dramatically coincident a fashion to suggest anything but real life, a plainly-costumed notable stepped in.

Indbur half-rose. He had the curiously swirling sensation of unreality that comes upon those days when too much happens. After Mis' intrusion and wild fumings there now came the equally improper, hence disturbing, intrusion unannounced, of his secretary, who at least knew the rules.

The secretary kneeled low.

Indbur said, sharply, "Well!"

The secretary addressed the floor, "Excellence, Captain Han Pritcher of Information, returning from Kalgan, in disobedience to your orders, has according to prior instructions—your order X20-513—been imprisoned, and awaits execution.

125

Those accompanying him are being held for questioning. A full report has been filed."

Indbur, in agony, said, "A full report has been received. *Well!*"

"Excellence, Captain Pritcher has reported, vaguely, dangerous designs on the part of the new warlord of Kalgan. He has been given, according to prior instructions—your order X20-651—no formal hearing, but his remarks have been recorded and a full report filed."

Indbur screamed, "A full report has been received. *Well!*"

"Excellence, reports have within the quarter-hour been received from the Salinnian frontier. Ships identified as Kalganian have been entering Foundation territory, unauthorized. The ships are armed. Fighting has occurred."

The secretary was bent nearly double. Indbur remained standing. Ebling Mis shook himself, clumped up to the secretary, and tapped him sharply on the shoulder.

"Here, you'd better have them release this Captain Pritcher, and have him sent here. Get out."

The secretary left, and Mis turned to the mayor, "Hadn't you better get the machinery moving, Indbur? Four months, you know."

Indbur remained standing, glaze-eyed. Only one finger seemed alive—and it traced rapid jerky triangles on the smooth desk top before him.

16. Conference

WHEN the twenty-seven independent Trading worlds, united
only by their distrust of the mother planet of the
Foundation, concert an assembly among themselves, and each
is big with a pride grown of its smallness, hardened by its own
insularity and embittered by eternal danger—there are
preliminary negotiations to be overcome of a pettiness
sufficiently staggering to heart-sicken the most persevering.

It is not enough to fix in advance such details as methods
of voting, type of representation—whether by world or by
population. These are matters of involved political importance.
It is not enough to fix matters of priority at the table, both
council and dinner, those are matters of involved social importance.

It was the place of meeting—since that was a matter of
overpowering provincialism. And in the end the devious routes
of diplomacy led to the world of Radole, which some com-
mentators had suggested at the start for logical reason of
central position.

Radole was a small world—and, in military potential, perhaps the weakest of the twenty-seven. That, by the way, was
another factor in the logic of the choice.

It was a ribbon world—of which the Galaxy boasts sufficient, but among which, the inhabited variety is a rarity. It
was a world, in other words, where the two halves face the
monotonous extremes of heat and cold, while the region of
possible life is the birdling ribbon of the twilight zone.

Such a world invariably sounds uninviting to those who
have not tried it, but there exist spots, strategically placed—
and Radole City was located in such a one.

It spread along the soft slopes of the foothills before the

hacked-out mountains that backed it along the rim of the cold hemisphere and held off the frightful ice. The warm, dry air of the sun-half spilled over, and from the mountains was piped the water—and between the two, Radole City became a continuous garden, swimming in the eternal morning of an eternal June.

Each house nestled among its flower garden, open to the fangless elements. Each garden was a horticultural forcing ground, where luxury plants grew in fantastic patterns for the sake of the foreign exchange they brought—until Radole had almost become a producing world, rather than a typical Trading world.

So, in its way, Radole City was a little point of softness and luxury on a horrible planet—a tiny scrap of Eden— and that, too, was a factor in the logic of the choice.

The strangers came from each of the twenty-six other Trading worlds: delegates, wives, secretaries, newsmen, ships, and crews—and Radole's population nearly doubled and Radole's resources strained themselves to the limit. One ate at will, and drank at will, and slept not at all.

Yet there were few among the roisterers who were not intensely aware that all that volume of the Galaxy burnt slowly in a sort of quiet, slumbrous war. And of those who were aware, there were three classes. First, there were the many who knew little and were very confident—

Such as the young space pilot who wore the Haven cockade on the clasp of his cap, and who managed, in holding his glass before his eyes, to catch those of the faintly smiling Radolian girl opposite. He was saying:

"We came right through the war-zone to get here—on purpose. We traveled about a light-minute or so, in neutral, right past Horleggor—"

"Horleggor?" broke in a long-legged native, who was playing host to that particular gathering. "That's where the Mule got the guts beat out of him last week, wasn't it?"

"Where'd you hear that the Mule got the guts beat out of him?" demanded the pilot, loftily.

"Foundation radio."

"Yeah? Well, the Mule's *got* Horleggor. We almost ran into a convoy of his ships, and that's where they were coming from. It isn't a gut-beating when you stay where you fought, and the gut-beater leaves in a hurry."

Someone else said in a high, blurred voice, "Don't talk like

128

that. Foundation always takes it on the chin for a while. You watch; just sit tight and watch. Ol' Foundation knows when to come back. And then—*pow!*" The thick voice concluded and was succeeded by a bleary grin.

"Anyway," said the pilot from Haven, after a short pause, "as I say, we saw the Mule's ships, and they looked pretty good, pretty good. I tell you what—they looked new."

"New?" said the native, thoughtfully. "They build them themselves?" He broke a leaf from an overhanging branch, sniffed delicately at it, then crunched it between his teeth, the bruised tissues bleeding greenly and diffusing a minty odor. He said, "You trying to tell me they beat Foundation ships with home-built jobs? Go on."

"We saw them, doc. And I can tell a ship from a comet, too, you know."

The native leaned close. "You know what I think. Listen, don't kid yourself. Wars don't just start by themselves, and we have a bunch of shrewd apples running things. They know what they're doing."

The well-unthirsted one said with a sudden loudness, "You watch ol' Foundation. They wait for the last minute, then— *pow!*" He grinned with vacuously open mouth at the girl, who moved away from him.

The Radolian was saying, "For instance, old man, you think maybe that this Mule guy's running things. No-o-o." And he wagged a finger horizontally. "The way I hear it, and from pretty high up, mind you, he's our boy. We're paying him off, and we probably built those ships. Let's be realistic about it —we probably did. Sure, he can't beat the Foundation in the long run, but he can get them shaky, and when he does— *we get in.*"

The girl said, "Is that all you can talk about, Klev? The war? You make me tired."

The pilot from Haven said, in an access of gallantry, "Change the subject. Can't make the girls tired."

The bedewed one took up the refrain and banged a mug to the rhythm. The little groups of two that had formed broke up with giggles and swagger, and a few similar groups of twos emerged from the sun-house in the background.

The conversation became more general, more varied, more meaningless—

Then there were those who knew a little more and were less confident.

129

Such as the one-armed Fran, whose large bulk represented Haven as official delegated, and who lived high in consequence, and cultivated new friendships—with women when he could and with men when he had to.

It was on the sun platform of the hilltop home, of one of these new friends, that he relaxed for the first of what eventually proved to be a total of two times while on Radole. The new friend was Iwo Lyon, a kindred soul of Radole. Iwo's house was apart from the general cluster, apparently alone in a sea of floral perfume and insect chatter. The sun platform was a grassy strip of lawn set at a forty-five degree angle, and upon it Fran stretched out and fairly sopped up sun.

He said, "Don't have anything like this on Haven."

Iwo replied, sleepily, "Ever seen the cold side. There's a spot twenty miles from here where the oxygen runs like water."

"Go on."

"Fact."

"Well, I'll tell you, Iwo— In the old days before my arm was chewed off I knocked around, see—and you won't believe this, but"— The story that followed lasted considerably, and Iwo didn't believe it.

Iwo said, through yawns, "They don't make them like in the old days, that's the truth."

"No, guess they don't. Well, now," Fran fired up. "don't say that. I told you about my son, didn't I? *He's* one of the old school, if you like. He'll make a great Trader, blast it. He's his old man up and down. Up and down, except that he gets married."

"You mean legal contract? With a girl?"

"That's right. Don't see the sense in it myself. They went to Kalgan for their honeymoon."

"Kalgan? *Kalgan?* When the Galaxy was this?"

Fran smiled broadly, and said with slow meaning, "Just before the Mule declared war on the Foundation."

"That so?"

Fran nodded and motioned Iwo closer with his head. He said, hoarsely, "In fact, I can tell you something, if you don't let it go any further. My boy was sent to Kalgan for a purpose. Now I wouldn't like to let it out, you know, just what the purpose was, naturally, but you look at the situation now, and I suppose you can make a pretty good guess. In any case, my boy was the man for the job. We Traders needed some sort of ruckus." He smiled, craftily. "It's here. I'm not saying how we did it, but—my boy went to Kalgan, and the Mule sent out his ships. My son!"

Iwo was duly impressed. He grew confidential in his turn, "That's good. You know, they say we've got five hundred ships ready to pitch in on our own at the right time."

Fran said authoritatively, "More than that, maybe. This is real strategy. This is the kind I like." He clawed loudly at the skin of his abdomen. "But don't you forget that the Mule is a smart boy, too. What happened at Horleggor worries me."

"I heard he lost about ten ships."

"Sure, but he had a hundred more, and the Foundation had to get out. It's all to the good to have those tyrants beaten, but not so quickly as all that." He shook his head.

"The question I ask is where does the Mule get his ships? There's a widespread rumor we're making them for him."

"We? The Traders? Haven has the biggest ship factories anywhere in the independent worlds, and we haven't made one for anyone but ourselves. Do you suppose any world is building a fleet for the Mule on its own, without taking the precaution of united action? That's a . . . a fairy tale."

"Well, where does he get them?"

And Fran shrugged, "Makes them himself, I suppose. That worries me, too."

Fran blinked at the sun and curled his toes about the smooth wood of the polished foot-rest. Slowly, he fell asleep and the soft burr of his breathing mingled with the insect sibilance.

Lastly, there were the very few who knew considerable and were not confident at all.

Such as Randu, who on the fifth day of the all-Trader convention entered the Central Hall and found the two men he had asked to be there, waiting for him. The five hundred seats were empty—and were going to stay so.

Randu said quickly, almost before he sat down, "We three represent about half the military potential of the Independent Trading Worlds."

"Yes," said Mangin of Iss, "my colleague and I have already commented upon the fact."

"I am ready," said Randu, "to speak quickly and earnestly.

I am not interested in bargaining or sublety. Our position is radically in the worse."

"As a result of—" urged Ovall Gri of Mnemon.

"Of developments of the last hour. Please! From the beginning. First, our position is not of our doing, and but doubtfully of our control. Our original dealings were not with the Mule, but with several others; notably the ex-warlord of Kalgan, whom the Mule defeated at the most inconvenient time for us."

"Yes, but this Mule is a worthy substitute," said Mangin. "I do not cavil at details."

"You may when you know *all* the details." Randu leaned forward and placed his hands upon the table palms-up in an obvious gesture.

He said, "A month ago I sent my nephew and my nephew's wife to Kalgan."

"Your nephew!" cried Ovall Gri, in surprise. "I did not know he was your nephew."

"With what purpose," asked Mangin, dryly. "This?" And his thumb drew an inclusive circle high in the air.

"No. If you mean the Mule's war on the Foundation, no. How could I aim so high. The young man knew nothing—neither of our organization nor of our aims. He was told I was a minor member of an intra-Haven patriotic society, and his function at Kalgan was nothing but that of an amateur observer. My motives were, I must admit, rather obscure. Mainly, I was curious about the Mule. He is a strange phenomenon—but that's a chewed cud; I'll not go into it. Secondly, it would make an interesting and educational training project for a man who had experience with the Foundation and the Foundation underground and showed promise of future usefulness to us. You see—"

Ovall's long face fell into vertical lines as he showed his large teeth, "You must have been surprised at the outcome, then, since there is not a world among the Traders, I believe, that does not know that this nephew of yours abducted a Mule underling in the name of the Foundation and furnished the Mule with a *casus belli*. Galaxy, Randu, you spin romances. I find it hard to believe you had no hand in that. Come, it was a skillful job."

Randu shook his white head, "Not of my doing. Nor, willfully, of my nephew's, who is now held prisoner at the

Foundation, and may not live to see the completion of this so-skillful job. I have just heard from him. The Personal Capsule has been smuggled out somehow, come through the war zone, gone to Haven, and traveled from there to here. It has been a month on its travels."

"And?—"

Randu leaned a heavy hand upon the heel of his palm and said, sadly, "I'm afraid we are cast for the same role that the onetime warlord of Kalgan played. The Mule is a mutant!"

There was a momentary qualm; a faint impression of quickened heartbeats. Randu might easily have imagined it.

When Mangin spoke, the evenness of his voice was unchanged, "How do you know?"

"Only because my nephew says so, but he was on Kalgan."

"What kind of a mutant? There are all kinds, you know."

Randu forced the rising impatience down, "All kinds of mutants, yes, Mangin. All kinds! But only one kind of Mule. What kind of a mutant would start as an unknown, assemble an army, establish, they say, a five-mile asteroid as original base, capture a planet, then a system, then a region—and then attack the Foundation, and *defeat* them at Horleggor. *And all in two or three years!*"

Ovall Gri shrugged, "So you think he'll beat the Foundation?"

"I don't know. Suppose he does?"

"Sorry, I can't go that far. You *don't* beat the Foundation. Look, there's not a new fact we have to go on except for the statements of a . . . well, of an inexperienced boy. Suppose we shelve it for a while. With all the Mule's victories, we weren't worried until now, and unless he goes a good deal further than he has, I see no reason to change that. Yes?"

Randu frowned and despaired at the cobweb texture of his argument. He said to both, "Have we yet made any contact with the Mule?"

"No," both answered.

"It's true, though, that we've tried, isn't it? It's true that there's not much purpose to our meeting unless we do reach him, isn't it? It's true that so far there's been more drinking than thinking, and more wooing than doing—I quote from an editorial in today's Radole Tribune—and all because we can't reach the Mule. Gentlemen, we have nearly a thousand ships waiting to be thrown into the fight at the proper moment

133

to seize control of the Foundation. I say we should change that. I say, throw those thousand onto the board now— *against the Mule.*"

"You mean for the Tyrant Indbur and the bloodsuckers of the Foundation?" demanded Mangin, with quiet venom.

Randu raised a weary hand, "Spare me the adjectives. Against the Mule, I say, and for I-don't-care-who."

Ovall Gri rose, "Randu, I'll have nothing to do with that. You present it to the full council tonight if you particularly hunger for political suicide."

He left without another word and Mangin followed silently, leaving Randu to drag out a lonely hour of endless, insoluble consideration.

At the full council that night, he said nothing.

But it was Ovall Gri who pushed into his room the next morning; an Ovall Gri only sketchily dressed and who had neither shaved nor combed his hair.

Randu stared at him over a yet-uncleared breakfast table with an astonishment sufficiently open and strenuous to cause him to drop his pipe.

Ovall said baldly, harshly. "Mnemon has been bombarded from space by treacherous attack."

Randu's eyes narrowed, "The Foundation?"

"The Mule!" exploded Ovall. "The Mule!" His words raced, "It was unprovoked and deliberate. Most of our fleet had joined the international flotilla. The few left as Home Squadron were insufficient and were blown out of the sky. There have been no landings yet, and there may not be, for half the attackers are reported destroyed—but it is war—and I have come to ask how Haven stands on the matter."

"Haven, I am sure, will adhere to the spirit of the Charter of Federation. But, you see? He attacks us as well."

"This Mule is a madman. Can he defeat the universe?" He faltered and sat down to seize Randu's wrist, "Our few survivors have reported the Mule's poss . . . enemy's possession of a new weapon. An atomic-field depressor."

"A what?"

Ovall said, "Most of our ships were lost because their atomic weapons failed them. It could not have happened by either accident or sabotage. It must have been a weapon of the Mule. It didn't work perfectly; the effect was intermittent; there were ways to neutralize—my dispatches are not detailed. But you see that such a tool would change the nature of war and, possibly, make our entire fleet obsolete."

Randu felt an old, old man. His face sagged hopelessly, "I am afraid a monster is grown that will devour all of us. Yet we must fight him."

17. The Visi-Sonor

EBLING MIS' HOUSE in a not-so-pretentious neighborhood of Terminus City was well known to the intelligentsia, literati, and just-plain-well-read of the Foundation. Its notable characteristics depended, subjectively, upon the source material that was read. To a thoughtful biographer, it was the "symbolization of a retreat from a nonacademic reality," a society columnist gushed silkily at its "frightfully masculine atmosphere of careless disorder," a University Ph. D. called it brusquely, "bookish, but unorganized," a nonuniversity friend said, "good for a drink anytime and you can put your feet on the sofa," and a breezy newsweekly broadcast, that went in for color, spoke of the "rocky, down-to-earth no-nonsense living quarters of blaspheming, Leftish, balding Ebling Mis."

To Bayta, who thought for no audience but herself at the moment, and who had the advantage of first-hand information, it was merely sloppy.

Except for the first few days, her imprisonment had been a light burden. Far lighter, it seemed, than this half-hour wait in the psychologist's home—under secret observation, perhaps? She had been with Toran then, at least—

Perhaps she might have grown wearier of the strain, had not Magnifico's long nose drooped in a gesture that plainly showed his own far greater tension.

Magnifico's pipe-stem legs were folded up under a pointed, sagging chin, as if he were trying to huddle himself into disappearance, and Bayta's hand went out in a gentle and automatic gesture of reassurance. Magnifico winced, then smiled.

"Surely, my lady, it would seem that even yet my body

denies the knowledge of my mind and expects of others' hands a blow."

"There's no need for worry, Magnifico. I'm with you, and I won't let anyone hurt you."

The clown's eyes sidled towards her, then drew away quickly. "But they kept me away from you earlier—and from your kind husband—and, on my word, you may laugh, but I was lonely for missing friendship."

"I wouldn't laugh at that. I was, too."

The clown brightened, and he hugged his knees closer. He said, "You have not met this man who will see us?" It was a cautious question.

"No. But he is a famous man. I have seen him in the newscasts and heard quite a good deal of him. I think he's a good man, Magnifico, who means us no harm."

"Yes?" The clown stirred uneasily. "That may be, my lady, but he has questioned me before, and his manner is of an abruptness and loudness that bequivers me. He is full of strange words, so that the answers to his questions could not worm out of my throat. Almost, I might believe the romancer who once played on my ignorance with a tale that, at such moments, the heart lodged in the windpipe and prevented speech."

"But it's different now. We're two to his one, and he won't be able to frighten the both of us, will he?"

"No, my lady."

A door slammed somewhere, and the roaring of a voice entered the house. Just outside the room, it coagulated into words with a fierce, "Get the Ga-LAX-y out of here!" and two uniformed guards were momentarily visible through the opening door, in quick retreat.

Ebling Mis entered frowning, deposited a carefully wrapped bundle on the floor, and approached to shake Bayta's hand with careless pressure. Bayta returned it vigorously, man-fashion. Mis did a double-take as he turned to the clown, and favored the girl with a longer look.

He said, "Married?"

"Yes. We went through the legal formalities."

Mis paused. Then, "Happy about it?"

"So far."

Mis shrugged, and turned again to Magnifico. He unwrapped the package, "Know what this is, boy?"

Magnifico fairly hurled himself out of his seat and caught

137

the multi-keyed instrument. He fingered the myriad knobby contacts and threw a sudden back somersault of joy, to the imminent destruction of the nearby furniture.

He croaked, "A Visi-Sonor—and of a make to distill joy out of a dead man's heart." His long fingers caressed softly and slowly, pressing lightly on contacts with a rippling motion, resting momentarily on one key then another— and in the air before them there was a soft glowing rosiness, just inside the range of vision.

Ebling Mis said, "All right, boy, you said you could pound on one of those gadgets, and there's your chance. You'd better tune it, though. It's out of a museum." Then, in an aside to Bayta, "Near as I can make it, no one on the Foundation can make it talk right."

He leaned closer and said quickly, "The clown won't talk without you. Will you help?"

She nodded.

"Good!" he said. "His state of fear is almost fixed, and I doubt that his mental strength would possibly stand a psychic probe. If I'm to get anything out of him otherwise, he's got to feel absolutely at ease. You understand?"

She nodded again.

"This Visi-Sonor is the first step in the process. He says he can play it; and his reaction now makes it pretty certain that it's one of the great joys of his life. So whether the playing is good or bad, be interested and appreciative. Then exhibit friendliness and confidence in me. Above all, follow my lead in everything." There was a swift glance at Magnifico, huddled in a corner of the sofa, making rapid adjustments in the interior of the instrument. He was completely absorbed.

Mis said in a conversational tone to Bayta, "Ever hear a Visi-Sonor?"

"Once," said Bayta, equally casually, "at a concert of rare instruments. I wasn't impressed."

"Well, I doubt that you came across good playing. There are very few really good players. It's not so much that it requires physical co-ordination—a multi-bank piano requires more, for instance—as a certain type of free-wheeling mentality." In a lower voice, "That's why our living skeleton there might be better than we think. More often than not, good players are idiots otherwise. It's one of those queer setups that makes psychology interesting."

He added, in a patent effort to manufacture light conversation. "You know how the beblistered thing works? I looked it up for this purpose, and all I've made out so far is that its radiations stimulate the optic center of the brain directly, without ever touching the optic nerve. It's actually the utilization of a sense never met with in ordinary nature. Remarkable, when you come to think of it. What you hear is all right. That's ordinary. Eardrum, cochlea, all that. But— Shh! He's ready. Will you kick that switch. It works better in the dark."

In the darkness, Magnifico was a mere blob, Ebling Mis a heavy-breathing mass. Bayta found herself straining her eyes anxiously, and at first with no effect. There was a thin, reedy quaver in the air, that wavered raggedly up the scale. It hovered, dropped and caught itself, gained in body, and swooped into a booming crash that had the effect of a thunderous split in a veiling curtain.

A little globe of pulsing color grew in rhythmic spurts and burst in midair into formless gouts that swirled high and came down as curving streamers in interlacing patterns. They coalesed into little spheres, no two alike in color—and Bayta began discovering things.

She noticed that closing her eyes made the color pattern all the clearer; that each little movement of color had its own little pattern of sound; that she could not identify the colors; and, lastly, that the globes were not globes but little figures.

Little figures; little shifting flames, that danced and flickered in their myriads; that dropped out of sight and returned from nowhere; that whipped about one another and coalesced then into a new color.

Incongruously, Bayta thought of the little blobs of color that come at night when you close your eyelids till they hurt, and stare patiently. There was the old familiar effect of the marching polka dots of shifting color, of the contracting concentric circles, of the shapeless masses that quiver momentarily. All that, larger, multivaried—and each little dot of color a tiny figure.

They darted at her in pairs, and she lifted her hands with a sudden gasp, but they tumbled and for an instant she was the center of a brilliant snowstorm, while cold light slipped off her shoulders and down her arm in a luminous ski-slide, shooting off her stiff fingers and meeting slowly in a shining midair focus. Beneath it all, the sound of a hundred instruments flowed in liquid streams until she could not tell it from the light.

She wondered if Ebling Mis were seeing the same thing, and if not, what he did see. The wonder passed, and then—

She was watching again. The little figures—were they little figures?—little tiny women with burning hair that turned and bent too quickly for the mind to focus?—seized one another in star-shaped groups that turned—and the music was faint laughter—girls' laughter that began inside the ear.

The stars drew together, sparked toward one another, grew slowly into structure—and from below, a palace shot upward in rapid evolution. Each brick a tiny color, each color a tiny spark, each spark a stabbing light that shifted patterns and led the eye skyward to twenty jeweled minarets.

A glittering carpet shot out and about, whirling, spinning an insubstantial web that engulfed all space, and from it luminous shoots stabbed upward and branched into trees that sang with a music all their own.

Bayta sat inclosed in it. The music welled about her in rapid, lyrical flights. She reached out to touch a fragile tree and blossoming spicules floated downwards and faded, each with its clear, tiny tinkle.

The music crashed in twenty cymbals, and before her an area flamed up in a spout and cascaded down invisible steps into Bayta's lap, where it spilled over and flowed in rapid current, raising the fiery sparkle to her waist, while across her lap was a rainbow bridge and upon it the little figures—

A place, and a garden, and tiny men and women on a bridge, stretching out as far as she could see, swimming through the stately swells of stringed music converging in upon her—

And then—there seemed a frightened pause, a hesitant, indrawn motion, a swift collapse. The colors fled, spun into a globe that shrank, and rose, and disappeared.

And it was merely dark again.

A heavy foot scratched for the pedal, reached it, and the light flooded in; the flat light of a prosy sun. Bayta blinked until the tears came, as though for the longing of what was gone. Ebling Mis was a podgy inertness with his eyes still round and his mouth still open.

Only Magnifico himself was alive, and he fondled his Visi-Sonor in a crooning ecstasy.

"My lady," he gasped, "it is indeed of an effect the most
140

magical. It is of balance and response almost beyond hope in its delicacy and stability. On this, it would seem I could work wonders. How liked you my composition, my lady?"

"Was it yours?" breathed Bayta. "Your own?"

At her awe, his thin face turned a glowing red to the tip of his mighty nose. "My very own, my lady. The Mule liked it not, but often and often I have played it for my own amusement. It was once, in my youth, that I saw the palace—a gigantic place of jeweled riches that I saw from a distance at a time of high carnival. There were people of a splendor undreamed of—and magnificence more than ever I saw afterwards, even in the Mule's service. It is but a poor makeshift I have created, but my mind's poverty precludes more. I call it, 'The Memory of Heaven.'"

Now through the midst of the chatter, Mis shook himself to active life. "Here," he said, "here, Magnifico, would you like to do that same thing for others?"

For a moment, the clown drew back. "For others?" he quavered.

"For thousands," cried Mis, "in the great Halls of the Foundation. Would you like to be your own master, and honored by all, wealthy, and . . . and—" his imagination failed him. "And all that? Eh? What do you say?"

"But how may I be all that, mighty sir, for indeed I am but a poor clown ungiven to the great things of the world?"

The psychologist puffed out his lips, and passed the back of his hand across his brow. He said, "But your playing, man. The world is yours if you would play so for the mayor and his Trading Trusts. Wouldn't you like that?"

The clown glanced briefly at Bayta, "Would *she* stay with me?"

Bayta laughed, "Of course, silly. Would it be likely that I'd leave you now that you're on the point of becoming rich and famous?"

"It would all be yours," he replied earnestly, "and surely the wealth of Galaxy itself would be yours before I could repay my debt to your kindness."

"But," said Mis, casually, "if you would first help me—"

"What is that?"

The psychologist paused, and smiled, "A little surface probe that doesn't hurt. It wouldn't touch but the peel of your brain."

There was a flare of deadly fear in Magnifico's eyes. "Not a

141

probe. I have seen it used. It drains the mind and leaves an empty skull. The Mule did use it upon traitors and let them wander mindless through the streets, until out of mercy, they were killed." He held up his hand to push Mis away.

"That was a psychic probe," explained Mis, patiently, "and even that would only harm a person when misused. This probe I have is a surface probe and wouldn't hurt a baby."

"That's right, Magnifico," urged Bayta. "It's only to help beat the Mule and keep him far away. Once that's done, you and I will be rich and famous all our lives."

Magnifico held out a trembling hand, "Will you hold my hand, then?"

Bayta took it in both her own, and the clown watched the approach of the burnished terminal plates with large eyes.

Ebling Mis rested carelessly on the too-lavish chair in Mayor Indbur's private quarters, unregenerately unthankful for the condescension shown him and watched the small mayor's fidgeting unsympathetically. He tossed away a cigar stub and spat out a shred of tobacco.

"And, incidentally, if you want something for your next concert at Mallow Hall, Indbur," he said, "you can dump out those electronic gadgeteers into the sewers they came from and have this little freak play the Visi-Sonor for you. Indbur—it's out of this world."

Indbur said peevishly, "I did not call you here to listen to your lectures on music. What of the Mule? Tell me that. What of the Mule?"

"The Mule? Well, I'll tell you—I used a surface probe and got little. Can't use the psychic probe because the freak is scared blind of it, so that his resistance will probably blow his unprintable mental fuses as soon as contact is made. But this is what I've got, if you'll just stop tapping your fingernails—

"First place, de-stress the Mule's physical strength. He's probably strong, but most of the freak's fairy tales about it are probably considerably blown up by his own fearful memory. He wears queer glasses and his eyes kill, he evidently has mental powers."

"So much we had at the start," commented the mayor, sourly.

"Then the probe confirms it, and from there on I've been working mathematically."

"So? And how long will all this take? Your word-rattling will deafen me yet."

"About a month, I should say, and I may have something for you. And I may not, of course. But what of it? If this is all outside Seldon's plans, our chances are precious little, unprintable little."

Indbur whirled on the psychologist fiercely, "Now I have you, traitor. Lie! Say you're not one of these criminal rumormongers that are spreading defeatism and panic through the Foundation, and making my work doubly hard."

"I? I?" Mis gathered anger slowly.

Indbur swore at him, "Because by the dust-clouds of space, the Foundation will win—the Foundation *must* win."

"Despite the loss at Horleggor?"

"It was not a loss. You have swallowed that spreading lie, too? We were outnumbered and betreasoned—"

"By whom?" demanded Mis, contemptuously.

"By the lice-ridden democrats of the gutter," shouted Indbur back at him, "I have known for long that the fleet has been riddled by democratic cells. Most have been wiped out, but enough remain of the unexplained surrender of twenty ships in the thickest of the swarming fight. Enough to force an apparent defeat.

"For that matter, my rough-tongued, simple patriot and epitome of the primitive virtues, what are your own connections with the democrats?"

Ebling Mis shrugged it off, "You rave, do you know that? What of the retreat since, and the loss of half of Siwenna? Democrats again?"

"No. Not democrats," the little man smiled sharply. "We retreat—as the Foundation has always retreated under attack, until the inevitable march of history turns with us. Already, I see the outcome. Already, the so-called underground of the democrats has issued manifestoes swearing aid and allegiance to the Government. It could be a feint, a cover for a deeper treachery, but I make good use of it, and the propaganda distilled from it will have its effect, whatever the crawling traitors scheme. And better than that—"

"Even better than that, Indbur?"

"Judge for yourself. Two days ago, the so-called Association of Independent Traders declared war on the Mule, and the Foundation fleet is strengthened, at a stroke, by a thousand ships. You see, this Mule goes too far. He finds us divided and

143

quarreling among ourselves and under the pressure of his attack we unite and grow strong. He *must* lose. It is inevitable— as always."

Mis still exuded skepticism, "Then you tell me that Seldon planned even for the fortuitous occurrence of a mutant."

"A mutant! I can't tell him from a human, nor could you but for the ravings of a rebel captain, some outland youngsters, and an addled juggler and clown. You forget the most conclusive evidence of all—your own."

"My own?" For just a moment, Mis was startled.

"Your own," sneered the mayor. "The Time Vault opens in nine weeks. What of that? It opens for a crisis. If this attack of the Mule is *not* the crisis, where is the 'real' one, the one the Vault is opening for? Answer me, you lardish ball."

The psychologist shrugged, "All right. If it keeps you happy. Do me a favor, though. Just in case . . . just in *case* old Seldon makes his speech and it *does* go sour, suppose you let me attend the Grand Opening."

"All right. Get out of here. And stay out of my sight for nine weeks."

"With unprintable pleasure, you wizened horror," muttered Mis to himself as he left.

18. Fall of the Foundation

THERE WAS an atmosphere about the Time Vault that just missed definition in several directions at once. It was not one of decay, for it was well lit and well conditioned, with the color scheme of the walls lively, and the rows of fixed chairs comfortable and apparently designed for eternal use. It was not even ancient, for three centuries had left no obvious mark. There was certainly no effort at the creation of awe or reverence, for the appointments were simple and everyday—next door to bareness, in fact.

Yet after all the negatives were added and the sum disposed of, something was left—and that something centered about the glass cubicle that dominated half the room with its clear emptiness. Four times in three centuries, the living simulacrum of Hari Seldom himself had sat there and spoken. Twice he had spoken to no audience.

Through three centuries and nine generations, the old man who had seen the great days of universal empire projected himself—and still he understood more of the Galaxy of his great-ultra-great-grandchildren, than did those grandchildren themselves.

Patiently that empty cubicle waited.

The first to arrive was Mayor Indbur III, driving his ceremonial ground car through the hushed and anxious streets. Arriving with him was his own chair, higher than those that belonged there, and wider. It was placed before all the others, and Indbur dominated all but the empty glassiness before him.

The solemn official at his left bowed a reverent head. "Excellence, arrangements are completed for the widest possible subetheric spread for the official announcement by your excellence tonight."

"Good. Meanwhile, special interplanetary programs concerning the Time Vault are to continue. There will, of course, be no predictions or speculations of any sort on the subject. Does popular reaction continue satisfactory?"

"Excellence, very much so. The vicious rumors prevailing of late have decreased further. Confidence is widespread."

"Good!" He gestured the man away and adjusted his elaborate neckpiece to a nicety.

It was twenty minutes of noon!

A select group of the great props of the mayoralty—the leaders of the great Trading organizations—appeared in ones and twos with the degree of pomp appropriate to their financial status and place in mayoral favor. Each presented himself to the mayor, received a gracious word or two, took an asigned seat.

Somewhere, incongruous among the stilted ceremony of all this, Randu of Haven made his appearance and wormed his way unannounced to the mayor's seat.

"Excellence!" he muttered, and bowed.

Indbur frowned. "You have not been granted an audience."

"Excellence, I have requested one for a week."

"I regret that the matters of State involved in the appearance of Seldon have—"

"Excellence, I regret them, too, but I must ask you to rescind your order that the ships of the Independent Traders be distributed among the fleets of the Foundation."

Indbur had flushed red at the interruption. "This is not the time for discussion."

"Excellence, it is the only time," Randu whispered urgently. "As representative of the Independent Trading Worlds, I tell you such a move can not be obeyed. It must be rescinded before Seldon solves our problem for us. Once the emergency is passed, it will be too late to conciliate and our alliance will melt away."

Indbur stared at Randu coldly. "You realize that I am head of the Foundation armed forces? Have I the right to determine military policy or have I not?"

"Excellence, you have, but some things are inexpedient."

"I recognize no inexpediency. It is dangerous to allow your people separate fleets in this emergency. Divided action plays into the hands of the enemy. We must unite, ambassador, militarily as well as politically."

Randu felt his throat muscles tighten. He omitted the courtesy of the opening title. "You feel safe now that Seldon will speak, and you move against us. A month ago you were soft and yielding, when our ships defeated the Mule at Terel. I might remind you, sir, that it is the Foundation Fleet that has been defeated in open battle five times, and that the ships of the Independent Trading Worlds have won your victories for you."

Indbur frowned dangerously, "You are no longer welcome upon Terminus, ambassador. Your return will be requested this evening. Furthermore, your connection with subversive democratic forces on Terminus will be—and has been—investigated."

Randu replied, "When I leave, our ships will go with me. I know nothing of your democrats. I know only that your Foundation's ships have surrendered to the Mule by the treason of their high officers, not their sailors, democratic or otherwise. I tell you that twenty ships of the Foundation surrendered at Horleggor at the orders of their rear admiral, when they were unharmed and unbeaten. The rear admiral was your own close associate—he presided at the trial of my nephew when he first arrived from Kalgan. It is not the only case we know of and our ships and men will not be risked under potential traitors."

Indbur said, "You will be placed under guard upon leaving here."

Randu walked away under the silent stares of the contemptuous coterie of the rulers of Terminus.

It was ten minutes of twelve!

Bayta and Toran had already arrived. They rose in their back seats and beckoned to Randu as he passed.

Randu smiled gently, "You are here after all. How did you work it?"

"Magnifico was our politician," grinned Toran. "Indbur insists upon his Visi-Sonor composition based on the Time Vault, with himself, no doubt, as hero. Magnifico refused to attend without us, and there was no arguing him out of it. Ebling Mis is with us, or was. He's wandering about somewhere." Then, with a sudden access of anxious gravity, "Why, what's wrong, uncle? You don't look well."

Randu nodded, "I suppose not. We're in for bad times, Toran. When the Mule is disposed of, our turn will come, I'm afraid."

147

A straight solemn figure in white approached, and greeted them with a stiff bow.

Bayta's dark eyes smiled, as she held out her hand, "Captain Pritcher! Are you on space duty then?"

The captain took the hand and bowed lower, "Nothing like it. Dr. Mis, I understand, has been instrumental in bringing me here, but it's only temporary. Back to home guard tomorrow. What time is it?"

It was three minutes of twelve!

Magnifico was the picture of misery and heartsick depression. His body curled up, in his eternal effort at self-effacement. His long nose was pinched at the nostrils and his large, down-slanted eyes darted uneasily about.

He clutched at Bayta's hand, and when she bent down, he whispered, "Do you suppose, my lady, that all these great ones were in the audience, perhaps, when I . . . when I played the Visi-Sonor?"

"Everyone, I'm sure," Bayta assured him, and shook him gently. "And I'm sure they all think you're the most wonderful player in the Galaxy and that your concert was the greatest ever seen, so you just straighten yourself and sit correctly. We must have dignity."

He smiled feebly at her mock-frown and unfolded his long-boned limbs slowly.

It was noon—

—and the glass cubicle was no longer empty.

It was doubtful that anyone had witnessed the appearance. It was a clean break; one moment not there and the next moment there.

In the cubicle was a figure in a wheelchair, old and shrunken, from whose wrinkled face bright eyes shone, and whose voice, as it turned out, was the livest thing about him. A book lay face downward in his lap, and the voice came softly.

"I am Hari Seldon!"

He spoke through a silence, thunderous in its intensity.

"I am Hari Seldon! I do not know if anyone is here at all by mere sense-perception but that is unimportant. I have few fears as yet of a breakdown in the Plan. For the first three centuries the percentage probability of nondeviation is nine-four point two."

He paused to smile, and then said genially, "By the way, if any of you are standing, you may sit. If any would like to

148

smoke, please do. I am not here in the flesh. I require no ceremony."

"Let us take up the problem of the moment, then. For the first time, the Foundation has been faced, or perhaps, is in the last stages of facing, civil war. Till now, the attacks from without have been adequately beaten off, and inevitably so, according to the strict laws of psychohistory. The attack at present is that of a too-undisciplined outer group of the Foundation against the too-authoritarian central government. The procedure was necessary, the result obvious."

The dignity of the high-born audience was beginning to break. Indbur was half out of his chair.

Bayta leaned forward with troubled eyes. What was the great Seldon talking about? She had missed a few of the words—

"—that the compromise worked out is necessary in two re spects. The revolt of the Independent Traders introduces an element of new uncertainty in a government perhaps grown over-confident. The element of striving is restored. Although beaten, a healthy increase of democracy—"

There were raised voices now. Whispers had ascended the scale of loudness, and the edge of panic was in them.

Bayta said in Toran's ear, "Why doesn't he talk about the Mule? The Traders never revolted."

Toran shrugged his shoulders.

The seated figure spoke cheerfully across and through the increasing disorganization:

"—a new and firmer coalition government was the necessary and beneficial outcome of the logical civil war forced upon the Foundation. And now only the remnants of the old Empire stand in the way of further expansion, and in them, for the next few years, at any rate, is no problem. Of course, I can not reveal the nature of the next prob—"

In the complete uproar, Seldon's lips moved soundlessly.

Ebling Mis was next to Randu, face ruddy. He was shouting. "Seldon is off his rocker. He's got the wrong crisis. Were your Traders ever planning civil war?"

Randu said thinly, "We planned one, yes. We called it off in the face of the Mule."

"Then the Mule is an added feature, unprepared for in Seldon's psycho-history. Now what's happened?"

In the sudden, frozen silence, Bayta found the cubicle once

149

again empty. The atomic glow of the walls was dead, the soft current of conditioned air absent.

Somewhere the sound of a shrill siren was rising and falling in the scale and Randu formed the words with his lips, "Space raid!"

And Ebling Mis held his wrist watch to his ears and shouted suddenly, "Stopped, by the Ga-LAX-y! Is there a watch in the room that is going?" His voice was a roar.

Twenty wrists went to twenty ears. And in far less than twenty seconds, it was quite certain that none were.

"Then," said Mis, with a grim and horrible finality, "something has stopped all atomic power in the Time Vault—and the Mule is attacking."

Indbur's wail rose high above the noise, "Take your seats! The Mule is fifty parsecs distant."

"He was," shouted back Mis, "a week ago. Right now, Terminus is being bombarded."

Bayta felt a deep depression settle softly upon her. She felt its folds tighten close and thick, until her breath forced its way only with pain past her tightened throat.

The outer noise of a gathering crowd was evident. The doors were thrown open and a harried figure entered, and spoke rapidly to Indbur, who had rushed to him.

"Excellence," he whispered, "not a vehicle is running in the city, not a communication line to the outside is open. The Tenth Fleet is reported defeated and the Mule's ships are outside the atmosphere. The general staff—"

Indbur crumpled, and was a collapsed figure of impotence upon the floor. In all that hall, not a voice was raised now. Even the growing crowd without was fearful, but silent, and the horror of cold panic hovered dangerously.

Indbur was raised. Wine was held to his lips. His lips moved before his eyes opened, and the word they formed was, "Surrender!"

Bayta found herself near to crying—not for sorrow or humiliation, but simply and plainly out of a vast frightened despair. Ebling Mis plucked at her sleeve. "Come, young lady—"

She was pulled out of her chair, bodily.

"We're leaving," he said, "and take your musician with you." The plump scientist's lips were trembling and colorless.

"Magnifico," said Bayta, faintly. The clown shrank in horror. His eyes were glassy.

"The Mule," he shrieked. "The Mule is coming for me."

He thrashed wildly at her touch. Toran leaned over and brought his fist up sharply. Magnifico slumped into unconsciousness and Toran carried him out potato-sack fashion.

The next day, the ugly, battle-black ships of the Mule poured down upon the landing fields of the planet Terminus. The attacking general sped down the empty main street of Terminus City in a foreign-made ground car that ran where a whole city of atomic cars still stood useless.

The proclamation of occupation was made twenty-four hours to the minute after Seldon had appeared before the former mighty of the Foundation.

Of all the Foundation planets, only the Independent Traders still stood, and against them the power of the Mule—conqueror of the Foundation—now turned itself.

19. Start of the Search

THE LONELY PLANET, Haven—only planet of an only sun
of a Galactic Sector that trailed raggedly off into intergalac-
tic vacuum—was under siege.

In a strictly military sense, it was certainly under siege,
since no area of space on the Galactic side further than
twenty parsecs distance was outside range of the Mule's
advance bases. In the four months since the shattering fall
of the Foundation, Haven's communications had fallen apart
like a spiderweb under the razor's edge. The ships of Haven
converged inwards upon the home world, and only Haven
itself was now a fighting base.

And in other respects, the siege was even closer; for the
shrouds of helplessness and doom had already invaded—

Bayta plodded her way down the pink-waved aisle past
the rows of milky plastic-topped tables and found her seat
by blind reckoning. She eased on to the high, armless chair,
answered half-heard greetings mechanically, rubbed a wearily-
itching eye with the back of a weary hand, and reached for
her menu.

She had time to register a violent mental reaction of distaste
to the pronounced presence of various cultured-fungus dishes,
which were considered high delicacies at Haven, and which
her Foundation taste found highly inedible—and then she
was aware of the sobbing near her and looked up.

Until then, her notice of Juddee, the plain, snub-nosed, indifferent blonde at the dining unit diagonally across had
been the superficial one of the nonacquaintance. And now
Juddee was crying, biting woefully at a moist handkerchief,
and choking back sobs until her complexion was blotched
with turgid red. Her shapeless radiation-proof costume was

thrown back upon her shoulders, and her transparent face shield had tumbled forward into her dessert, and there remained.

Bayta joined the three girls who were taking turns at the eternally applied and eternally inefficacious remedies of shoulder-patting, hair-smoothing, and incoherent murmuring.

"What's the matter?" she whispered.

One turned to her and shrugged a discreet, "I don't know." Then, feeling the inadequacy of the gesture, she pulled Bayta aside.

"She's had a hard day, I guess. And she's worrying about her husband."

"Is he on space patrol?"

"Yes."

Bayta reached a friendly hand out to Juddee.

"Why don't you go home, Juddee?" Her voice was a cheerfully businesslike intrusion on the soft, flabby inanities that had preceded.

Juddee looked up half in resentment. "I've been out once this week already——"

"Then you'll be out twice. If you try to stay on, you know, you'll just be out three days next week—so going home now amounts to patriotism. Any of you girls work in her department? Well, then, suppose you take care of her card. Better go to the washroom first, Juddee, and get the peaches and cream back where it belongs. Go ahead! Shoo!"

Bayta returned to her seat and took up the menu again with a dismal relief. These moods were contagious. One weeping girl would have her entire department in a frenzy these nerve-torn days.

She made a distasteful decision, pressed the correct buttons at her elbow and put the menu back into its niche.

The tall, dark girl opposite her was saying, "Isn't much any of us can do except cry, is there?"

Her amazingly full lips scarcely moved, and Bayta noticed that their ends were carefully touched to exhibit that artificial, just-so half-smile that was the current last word in sophistication.

Bayta investigated the insinuating thrust contained in the words with lashed eyes and welcomed the diversion of the arrival of her lunch, as the tile-top of her unit moved inward and the food lifted. She tore the wrappings carefully off her cutlery and handled them gingerly till they cooled.

153

She said, "Can't *you* think of anything else to do, Hella?"

"Oh, yes," said Hella. "*I* can!" She flicked her cigarette with a casual and expert finger-motion into the little recess provided and the tiny atom-flash caught it before it hit shallow bottom.

"For instance," and Hella clasped slender, well-kept hands under her chin, "I think we could make a very nice arrangement with the Mule and stop all this nonsense. But then *I* don't have the . . . uh . . . facilities to manage to get out of places quickly when the Mule takes over."

Bayta's clear forehead remained clear. Her voice was light and indifferent. "You don't happen to have a brother or husband in the fighting ships, do you?"

"No. All the more credit that I see no reason for the sacrifice of the brothers and husbands of others."

"The sacrifice will come the more surely for surrender."

"The Foundation surrendered and is at peace. Our men are away and the Galaxy is against us."

Bayta shrugged, and said sweetly, "I'm afraid it is the first of the pair that bothers you." She returned to her vegetable platter and ate it with the clammy realization of the silence about her. No one in ear-shot had cared to answer Hella's cynicism.

She left quickly, after stabbing at the button which cleared her dining unit for the next shift's occupant.

A new girl, three seats away, stage-whispered to Hella, "Who was she?"

Hella's mobile lips curled in indifference. "She's our coordinator's niece. Didn't you know that?"

"Yes?" Her eyes sought out the last glimpse of disappearing back. "What's she doing here?"

"Just an assembly girl. Don't you know it's fashionable to be patriotic? It's all so democratic, it makes me retch."

"Now, Hella," said the plump girl to her right. "She's never pulled her uncle on us yet. Why don't you lay off?"

Hella ignored her neighbor with a glazed sweep of eyes and lit another cigarette.

The new girl was listening to the chatter of the bright-eyes accountant opposite. The words were coming quickly, "—and she's supposed to have been in the Vault—actually in the Vault, you know—when Seldon spoke—and they say the mayor was in frothing furies and there were riots, and all of that sort of thing, you know. She got away before the

154

Mule landed, and they say she had the most tha-rilling escape—had to go through the blockade, and all—and I do wonder she doesn't write a book about it, these war books being so popular these days, you know. And she was supposed to be on this world of the Mule's, too—Kalgan, you know—and—."

The time bell shrilled and the dining room emptied slowly. The accountant's voice buzzed on, and the new girl interrupted only with the conventional and wide-eyed, "Really-y-y-y?" at appropriate points.

The huge cave lights were being shielded group-wise in the gradual descent towards the darkness that meant sleep for the righteous and hard-working, when Bayta returned home.

Toran met her at the door, with a slice of buttered bread in his hand.

"Where've you been?" he asked, food-muffled. Then, more clearly, "I've got a dinner of sorts rassled up. If it isn't much, don't blame me."

But she was circling him, wide-eyed. "Torie! Where's your uniform? What are you doing in civvies?"

"Orders, Bay. Randu is holed up with Ebling Mis right now, and what it's all about, I don't know. So there you have everything."

"Am I going?" She moved towards him impulsively.

He kissed her before he answered, "I believe so. It will probably be dangerous."

"What isn't dangerous?"

"Exactly. Oh, yes, and I've already sent for Magnifico, so he's probably coming too."

"You mean his concert at the Engine Factory will have to be cancelled."

"Obviously."

Bayta passed into the next room and sat down to a meal that definitely bore signs of having been "rassled-up." She cut the sandwiches in two with quick efficiency and said:

"That's too bad about the concert. The girls at the factory were looking forward to it. Magnifico, too, for that matter. Darn it, he's such a queer thing."

"Stirs your mother-complex, Bay, that's what he does. Some day we'll have a baby, and then you'll forget Magnifico."

Bayta answered from the depths of her sandwich, "Strikes me that you're all the stirring my mother-complex can stand."

And then she laid the sandwich down, and was gravely serious in a moment.

"Torie."

"M-m-m?"

"Torie, I was at City Hall today—at the Bureau of Production. That is why I was so late today."

"What were you doing there?"

"Well . . ." she hesitated, uncertainly. "It's been building up. I was getting so I couldn't stand it at the factory. Morale —just doesn't exist. The girls go on crying jags for no particular reason. Those who don't get sick become sullen. Even the little mousie types pout. In my particular section, production isn't a quarter what it was when I came, and there isn't a day that we have a full roster of workers."

"All right," said Toran, "tie in the B. of P. What did you do there?"

"Asked a few questions. And it's so, Torie, it's so all over Haven. Dropping production, increasing sedition and disaffection. The bureau chief just shrugged his shoulders—after I had sat in the anteroom an hour to see him, and only got in because I was the co-ordinator's niece—and said it was beyond him. Frankly, I don't think he cared."

"Now, don't go off base, Bay."

"I don't think he did." She was strenuously fiery. "I tell you there's something wrong. It's that same horrible frustration that hit me in the Time Vault when Seldon deserted us. You felt it yourself."

"Yes, I did."

"Well, it's back," she continued savagely. "And we'll never be able to resist the Mule. Even if we had the material, we lack the heart, the spirit, the will—Torie, there's no use fighting—"

Bayta had never cried in Toran's memory, and she did not cry now. Not really. But Toran laid a light hand on her shoulder and whispered, "Suppose you forget it, baby. I know what you mean. But there's nothing—"

"Yes, there's nothing we can do! Everyone says that—and we just sit and wait for the knife to come down."

She returned to what was left of her sandwich and tea. Quietly, Toran was arranging the beds. It was quite dark outside.

Randu, as newly-appointed co-ordinator—in itself a wartime post—of the confederation of cities on Haven, had been assigned, at his own request, to an upper room, out of the window of which he could brood over the roof tops and greenery of the city. Now, in the fading of the cave lights, the city receded into the level lack of distinction of the shades. Randu did not care to meditate upon the symbolism.

He said to Ebling Mis—whose clear, little eyes seemed to have no further interest than the red filled goblet in his hand —"There's a saying on Haven that when the cave lights go out, it is time for the righteous and hard-working to sleep."

"Do you sleep much lately?"

"No! Sorry to call you so late, Mis. I like the night better somehow these days. Isn't that strange? The people on Haven condition themselves pretty strictly on the lack of light meaning sleep. Myself, too. But it's different now—"

"You're hiding," said Mis, flatly. "You're surrounded by people in the waking period, and you feel their eyes and their hopes on you. You can't stand up under it. In the sleep period, you're free."

"Do you feel it, too, then? This miserable sense of de feat?"

Ebling Mis nodded slowly, "I do. It's a mass psychosis, an unprintable mob panic. Ga-LAX-y, Randu, what do you expect? Here you have a whole culture brought up to a blind, blubbering belief that a folk hero of the past has everything all planned out and is taking care of every little piece of their unprintable lives. The thought-pattern evoked has characteristics *ad religio*, and you know what that means."

"Not a bit."

Mis was not enthusiastic about the necessity of explanation. He never was. So he growled, stared at the long cigar he rolled thoughtfully between his fingers and said, "Characterized by strong faith reactions. Beliefs can't be shaken short of a major shock, in which case, a fairly complete mental disruption results. Mild cases—hysteria, morbid sense of insecurity. Advanced cases—madness and suicide."

Randu bit at a thumbnail. "When Seldon fails us, in other words, our prop disappears, and we've been leaning upon it so long, our muscles are atrophied to where we can not stand without it."

"That's it. Sort of a clumsy metaphor, but that's it."

"And you, Ebling, what of your own muscles?"

The psychologist filtered a long draught of air through his cigar, and let the smoke laze out. "Rusty, but not atrophied.

157

My profession has resulted in just a bit of independent thinking."

"And you see a way out?"

"No, but there must be one. Maybe Seldon made no provisions for the Mule. Maybe he didn't guarantee our victory. But, then, neither did he guarantee defeat. He's just out of the game and we're on our own. The Mule can be licked."

"How?"

"By the only way anyone can be licked—by attacking in strength at weakness. See here, Randu, the Mule isn't a superman. If he is finally defeated, everyone will see that for himself. It's just that he's an unknown, and the legends cluster quickly. He's supposed to be a mutant. Well, what of that? A mutant means a 'superman' to the ignoramuses of humanity. Nothing of the sort.

"It's been estimated that several million mutants are born in the Galaxy every day. Of the several million, all but one or two percent can be detected only by means of microscopes and chemistry. Of the one or two percent macromutants, that is, those with mutations detectable to the naked eye or naked mind, all but one or two percent are freaks, fit for the amusement centers, the laboratories, and death. Of the few macromutants whose differences are to the good, almost all are harmless curiosities, unusual in some single respect, normal—and often subnormal—in most others. You see that, Randu?"

"I do. But what of the Mule?"

"Supposing the Mule to be a mutant then, we can assume that he has some attribute, undoubtedly mental, which can be used to conquer worlds. In other respects, he undoubtedly has his shortcomings, which we must locate. He would not be so secretive, so shy of others' eyes, if these shortcomings were not apparent and fatal. *If* he's a mutant."

"Is there an alternative?"

"There might be. Evidence for mutation rests on Captain Han Pritcher of what used to be Foundation's Intelligence. He drew his conclusions from the feeble memories of those who claimed to know the Mule—or somebody who might have been the Mule—in infancy and early childhood. Pritcher worked on slim pickings there, and what evidence he found might easily have been planted by the Mule for his own purposes, for it's certain that the Mule has been vastly aided by his reputation as a mutant-superman."

"This is interesting. How long have you thought that?"

"I never thought that, in the sense of believing it. It is merely an alternative to be considered. For instance, Randu, suppose the Mule has discovered a form of radiation capable of depressing mental energy just as he is in possession of one which depresses atomic reactions. What then, eh? Could that explain what's hitting us now—and what did hit the Foundation?"

Randu seemed immersed in a near-wordless gloom.

He said, "What of your own researches on the Mule's clown."

And now Ebling Mis hesitated. "Useless as yet. I spoke bravely to the mayor previous to the Foundation's collapse, mainly to keep his courage up partly to keep my own up as well. But, Randu, if my mathematical tools were up to it, then from the clown alone I could analyze the Mule completely. Then we would have him. Then we could solve the queer anomalies that have impressed me already."

"Such as?"

"Think, man. The Mule defeated the navies of the Foundation at will, but he has not once managed to force the much weaker fleets of the Independent Traders to retreat in open combat. The Foundation fell at a blow; the Independent Traders hold out against all his strength. He first used his Extinguishing Field upon the atomic weapons of the Independent Traders of Mnemon. The element of surprise lost them that battle but they countered the Field. He was never able to use it successfully against the Independents again.

"But over and over again, it worked against Foundation forces. It worked on the Foundation itself. Why? With our present knowledge, it is all illogical. So there must be factors of which we are not aware."

"Treachery?"

"That's rattle-pated nonsense, Randu. Unprintable twaddle. There wasn't a man on the Foundation who wasn't sure of victory. Who would betray a certain-to-win side."

Randu stepped to the curved window and stared unseeingly out into the unseeable. He said, "But we're certain to lose now, if the Mule had a thousand weaknesses; if he were a network of holes——"

He did not turn. It was as if the slump of his back, the

159

nervous groping for one another of the hands behind him that spoke. He said, "We escaped easily after the Time Vault episode, Ebling. Others might have escaped as well. A few did. Most did not. The Extinguishing Field could have been counteracted. It asked ingenuity and a certain amount of labor. All the ships of the Foundation Navy could have flown to Haven or other nearby planets to continue the fight as we did. Not one per cent did so. In effect, they deserted to the enemy.

"The Foundation underground, upon which most people here seem to rely so heavily, has thus far done nothing of consequence. The Mule has been politic enough to promise to safeguard the property and profits of the great Traders and they have gone over to him."

Ebling Mis said stubbornly, "The plutocrats have always been against us."

"They always held the power, too. Listen, Ebling. We have reason to believe that the Mule or his tools have already been in contact with powerful men among the Independent Traders. At least ten of the twenty-seven Trading Worlds are known to have gone over to the Mule. Perhaps ten more waver. There are personalities on Haven itself who would not be unhappy over the Mule's domination. It's apparently an insurmountable temptation to give up endangered political power, if that will maintain your hold over economic affairs."

"You don't think Haven can fight the Mule?"

"I don't think Haven will." And now Randu turned his troubled face full upon the psychologist. "I think Haven is waiting to surrender. It's what I called you here to tell you. I want you to leave Haven."

Ebling Mis puffed up his plump cheeks in amazement. "Already?"

Randu felt horribly tired. "Ebling, you are the Foundation's greatest psychologist. The real master-psychologists went out with Seldon, but you're the best we have. You're our only chance of defeating the Mule. You can't do that here; you'll have to go to what's left of the Empire."

"To Trantor?"

"That's right. What was once the Empire is bare bones today, but something must still be at the center. They've got the records there, Ebling. You may learn more of mathematical psychology; perhaps enough to be able to interpret the clown's mind. He will go with you, of course."

160

Mis responded dryly, "I doubt if he'd be willing to, even for fear of the Mule, unless your niece went with him."

"I know that. Toran and Bayta are leaving with you for that very reason. And, Ebling, there's another, greater purpose. Hari Seldon founded *two* Foundations three centuries ago; one at each end of the Galaxy. *You must find that Second Foundation.*"

20. Conspirator

THE MAYOR'S PALACE—what was once the mayor's palace—
was a looming smudge in the darkness. The city was quiet
under its conquest and curfew, and the hazy milk of the
great Galactic Lens, with here and there a lonely star,
dominated the sky of the Foundation.

In three centuries the Foundation had grown from a private project of a small group of scientists to a tentacular
trade empire sprawling deep into the Galaxy and half a
year had flung it from its heights to the status of another
conquered province.

Captain Han Pritcher refused to grasp that.

The city's sullen nighttime quiet, the darkened palace, in-
truder-occupied, were symbolic enough, but Captain Han
Pritcher, just within the outer gate of the palace, with the
tiny atomic bomb under his tongue, refused to understand.

A shape drifted closer—the captain bent his head.

The whisper came deathly low, "The alarm system is as it
always was, captain. Proceed! It will register nothing."

Softly, the captain ducked through the low archway, and
down the fountain-lined path to what had been Indbur's
garden.

Four months ago had been the day in the Time Vault, the
fullness of which his memory balked at. Singly and separately
the impressions would come back, unwelcome, mostly at
night.

Old Seldon speaking his benevolent words that were so
shatteringly wrong—the jumbled confusion—Indbur, with his
mayoral costume incongruously bright about his pinched, unconscious face—the frightened crowds gathering quickly,
waiting noiselessly for the inevitable word of surrender—the
young man, Toran, disappearing out of a side door with
the Mule's clown dangling over his shoulder.

And himself, somehow out of it all afterward, with his
car unworkable.

Shouldering his way along and through the leaderless mob
that was already leaving the city—destination unknown.

Making blindly for the various rat holes which were—which had once been—the headquarters for a democratic underground that for eighty years had been failing and dwindling.

And the rat holes were empty.

The next day, black alien ships were momentarily visible in the sky, sinking gently into the clustered buildings of the nearby city. Captain Han Pritcher felt an accumulation of helplessness and despair drown him.

He started his travels in earnest.

In thirty days he had covered nearly two hundred miles on foot, changed to the clothing of a worker in the hydroponic factories whose body he found newly-dead by the side of the road, grown a fierce beard of russet intensity—

And found what was left of the underground.

The city was Newton, the district a residential one of one-time elegance slowly edging towards squalor, the house an undistinguished member of a row, and the man a small-eyed, big-bones whose knotted fists bulged through his pockets and whose wiry body remained unbudgingly in the narrow door opening.

The captain mumbled, "I come from Miran."

The man returned the gambit, grimly. "Miran is early this year."

The captain said, "No earlier than last year."

But the man did not step aside. He said, "Who are you?"

"Aren't you Fox?"

"Do you always answer by asking?"

The captain took an imperceptibly longer breath, and then said calmly, "I am Han Pritcher, Captain of the Fleet, and member of the Democratic Underground Party. Will you let me in?"

The Fox stepped aside. He said, "My real name is Orum Palley."

He held out his hand. The captain took it.

The room was well-kept, but not lavish. In one corner stood a decorative book-film projector, which to the captain's military eyes might easily have been a camouflaged blaster of respectable caliber. The projecting lens covered the doorway, and such could be remotely controlled.

The Fox followed his bearded guest's eyes, and smiled tightly. He said, "Yes! But only in the days of Indbur and his lackey-hearted vampires. It wouldn't do much against the

163

Mule, eh? Nothing would help against the Mule. Are you hungry?"

The captain's jaw muscles tightened beneath his beard, and he nodded.

"It'll take a minute if you don't mind waiting." The Fox removed cans from a cupboard and placed two before Captain Pritcher. "Keep your finger on it, and break them when they're hot enough. My heat-control unit's out of whack. Things like that remind you there's a war on—or was on, eh?"

His quick words had a jovial content, but were said in anything but a jovial tone—and his eyes were coldly thoughtful. He sat down opposite the captain and said, "There'll be nothing but a burn-spot left where you're sitting, if there's anything about you I don't like. Know that?"

The captain did not answer. The cans before him opened at a pressure.

The Fox said, shortly, "Stew! Sorry, but the food situation is short."

"I know," said the captain. He ate quickly; not looking up.

The Fox said, "I once saw you. I'm trying to remember, and the beard is definitely out of the picture."

"I haven't shaved in thirty days." Then, fiercely, "What do you want? I had the correct passwords. I have identification."

The other waved a hand, "Oh, I'll grant you're Pritcher all right. But there are plenty who have the passwords, and the identifications, and the *identities*—who are with the Mule. Ever hear of Levvaw, eh?"

"Yes."

"He's with the Mule."

"What? He——"

"Yes. He was the man they called 'No Surrender.'" The Fox's lips made laughing motions, with neither sound nor humor. "Then there's Willig. With the Mule! Garre and Noth. With the Mule! Why not Pritcher as well, eh? How would I know?"

The captain merely shook his head.

"But it doesn't matter," said the Fox, softly. "They must have my name, if Noth has gone over—so if you're legitimate, you're in more new danger than I am over our acquaintanceship."

The captain had finished eating. He leaned back, "If you have no organization here, where can I find one? The Foundation may have surrendered, but I haven't."

"So! You can't wander forever, captain. Men of the Foundation must have travel permits to move from town to town these days. You know that? Also identity cards. You have one? Also, all officers of the old Navy have been requested to report to the nearest occupation headquarters. That's you, eh?"

"Yes." The Captain's voice was hard. "Do you think I run through fear. I was on Kalgan not long after *its* fall to the Mule. Within a month, not one of the old warlord's officers was at large, because they were the natural military leaders of any revolt. It's always been the underground's knowledge that no revolution can be successful without the control of at least part of the Navy. The Mule evidently knows it, too."

The Fox nodded thoughtfully, "Logical enough. The Mule is thorough."

"I discarded the uniform as soon as I could. I grew the beard. Afterwards there may be a chance that others have taken the same action."

"Are you married?"

"My wife is dead. I have no children."

"You're hostage-immune, then."

"Yes."

"You want my advice?"

"If you have any."

"I don't know what the Mule's policy is or what he intends, but skilled workers have not been harmed so far. Pay rates have gone up. Production of all sorts of atomic weapons is booming."

"Yes? Sounds like a continuing offensive."

"I don't know. The Mule's a subtle son of a drab, and he may merely be soothing the workers into submission. If Seldon couldn't figure him out with all his psycho-history, I'm not going to try. But you're wearing work clothes. That suggests something, eh?"

"I'm not a skilled worker."

"You've had a military course in atomics, haven't you?"

"Certainly."

"That's enough. The Atom-Field Bearings, Inc., is locat-

165

ed here in town. Tell them you've had experience. The stinkers who used to run the factory for Indbur are still running it—for the Mule. They won't ask questions, as long as they need more workers to make their fat hunk. They'll give you an identity card and you can apply for a room in the Corporation's housing district. You might start now."

In that manner, Captain Han Pritcher of the National Fleet became Shield-man Lo Moro of the 45 Shop of Atom-Field Bearings, Inc. And from an Intelligence agent, he descended the social scale to "conspirator"—a calling which led ... months later to what had been Indbur's private garden.

In the garden, Captain Pritcher consulted the radometer in the palm of his hand. The inner warning field was still in operation, and he waited. Half an hour remained to the life of the atomic bomb in his mouth. He rolled it gingerly with his tongue.

The radometer died into an ominous darkness and the captain advanced quickly.

So far, matters had progressed well.

He reflected objectively that the life of the atomic bomb was his as well; that its death was his death—and the Mule's death.

And the grand climacteric of a four-month's private war would be reached; a war that had passed from flight through a Newton factory—

For two months, Captain Pritcher wore leaden aprons and heavy face shields, till all things military had been frictioned off his outer bearing. He was a laborer, who collected his pay, spent his evenings in town, and never discussed politics.

For two months, he did not see the Fox.

And then, one day, a man stumbled past his bench, and there was a scrap of paper in his pocket. The word "Fox" was on it. He tossed it into the atom chamber, where it vanished in a sightless puff, sending the energy output up a millimicrovolt—and turned back to his work.

That night he was at the Fox's home, and took a hand in a game of cards with two other men he knew by reputation and one by name and face.

Over the cards and the passing and repassing tokens, they spoke.

The captain said, "It's a fundamental error. You live in the

166

exploded past. For eighty years our organization has been waiting, for the correct historical moment. We've been blinded by Seldon's psycho-history, one of the first propositions of which is that the individual does not count, does not make history, and that complex social and economic factors override him, make a puppet out of him." He adjusted his cards carefully, appraised their value and said, as he put out a token, "Why not kill the Mule?"

"Well, now, and what good would that do?" demanded the man at his left, fiercely.

"You see," said the captain, discarding two cards, "that's the attitude. What is one man—out of trillions. The Galaxy won't stop rotating because one man dies. But the Mule is not a man, he is a Mutant. Already, he had upset Seldon's plan, and if you'll stop to analyze the implications, it means that he—one man—one mutant upset all of Seldon's psycho-history. If he had never lived, the Foundation would not have fallen. If he ceased living, it would not remain fallen.

"Come, the democrats have fought the mayors and the traders for eighty years by connivery. Let's try assassination."

"How?" interposed the Fox, with cold common sense.

The captain said, slowly, "I've spent three months of thought on that with no solution. I came here and had it in five minutes." He glanced briefly at the man whose broad, pink melon of a face smiled from the place at his right. "You were once Mayor Indbur's chamberlain. I did not know you were of the underground."

"Nor I, that you were."

"Well, then, in your capacity as chamberlain you periodically checked the working of the alarm system of the palace."

"I did."

"And the Mule occupies the palace now."

"So it has been announced—though he is a modest conqueror who makes no speeches, proclamations nor public appearances of any sort."

"That's an old story, and affects nothing. You, my ex-chamberlain, are all we need."

The cards were shown and the Fox collected the stakes. Slowly, he dealt a new hand.

The man who had once been chamberlain picked up his cards, singly, "Sorry, captain. I checked the alarm system, but it was routine. I know nothing about it."

"I expected that, but your mind carries an eidetic memory of the controls if it can be probed deeply enough—with a psychic probe."

The chamberlain's ruddy face paled suddenly and sagged. The cards in his hand crumpled under sudden fist-pressure, "A psychic probe?"

"You needn't worry," said the captain, sharply. "I know how to use one. It will not harm you past a few days' weakness. And if it did, it is the chance you take and the price you pay. There are some among us, no doubt, who from the controls of the alarm could determine the wave-length combinations. There are some among us who could manufacture a small bomb under time-control and I myself will carry it to the Mule."

The men gathered over the table.

The captain continued, "On a given evening, a riot will start in Terminus City in the neighborhood of the palace. No real fighting. Disturbance—then flight. As long as the palace guard is attracted . . . or, at the very least, distracted—"

From that day for a month the preparations went on, and Captain Han Pritcher of the National Fleet having become conspirator descended further in the social scale and became an "assassin."

Captain Pritcher, assassin, was in the palace itself, and found himself grimly pleased with his psychology. A thorough alarm system outside meant few guards within. In this case, it meant none at all.

The floor plan was clear in his mind. He was a blob moving noiselessly up the well-carpeted ramp. At its head, he flattened against the wall and waited.

The small closed door of a private room was before him. Behind that door must be the mutant who had beaten the unbeatable. He was early—the bomb had ten minutes of life in it.

Five of these passed, and still in all the world there was no sound. The Mule had five minutes to live— So had Captain Pritcher—

He stepped forward on sudden impulse. The plot could no longer fail. When the bomb went, the palace would go with it —all the palace. A door between—ten yards between—was nothing. But he wanted to see the Mule as they died together.

168

In a last, insolent gesture, he thundered upon the door—
And it opened and let out the blinding light.

Captain Pritcher staggered, then caught himself. The solemn man, standing in the center of the small room before a suspended fish bowl, looked up mildly.

His uniform was a somber black, and as he tapped the bowl in an absent gesture, it bobbed quickly and the feather-finned orange and vermilion fish within darted wildly.

He said, "Come in, captain!"

To the captain's quivering tongue the little metal globe beneath was swelling ominously—a physical impossibility, the captain knew. But it was in its last minute of life.

The uniformed man said, "You had better spit out the foolish pellet and free yourself for speech. It won't blast."

The minute passed and with a slow, sodden motion the captain bent his head and dropped the silvery globe into his palm. With a furious force it was flung against the wall. It rebounded with a tiny, sharp clangor, gleaming harmlessly as it flew.

The uniformed man shrugged. "So much for that, then. It would have done you no good in any case, captain. I am not the Mule. You will have to be satisfied with his viceroy."

"How did you know?" muttered the captain, thickly.

"Blame it on an efficient counter-espionage system. I can name every member of your little gang, every step of their planning—"

"And you let it go this far?"

"Why not? It has been one of my great purposes here to find you and some others. Particularly you. I might have had you some months ago, while you were still a worker at the Newton Bearings Works, but this is much better. If you hadn't suggested the main outlines of the plot yourself, one of my own men would have advanced something of much the same sort for you. The result is quite dramatic, and rather grimly humorous."

The captain's eyes were hard. "I find it so, too. Is it all over now?"

"Just begun. Come, captain, sit down. Let us leave heroics for the fools who are impressed by it. Captain, you are a capable man. According to the information I have, you were the first on the Foundation to recognize the power of the

Mule. Since then you have interested yourself, rather daringly, in the Mule's early life. You have been one of those who carried off his clown, who, incidentally, has not yet been found, and for which there will yet be full payment. Naturally, your ability is recognized and the Mule is not of those who fear the ability of his enemies as long as he can convert it into the ability of a new friend."

"Is that what you're hedging up to? Oh, no!"

"Oh, yes! It was the purpose of tonight's comedy. You are an intelligent man, yet your little conspiracies against the Mule fail humorously. You can scarcely dignify it with the name of conspiracy. Is it part of your military training to waste ships in hopeless actions?"

"One must first admit them to be hopeless."

"One will," the viceroy assured him, gently. "The Mule has conquered the Foundation. It is rapidly being turned into an arsenal for accomplishment of his greater aims."

"What greater aims?"

"The conquest of the entire Galaxy. The reunion of all the torn worlds into a new Empire. The fulfillment, you dull-witted patriot, of your own Seldon's dream seven hundred years before he hoped to see it. And in the fulfillment, you can help us."

"I can, undoubtedly. But I won't, undoubtedly."

"I understand," reasoned the viceroy, "that only three of the Independent Trading Worlds yet resist. They will not last much longer. It will be the last of all Foundation forces. You still hold out."

"Yes."

"Yet you won't. A voluntary recruit is the most efficient. But the other kind will do. Unfortunately, the Mule is absent. He leads the fight, as always, against the resisting Traders. But he is in continual contact with us. You will not have to wait long."

"For what?"

"For your conversion."

"The Mule," said the captain, frigidly, "will find that beyond his ability."

"But he won't. *I* was not beyond it. You don't recognize me? Come, you were on Kalgan, so you have seen me. I wore a monocle, a fur-lined scarlet robe, a high-crowned hat—"

170

The captain stiffened in dismay. "You were the warlord of Kalgan."

"Yes. And now I am the loyal viceroy of the Mule. You see, he is persuasive."

21. Interlude in Space

THE BLOCKADE was run successfully. In the vast volume of space, not all the navies ever in existence could keep their watch in tight proximity. Given a single ship, a skillful pilot, and a moderate degree of luck, and there are holes and to spare.

With cold-eyed calm, Toran drove a protesting vessel from the vicinity of one star to that of another. If the neighborhood of great mass made an interstellar jump erratic and difficult, it also made the enemy detection devices useless or nearly so.

And once the girdle of ships had been passed the inner sphere of dead space, through whose blockaded sub-ether no message could be driven, was passed as well. For the first time in over three months Toran felt unisolated.

A week passed before the enemy news programs dealt with anything more than the dull, self-laudatory details of growing control over the Foundation. It was a week in which Toran's armored trading ship fleeted in from the Periphery with hasty jumps.

Ebling Mis called out to the pilot room and Toran rose blink-eyed from his charts.

"What's the matter?" Toran stepped down into the small central chamber which Bayta had inevitably devised into a living room.

Mis shook his head. "Bescuppered if I know. The Mule's newsmen are announcing a special bulletin. Thought you might want to get in on it."

"Might as well. Where's Bayta?"

"Setting the table in the diner and picking out a menu— or some such frippery."

Toran sat down upon the cot that served as Magnifico's bed, and waited. The propaganda routine of the Mule's "special bulletins" were monotonously similar. First the martial music, and then the buttery slickness of the announcer. The minor news items would come, following one another in patient lock step. Then the pause. Then the trumpets and the rising excitement and the climax.

Toran endured it. Mis muttered to himself.

The newscaster spilled out, in conventional war-correspondent phraseology, the unctuous words that translated into sound the molten metal and blasted flesh of a battle in space.

"Rapid cruiser squadrons under Lieutenant General Sammin hit back hard today at the task force striking out from Iss—" The carefully expressionless face of the speaker upon the screen faded into the blackness of a space cut through by the quick swaths of ships reeling across emptiness in deadly battle. The voice continued through the soundless thunder—

"The most striking action of the battle was the subsidiary combat of the heavy cruiser *Cluster* against three enemy ships of the 'Nova' class—"

The screen's view veered and closed in. A great ship sparked and one of the frantic attackers glowed angrily, twisted out of focus, swung back and rammed. The *Cluster* bowed wildly and survived the glancing blow that drove the attacker off in twisting reflection.

The newsman's smooth unimpassioned delivery continued to the last blow and the last hulk.

Then a pause, and a largely similar voice-and-picture of the fight off Mnemon, to which the novelty was added of a lengthy description of a hit-and-run landing—the picture of a blasted city—huddled and weary prisoners—and off again.

Mnemon had not long to live.

The pause again—and this time the raucous sound of the expected brasses. The screen faded into the long, impressively soldier-lined corridor up which the government spokesman in councilor's uniform strode quickly.

The silence was oppressive.

The voice that came at last was solemn, slow and hard:

"By order of our sovereign, it is announced that the planet, Haven, hitherto in warlike opposition to his will, has submitted to the acceptance of defeat. At this moment, the forces of our sovereign are occupying the planet. Opposition was scattered, unco-ordinated, and speedily crushed."

The scene faded out, the original newsman returned to state importantly that other developments would be transmitted as they occurred.

173

Then there was dance music, and Ebling Mis threw the shield that cut the power.

Toran rose and walked unsteadily away, without a word. The psychologist made no move to stop him.

When Bayta stepped out of the kitchen, Mis motioned silence.

He said, "They've taken Haven."

And Bayta said, "Already?" Her eyes were round, and sick with disbelief.

"Without a fight. Without an unprin—" He stopped and swallowed. "You'd better leave Toran alone. It's not pleasant for him. Suppose we eat without him this once."

Bayta looked once toward the pilot room, then turned hopelessly. "Very well!"

Magnifico sat unnoticed at the table. He neither spoke nor ate but stared ahead with a concentrated fear that seemed to drain all the vitality out of his thread of a body.

Ebling Mis pushed absently at his iced-fruit dessert and said, harshly, "Two Trading worlds fight. They fight, and bleed, and die and don't surrender. Only at Haven—just as at the Foundation—"

"But why? Why?"

The psychologist shook his head. "It's of a piece with all the problem. Every queer facet is a hint at the nature of the Mule. First, the problem of how he could conquer the Foundation, with little blood, and at a single blow essentially—while the Independent Trading Worlds held out. The blanket on atomic reactions was a puny weapon—we've discussed that back and forth till I'm sick of it—and it did not work on any but the Foundation.

"Randu suggested," and Ebling's grizzly eyebrows pulled together, "it might have been a radiant Will-Depresser. It's what might have done the work on Haven. But then why wasn't it used on Mnemon and Iss—which even now fight with such demonic intensity that it is taking half the Foundation fleet in addition to the Mule's forces to beat them down. Yes, I recognized Foundation ships in the attack."

Bayta whispered, "The Foundation, then Haven. Disaster seems to follow us, without touching. We always seem to get out by a hair. Will it last forever?"

Ebling Mis was not listening. To himself, he was making a point. "But there's another problem—another problem. Bayta, you remember the news item that the Mule's clown was not found on Terminus; that it was suspected he had fled to Haven, or been carried there by his original kidnapers, There is an importance attached to him, Bayta, that doesn't fade, and we have not located it yet. Magnifico must know something that is fatal to the Mule. I'm sure of it."

Magnifico, white and stuttering, protested, "Sire . . . noble lord . . . indeed, I swear it is past my poor reckoning to penetrate your wants. I have told what I know to the utter limits, and with your probe, you have drawn out of my meager wit that which I knew, but knew not that I knew."

"I know . . . I know. It is something small. A hint so small that neither you nor I recognize it for what it is. Yet I must find it—for Mnemon and Iss will go soon, and when they do, we are the last remnants, the last droplets of the independent Foundation."

The stars begin to cluster closely when the core of the Galaxy is penetrated. Gravitational fields begin to overlap at intensities sufficient to introduce perturbations in an interstellar jump, that can not be overlooked.

Toran became aware of that when a jump landed their ship in the full glare of a red giant which clutched viciously, and whose grip was loosed, then wrenched apart, only after twelve sleepless, soul-battering hours.

With charts limited in scope, and an experience not at all fully developed, either operationally or mathematically, Toran resigned himself to days of careful plotting between jumps.

It became a community project of a sort. Ebling Mis checked Toran's mathematics and Bayta tested possible routes, by the various generalized methods, for the presence of real solutions. Even Magnifico was put to work on the calculating machine for routine computations, a type of work, which, once explained, was a source of great amusement to him and at which he was surprisingly proficient.

So at the end of a month, or nearly, Bayta was able to survey the red line that wormed its way through the ship's trimensional model of the Galactic Lens halfway to its center, and say with satiric relish, "You know what it looks like. It looks like a ten-foot earth-worm with a terrific case of indigestion. Eventually, you'll land us back in Haven."

"I will," growled Toran, with a fierce rustle of his chart, "if you don't shut up."

"And at that," continued Bayta, "there is probably a route right through, straight as a meridian of longitude."

"Yeah? Well, in the first place, dimwit, it probably took five hundred ships five hundred years to work out that route by hit-and-miss, and my lousy half-credit charts don't give it. Besides, maybe those straight routes are a good thing to avoid. They're probably choked up with ships. And besides—"

"Oh, for Galaxy's sake, stop driveling and slavering so much righteous indignation." Her hands were in his hair.

He yowled, "Ouch! Let go!" seized her wrists and whipped downward, whereupon Toran, Bayta, and chair formed a tangled threesome on the floor. It degenerated into a panting wrestling match, composed mostly of choking laughter and various foul blows.

Toran broke loose at Magnifico's breathless entrance.

"What is it?"

The lines of anxiety puckered the clown's face and tightened the skin whitely over the enormous bridge of his nose. "The instruments are behaving queerly, sir. I have not, in the knowledge of my ignorance, touched anything—"

In two seconds, Toran was in the pilot room. He said quietly to Magnifico, "Wake up Ebling Mis. Have him come down here."

He said to Bayta, who was trying to get a basic order back to her hair by use of her fingers, "We've been detected, Bay."

"Detected?" And Bayta's arms dropped. "By whom?"

"Galaxy knows," muttered Toran, "but I imagine by someone with blasters already ranged and trained."

He sat down and in a low voice was already sending into the sub-ether the ship's identification code.

And when Ebling Mis entered, bathrobed and blear-eyed, Toran said with a desperate calm, "It seems we're inside the borders of a local Inner Kingdom which is called the Autarchy of Filia."

"Never heard of it," said Mis, abruptly.

"Well, neither did I," replied Toran, "but we're being stopped by a Filian ship just the same, and I don't know what it will involve."

The captain-inspector of the Filian ship crowded aboard with six armed men following him. He was short, thin-haired, thin-lipped, and dry-skinned. He coughed a sharp cough as

176

he sat down and threw open the folio under his arm to a blank page.

"Your passports and ship's clearance, please."

"We have none," said Toran.

"None, hey?" he snatched up a microphone suspended from his belt and spoke into it quickly, "Three men and one woman. Papers not in order." He made an accompanying notation in the folio.

He said, "Where are you from?"

"Siwenna," said Toran warily.

"Where is that?"

"A hundred thousand parsecs, eighty degrees west Trantor, forty degrees—"

"Never mind, never mind!" Toran could see that his inquisitor had written down: "Point of origin—Periphery."

The Filian continued, "Where are you going?"

Toran said, "Trantor sector."

"Purpose?"

"Pleasure trip."

"Carrying any cargo?"

"No."

"Hm-m-m. We'll check on that." He nodded and two men jumped to activity. Toran made no move to interfere.

"What brings you into Filian territory?" The Filian's eyes gleamed unamiably.

"We didn't know we were. I lack a proper chart."

"You will be required to pay a hundred credits for that lack—and, of course, the usual fees required for tariff duties, et cetera."

He spoke again into the microphone—but listened more than he spoke. Then, to Toran, "Know anything about atomic technology?"

"A little," replied Toran, guardedly.

"Yes?" The Filian closed his folio, and added, "The men of the Periphery have a knowledgeable reputation that way. Put on a suit and come with me."

Bayta stepped forward. "What are you going to do with him?"

Toran put her aside gently, and asked coldly, "Where do you want me to come?"

"Our power plant needs minor adjustments. He'll come with you." His pointing finger aimed directly at Magnifico, whose brown eyes opened wide in a blubbery dismay.

177

"What's he got to do with it?" demanded Toran fiercely.

The official looked up coldly. "I am informed of pirate activities in this vicinity. A description of one of the known thugs tallies roughly. It is a purely routine matter of identification."

Toran hesitated, but six men and six blasters are eloquent arguments. He reached into the cupboard for the suits.

An hour later, he rose upright in the bowels of the Filian ship and raged, "There's not a thing wrong with the motors that I can see. The busbars are true, the L-tubes are feeding properly and the reaction analysis checks. Who's in charge here?"

The head engineer said quietly, "I am."

"Well, get me out of here—"

He was led to the officers' level and the small anteroom held only an indifferent ensign.

"Where's the man who came with me?"

"Please wait," said the ensign.

It was fifteen minutes later that Magnifico was brought in.

"What did they do to you?" asked Toran quickly.

"Nothing. Nothing at all." Magnifico's head shook a slow negative.

It took two hundred and fifty credits to fulfill the demands of Filia—fifty credits of it for instant release—and they were in free space again.

Bayta said with a forced laugh, "Don't we rate an escort? Don't we get the usual figurative boot over the border?"

And Toran replied, grimly, "That was no Filian ship—and we're not leaving for awhile. Come in here."

They gathered about him.

He said, whitely, "That was a Foundation ship, and those were the Mule's men aboard."

Ebling bent to pick up the cigar he had dropped. He said, "Here? We're thirty thousand parsecs from the Foundation."

"And we're here. What's to prevent them from making the same trip. Galaxy, Ebling, don't you think I can tell ships apart? I saw their engines, and that's enough for me. I tell you it was a Foundation engine in a Foundation ship."

"And how did they get here?" asked Bayta, logically. "What are the chances of a random meeting of two given ships in space?"

"What's that to do with it?" demanded Toran, hotly. "It would only show we've been followed."

"Followed?" hooted Bayta. "Through hyperspace?"

Ebling Mis interposed wearily, "That can be done—given a good ship and a great pilot. But the possibility doesn't impress me."

"I haven't been masking my trail," insisted Toran. "I've been building up take-off speed on the straight. A blind man could have calculated our route."

"The blazes he could," cried Bayta. "With the cockeyed jumps you are making, observing our initial direction didn't mean a thing. We came out of the jump wrong-end forwards more than once."

"We're wasting time," blazed Toran, with gritted teeth. "It's a Foundation ship under the Mule. It's stopped us. It's searched us. It's had Magnifico—alone—with me as hostage to keep the rest of you quiet, in case you suspected. And we're going to burn it out of space right now."

"Hold on now," and Ebling Mis clutched at him. "Are you going to destroy us for one ship you think is an enemy? Think, man, would those scuppers chase us over an impossible route half through the bestinkered Galaxy, look us over, and then *let us go?*"

"They're still interested in where we're going."

"Then why stop us and put us on our guard? You can't have it both ways, you know."

"I'll have it my way. Let go of me, Ebling, or I'll knock you down."

Magnifico leaned forward from his balanced perch on his favorite chair back. His long nostrils flared with excitement. "I crave your pardon for my interruption, but my poor mind is of a sudden plagued with a queer thought."

Bayta anticipated Toran's gesture of annoyance, and added her grip to Ebling's. "Go ahead and speak, Magnifico. We will all listen faithfully."

Magnifico said, "In my stay in their ship what addled wits I have were bemazed and bemused by a chattering fear that befell me. Of a truth I have a lack of memory of most that happened. Many men staring at me, and talk I did not understand. But towards the last—as though a beam of sunlight had dashed through a cloud rift—there was a face I knew. A glimpse, the merest glimmer—and yet it glows in my memory even stronger and brighter."

Toran said, "Who was it?"

"That captain who was with us so long a time ago, when first you saved me from slavery."

It had obviously been Magnifico's intention to create a sensation, and the delighted smile that curled broadly in the shadow of his proboscis, attested to his realization of the intention's success.

"Captain . . . Han . . . Pritcher?" demanded Mis, sternly. "You're sure of that? Certain sure now?"

"Sir, I swear," and he laid a bone-thin hand upon his narrow chest. "I would uphold the truth of it before the Mule and swear it in his teeth, though all his power were behind him to deny it."

Bayta said in pure wonder, "Then what's it all about?"

The clown faced her eagerly, "My lady, I have a theory. It came upon me, ready made, as though the Galactic Spirit had gently laid it in my mind." He actually raised his voice above Toran's interrupting objection.

"My lady," he addressed himself exclusively to Bayta, "if this captain had, like us, escaped with a ship; if he, like us, were on a trip for a purpose of his own devising; if he blundered upon us—he would suspect us of following and waylaying him, as we suspect him of the like. What wonder he played this comedy to enter our ship?"

"Why would he want us in his ship, then?" demanded Toran. "That doesn't fit."

"Why, yes, it does," clamored the clown, with a flowing inspiration. "He sent an underling who knew us not, but who described us into his microphone. The listening captain would be struck at my own poor likeness—for, of a truth there are not many in this great Galaxy who bear a resemblance to my scantiness. I was the proof of the identity of the rest of you."

"And so he leaves us?"

"What do we know of this mission, and the secrecy thereof? He has spied us out for not an enemy and having it done, so must he needs think it wise to risk his plan by widening the knowledge thereof?"

Bayta said slowly, "Don't be stubborn, Torie. It does explain things."

"It could be," agreed Mis.

Toran seemed helpless in the face of united resistance. Something in the clown's fluent explanations bothered him.

Something was wrong. Yet he was bewildered and, in spite of himself, his anger ebbed.

"For a while," he whispered, "I thought we might have had *one* of the Mule's ships."

And his eyes were dark with the pain of Haven's loss.

The others understood.

22. Death on Neotrantor

NEOTRANTOR   *The small planet of Delicass, renamed after the Great Sack, was for nearly a century, the seat of the last dynasty of the First Empire. It was a shadow world and a shadow Empire and its existence is only of legalistic importance. Under the first of the Neotrantorian dynasty. . . .*

—Encyclopedia Galactica

NEOTRANTOR WAS THE NAME! New Trantor! And when you have said the name you have exhausted at a stroke all the resemblances of the new Trantor to the great original. Two parsecs away, the sun of Old Trantor still shone and the Galaxy's Imperial Capital of the previous century still cut through space in the silent and eternal repetition of its orbit.

Men even inhabited Old Trantor. Not many—a hundred million, perhaps, where fifty years before, forty billions had swarmed. The huge, metal world was in jagged splinters. The towering thrusts of the multi-towers from the single world-girdling base were torn and empty—still bearing the original blastholes and firegut—shards of the Great Sack of forty years earlier.

It was strange that a world which had been the center of a Galaxy for two thousand years—that had ruled limitless space and been home to legislators and rulers whose whims spanned the parsecs—could die in a month. It was strange that a world which had been untouched through the vast conquering sweeps and retreats of a millennium, and equally untouched by the civil wars and palace revolutions of another millennium— should lie dead at last. It was strange that the Glory of the Galaxy should be a rotting corpse.

And pathetic!

For centuries would yet pass before the mighty works of fifty generations of humans would decay past use. Only the declining powers of men, themselves, rendered them useless now.

The millions left after the billions had died tore up the

182

gleaming metal base of the planet and exposed soil that had not felt the touch of sun in a thousand years.

Surrounded by the mechanical perfections of human efforts, encircled by the industrial marvels of mankind freed of the tyranny of environment—they returned to the land. In the huge traffic clearings, wheat and corn grew. In the shadow of the towers, sheep grazed.

But Neotrantor existed—an obscure village of a planet drowned in the shadow of mighty Trantor, until a heart-throttled royal family, racing before the fire and flame of the Great Sack sped to it as its last refuge—and held out there, barely, until the roaring wave of rebellion subsided. There it ruled in ghostly splendor over a cadaverous remnant of Imperium.

Twenty agricultural worlds were a Galactic Empire!

Dagobert IX, ruler of twenty worlds of refractory squires and sullen peasants, was Emperor of the Galaxy, Lord of the Universe.

Dagobert IX had been twenty-five on the bloody day he arrived with his father upon Neotrantor. His eyes and mind were still alive with the glory and the power of the Empire that was. But his son, who might one day be Dagobert X, was born on Neotrantor.

Twenty worlds were all he knew.

Jord Commason's open air car was the finest vehicle of its type on all Neotrantor—and, after all, justly so. It did not end with the fact that Commason was the largest landowner on Neotrantor. It began there. For in earlier days he had been the companion and evil genius of a young crown prince, restive in the dominating grip of a middle-aged emperor. And now he was the companion and still the evil genius of a middle-aged crown prince who hated and dominated an old emperor.

So Jord Commason, in his air car, which in mother-of-pearl finish and gold-and-lumetron ornamentation needed no coat of arms as owner's identification, surveyed the lands that were his, and the miles of rolling wheat that were his, and the huge threshers and harvesters that were his, and the tenant-farmers and machine-tenders that were his—and considered his problems cautiously.

Beside him, his bent and withered chauffeur, guided the ship gently through the upper winds and smiled.

Jord Commason spoke to the wind, the air, and the sky, "You remember what I told you, Inchney?"

Inchney's thin gray hair wisped lightly in the wind. His gap-toothed smile widened in its thin-lipped fashion and the vertical wrinkles of his cheeks deepened as though he were keeping an eternal secret from himself. The whisper of his voice whistled between his teeth.

"I remember, sire, and I have thought."

"And what have you thought, Inchney?" There was an impatience about the question.

Inchney remembered that he had been young and handsome, and a lord on Old Trantor. Inchney remembered that he was a disfigured ancient on Neotrantor, who lived by grace of Squire Jord Commason, and paid for the grace by lending his subtlety on request. He sighed very softly.

He whispered again, "Visitors from the Foundation, sire, are a convenient thing to have. Especially, sire, when they come with but a single ship, and but a single fighting man. How welcome they might be?"

"Welcome?" said Commason, gloomily. "Perhaps so. But those men are magicians and may be powerful."

"*Pugh*," muttered Inchney, "the mistiness of distance hides the truth. The Foundation is but a world. Its citizens are but men. If you blast them, they die."

Inchney held the ship on its course. A river was a winding sparkle below. He whispered, "And is there not a man they speak of now who stirs the worlds of the Periphery?"

Commason was suddenly suspicious. "What do you know of this?"

There was no smile on his chauffeur's face. "Nothing, sire. It was but an idle question."

The squire's hesitation was short. He said, with brutal directness, "Nothing you ask is idle, and your method of acquiring knowledge will have your scrawny neck in a vise yet. But—have it! This man is called the Mule, and a subject of his had been here some months ago on a . . . matter of business. I await another . . . now . . . for its conclusion."

"And these newcomers? They are not the ones you want, perhaps?"

"They lack the identification they should have."

"It has been reported that the Foundation has been captured—"

"I did not tell you that."

"It has been so reported," continued Inchney, coolly, "and if that is correct, then these may be refugees from the destruction, and may be held for the Mule's man out of honest friendship."

"Yes?" Commason was uncertain.

"And, sire, since it is well-known that the friend of a conqueror is but the last victim, it would be but a measure of honest self-defense. For there are such things as psychic probes, and here we have four Foundation brains. There is much about the Foundation it would be useful to know, much even about the Mule. And then the Mule's friendship would be a trifle the less overpowering."

Commason, in the quiet of the upper air, returned with a shiver to his first thought. "But if the Foundation has not fallen. If the reports are lies. It is said that it has been foretold it can not fall."

"We are past the age of soothsayers, sire."

"And yet if it did not fall, Inchney. Think! If it did not fall. The Mule made me promises, indeed—" He had gone too far, and backtracked. "That is, he made boasts. But boasts are wind and deeds are hard."

Inchney laughed noiselessly. "Deeds are hard indeed, until begun. One could scarcely find a further fear than a Galaxy-end Foundation."

"There is still the prince," murmured Commason, almost to himself.

"He deals with the Mule also, then, sire?"

Commason could not quite choke down the complacent shift of features. "Not entirely. Not as *I* do. But he grows wilder, more uncontrollable. A demon is upon him. If I seize these people and he takes them away for his own use—for he does not lack a certain shrewdness—I am not yet ready to quarrel with him." He frowned and his heavy cheeks bent downwards with dislike.

"I saw those strangers for a few moments yesterday," said the gray chauffeur, irrelevantly, "and it is a strange woman, that dark one. She walks with the freedom of a man and she is of a startling paleness against the dark luster of hair." There was almost a warmth in the husky whisper of the withered voice, so that Commason turned toward him in sudden surprise.

Inchney continued, "The prince, I think, would not find his

185

shrewdness proof against a reasonable compromise. You could have the rest, if you left him the girl—"

A light broke upon Commason, "A thought! Indeed a thought! Inchney, turn back! And Inchney, if all turns well, we will discuss further this matter of your freedom."

It was with an almost superstitious sense of symbolism that Commason found a Personal Capsule waiting for him in his private study when he returned. It had arrived by a wave length known to few. Commason smiled a fat smile. The Mule's man was coming and the Foundation had indeed fallen.

Bayta's misty visions, when she had them, of an Imperial palace, did not jibe with the reality, and inside her, there was a vague sense of disappointment. The room was small, almost plain, almost ordinary. The palace did not even match the mayor's residence back at the Foundation—and Dagobert IX—

Bayta had *definite* ideas of what an emperor ought to look like. He ought *not* look like somebody's benevolent grandfather. He ought not be thin and white and faded—or serving cups of tea with his own hand in an expressed anxiety for the comfort of his visitors.

But so it was.

Dagobert IX chuckled as he poured tea into her stiffly outheld cup.

"This is a great pleasure for me, my dear. It is a moment away from ceremony and courtiers. I have not had the opportunity for welcoming visitors from my outer provinces for a time now. My son takes care of these details now that I'm older. You haven't met my son? A fine boy. Headstrong, perhaps. But then he's young. Do you care for a flavor capsule? No?"

Toran attempted an interruption, "Your imperial majesty—"

"Yes?"

"Your imperial majesty, it has not been our intention to intrude upon you—"

"Nonsense, there is no intrusion. Tonight there will be the official reception, but until then, we are free. Let's see, where did you say you were from? It seems a long time since we had an official reception. You said you were from the Province of Anacreon?"

"From the Foundation, your imperial majesty!"

"Yes, the Foundation. I remember now. I had it located.

186

It is in the Province of Anacreon. I have never been there. My doctor forbids extensive traveling. I don't recall any recent reports from my viceroy at Anacreon. How are conditions there?" he concluded anxiously.

"Sire," mumbled Toran, "I bring no complaints."

"That is gratifying. I will commend my viceroy."

Toran looked helplessly at Ebling Mis, whose brusque voice rose. "Sire, we have been told that it will require your permission for us to visit the Imperial University Library on Trantor."

"Trantor?" questioned the emperor, mildly, "Trantor?"

Then a look of puzzled pain crossed his thin face. "Trantor?" he whispered. "I remember now. I am making plans now to return there with a flood of ships at my back. You shall come with me. Together we will destroy the rebel, Gilmer. Together we shall restore the empire!"

His bent back had straightened. His voice had strengthened. For a moment his eyes were hard. Then, he blinked and said softly, "But Gilmer is dead. I seem to remember— Yes. Yes! Gilmer is dead! Trantor is dead— For a moment, it seemed— Where was it you said you came from?"

Magnifico whispered to Bayta, "Is this really an emperor? For somehow I thought emperors were greater and wiser than odirnary men."

Bayta motioned him quiet. She said, "If your imperial majesty would but sign an order permitting us to go to Trantor, it would avail greatly the common cause."

"To Trantor?" The emperor was blank and uncomprehending.

"Sire, the Viceroy of Anacreon, in whose name we speak, sends word that Gilmer is yet alive—"

"Alive! Alive!" thundered Dagobert. "Where? It will be war!"

"Your imperial majesty, it must not yet be known. His whereabouts are uncertain. The viceroy sends us to acquaint you of the fact, and it is only on Trantor that we may find his hiding place. Once discovered—"

"Yes, yes— He must be found—" The old emperor doddered to the wall and touched the little photocell with a trembling finger. He muttered, after an ineffectual pause, "My servants do not come. I can not wait for them."

He was scribbling on a blank sheet, and ended with a flourished "D." He said, "Gilmer will yet learn the power of his emperor. Where was it you came from? Anacreon? What are the conditions there? Is the name of the emperor powerful?"

Bayta took the paper from his loose fingers, "Your imperial majesty is beloved by the people. Your love for them is widely known."

"I shall have to visit my good people of Anacreon, but my doctor says . . . I don't remember what he says, but—" He looked up, his old gray eyes sharp, "Were you saying something of Gilmer?"

"No, your imperial majesty."

"He shall not advance further. Go back and tell your people that. Trantor shall hold! My father leads the fleet now, and the rebel vermin Gilmer shall freeze in space with his regicidal rabble."

He staggered into a seat and his eyes were blank once more. "What was I saying?"

Toran rose and bowed low. "Your imperial majesty has been kind to us, but the time allotted us for an audience is over."

For a moment, Dagobert IX looked like an emperor indeed as he rose and stood stiff-backed while, one by one, his visitors retreated backward through the door—

—to where twenty armed men intervened and locked a circle about them.

A hand-weapon flashed—

To Bayta, consciousness returned sluggishly, but without the "Where am I?" sensation. She remembered clearly the odd old man who called himself emperor, and the other men who waited outside. The arthritic tingle in her finger joints meant a stun pistol.

She kept her eyes closed, and listened with painful attention to the voices.

There were two of them. One was slow and cautious, with a slyness beneath the surface obsequity. The other was hoarse and thick, almost sodden, and blurted out in viscous spurts. Bayta liked neither.

The thick voice was predominant.

Bayta caught the last words, "He will live forever, that old madman. It wearies me. It annoys me. Commason, I will have it. I grow older, too."

"Your highness, let us first see of what use these people

are. It may be we shall have sources of strength other than your father still provides."

The thick voice was lost in a bubbling whisper. Bayta caught only the phrase, "—the girl—" but the other, fawning voice was a nasty, low, running chuckle followed by a comradely, near-patronizing, "Dagobert, you do not age. They lie who say you are not a youth of twenty."

They laughed together, and Bayta's blood was an icy trickle. Dagobert—your highness— The old emperor had spoken of a headstrong son, and the implication of the whispers now beat dully upon her. But such things didn't happen to people in real life—

Toran's voice broke upon her in a slow, hard current of cursing.

She opened her eyes, and Toran's, which were upon her, showed open relief. He said, fiercely, "This banditry will be answered by the emperor. Release us."

It dawned upon Bayta that her wrists and ankles were fastened to wall and floor by a tight attraction field.

Thick Voice approached Toran. He was paunchy, his lower eyelids puffed darkly, and his hair was thinning out. There was a gay feather in his peaked hat, and the edging of his doublet was embroidered with silvery metal-foam.

He sneered with a heavy amusement. "The emperor? The poor, mad emperor?"

"I have his pass. No subject may hinder our freedom."

"But I am no subject, space-garbage. I am the regent and crown prince and am to be addressed as such. As for my poor silly father, it amuses him to see visitors occasionally. And we humor him. It tickles his mock-Imperial fancy. But, of course, it has no other meaning."

And then he was before Bayta, and she looked up at him contemptuously. He leaned close and his breath was overpoweringly minted.

He said, "Her eyes suit well, Commason—she is even prettier with them open. I think she'll do. It will be an exotic dish for a jaded taste, eh?"

There was a futile surge upwards on Toran's part, which the crown prince ignored and Bayta felt the iciness travel outward to the skin. Ebling Mis was still out; head lolling weakly upon his chest, but, with a sensation of surprise, Bayta noted that Magnifico's eyes were open, sharply open, as though awake for many minutes. Those large brown eyes swiveled towards Bayta and stared at her out of a doughy face.

He whimpered, and nodded with his head towards the crown prince, "That one has my Visi-Sonor."

The crown prince turned sharply toward the new voice, "This is yours, monster?" He swung the instrument from his shoulder where it had hung, suspended by its green strap, unnoticed by Bayta.

He fingered it clumsily, tried to sound a chord and got nothing for his pains, "Can you play it, monster?"

Magnifico nodded once.

Toran said suddenly, "You've rifled a ship of the Foundation. If the emperor will not avenge, the Foundation will."

It was the other, Commason, who answered slowly, "*What* Foundation? Or is the Mule no longer the Mule?"

There was no answer to that. The prince's grin showed large uneven teeth. The clown's binding field was broken and he was nudged ungently to his feet. The Visi-Sonor was thrust into his hand.

"Play for us, monster," said the prince. "Play us a serenade of love and beauty for our foreign lady here. Tell her that my father's country prison is no palace, but that I can take her to one where she can swim in rose water—and know what a prince's love is. Sing of a prince's love, monster."

He placed one thick thigh upon a marble table and swung a leg idly, while his fatuous smiling stare swept Bayta into a silent rage. Toran's sinews strained against the field, in painful, perspiring effort. Ebling Mis stirred and moaned.

Magnifico gasped, "My fingers are of useless stiffness—"

"Play, monster!" roared the prince. The lights dimmed at a gesture to Commason and in the dimness he crossed his arms and waited.

Magnifico drew his fingers in rapid, rhythmic jumps from end to end of the multikeyed instrument—and a sharp, gliding rainbow of light jumped across the room. A low, soft tone sounded—throbbing, tearful. It lifted in sad laughter, and underneath it there sounded a dull tolling.

The darkness seemed to intensify and grow thick. Music reached Bayta through the muffled folds of invisible blankets. Gleaming light reached her from the depths as though a single candle glowed at the bottom of a pit.

Automatically, her eyes strained. The light brightened, but remained blurred. It moved fuzzily, in confused color, and the

190

music was suddenly brassy, evil—flourishing in high crescendo. The light flickered quickly, in swift motion to the wicked rhythm. Something writhed within the light. Something with poisonous metallic scales writhed and yawned. And the music writhed and yawned with it.

Bayta struggled with a strange emotion and then caught herself in a mental gasp. Almost, it reminded her of the time in the Time Vault, of those last days on Haven. It was that horrible, cloying, clinging spiderweb of horror and despair. She shrunk beneath it oppressed.

The music dinned upon her, laughing horribly, and the writhing terror at the wrong end of the telescope in the small circle of light was lost as she turned feverishly away. Her forehead was wet and cold.

The music died. It must have lasted fifteen minutes, and a vast pleasure at its absence flooded Bayta. Light glared, and Magnifico's face was close to hers, sweaty, wild-eyed, lugubrious.

"My lady," he gasped, "how fare you?"

"Well enough," she whispered, "but why did you play like that?"

She became aware of the others in the room. Toran and Mis were limp and helpless against the wall, but her eyes skimmed over them. There was the prince, lying strangely still at the foot of the table. There was Commason, moaning wildly through an open, drooling mouth.

Commason flinched, and yelled mindlessly, as Magnifico took a step towards him.

Magnifico turned, and with a leap, turned the others loose.

Toran lunged upwards and with eager, taut fists seized the landowner by the neck, "You come with us. We'll want you —to make sure we get to our ship."

Two hours later, in the ship's kitchen, Bayta served a walloping homemade pie, and Magnifico celebrated the return to space by attacking it with a magnificent disregard of table manners.

"Good, Magnifico?"

"Um-m-m-m!"

"Magnifico?"

"Yes, my lady?"

"What was it you played back there?"

The clown writhed, "I . . . I'd rather not say. I learned it once, and the Visi-Sonor is of an effect upon the nervous

191

system most profound. Surely, it was an evil thing, and not for your sweet innocence, my lady."

"Oh, now, come, Magnifico. I'm not as innocent as that. Don't flatter so. Did I see anything like what *they* saw?"

"I hope not. I played it for them only. If you saw, it was but the rim of it—from afar."

"And that was enough. Do you know you knocked the prince out?"

Magnifico spoke grimly through a large, muffled piece of pie. "I *killed* him, my lady."

"What?" She swallowed, painfully.

"He was dead when I stopped, or I would have continued. I cared not for Commason. His greatest threat was death or torture. But, my lady, this prince looked upon you wickedly, and—" he choked in a mixture of indignation and embarrassment.

Bayta felt strange thoughts come and repressed them sternly. "Magnifico, you've got a gallant soul."

"Oh, my lady." He bent a red nose into his pie, but, somehow did not eat.

Ebling Mis stared out the port. Trantor was near—its metallic shine fearfully bright. Toran was standing there, too.

He said with dull bitterness, "We've come for nothing, Ebling. The Mule's man precedes us."

Ebling Mis rubbed his forehead with a hand that seemed shriveled out of its former plumpness. His voice was an abstracted mutter.

Toran was annoyed. "I say those people know the Foundation has fallen. I say—"

"Eh?" Mis looked up, puzzled. Then, he placed a gentle hand upon Toran's wrist, in complete oblivion of any previous conversation, "Toran, I . . . I've been looking at Trantor. Do you know . . . I have the queerest feeling . . . ever since we arrived on Neotrantor. It's an urge, a driving urge that's pushing and pushing inside. Toran, I can do it; I know I can do it. Things are becoming clear in my mind—they have never been so clear."

Toran stared—and shrugged. The words brought him no confidence.

He said, tentatively, "Mis?"

"Yes?"

"You didn't see a ship come down on Neotrantor as we left?"

Consideration was brief. "No."

"I did. Imagination, I suppose, but it could have been that Filian ship."

"The one with Captain Han Pritcher on it?"

"The one with space knows who upon it. Magnifico's information— It followed us here, Mis."

Ebling Mis said nothing.

Toran said strenuously, "Is there anything wrong with you? Aren't you well?"

Mis' eyes were thoughtful, luminous, and strange. He did not answer.

23. The Ruins of Trantor

THE LOCATION of an objective upon the great world of Trantor presents a problem unique in the Galaxy. There are no continents or oceans to locate from a thousand miles distance. There are no rivers, lakes, and islands to catch sight of through the cloud rifts.

The metal-covered world was—had been—one colossal city, and only the old Imperial palace could be identified readily from outer space by a stranger. The *Bayta* circled the world at almost air-car height in repeated painful search.

From polar regions, where the icy coating of the metal spires were somber evidence of the breakdown or neglect of the weather-conditioning machinery, they worked southwards. Occasionally they could experiment with the correlations— (or presumable correlations)—between what they saw and what the inadequate map obtained at Neotrantor showed.

But it was unmistakable when it came. The gap in the metal coat of the planet was fifty miles. The unusual greenery spread over hundreds of square miles, inclosing the mighty grace of the ancient Imperial residences.

The *Bayta* hovered and slowly oriented itself. There were only the huge supercauseways to guide them. Long straight arrows on the map; smooth, gleaming ribbons there below them.

What the map indicated to be the University area was reached by dead reckoning, and upon the flat area of what once must have been a busy landing-field, the ship lowered itself.

It was only as they submerged into the welter of metal that the smooth beauty apparent from the air dissolved into the broken, twisted near-wreckage that had been left in the wake of the Sack. Spires were truncated, smooth walls gouted and twisted, and just for an instant there was the glimpse of a shaven area of earth—perhaps several hundred acres in extent—dark and plowed.

Lee Senter waited as the ship settled downward cautiously.

It was a strange ship, not from Neotrantor, and inwardly he sighed. Strange ships and confused dealings with the men of outer space could mean the end of the short days of peace, a return to the old grandiose times of death and battle. Senter was leader of the group; the old books were in his charge and he had read of those old days. He did not want them.

Perhaps ten minutes spent themselves as the strange ship came down to nestle upon the flatness, but long memories telescoped themselves in that time. There was first the great farm of his childhood—that remained in his mind merely as busy crowds of people. Then there was the trek of the young families to new lands. He was ten, then; an only child, puzzled, and frightened.

Then the new buildings; the great metal slabs to be uprooted and torn aside; the exposed soil to be turned, and freshened, and invigorated; neighboring buildings to be torn down and leveled; others to be transformed to living quarters.

There were crops to be grown and harvested; peaceful relations with neighboring farms to be established—

There was growth and expansion, and the quiet efficiency of self-rule. There was the coming of a new generation of hard, little youngsters born to the soil. There was the great day when he was chosen leader of the Group and for the first time since his eighteenth birthday he did not shave and saw the first stubble of his Leader's Beard appear.

And now the Galaxy might intrude and put an end to the brief idyll of isolation—

The ship landed. He watched wordlessly as the port opened. Four emerged, cautious and watchful. There were three men varied, old, young, thin and beaked. And a woman striding among them like an equal. His hand left the two glassy black tufts of his beard as he stepped forward.

He gave the universal gesture of peace. Both hands were before him; hard, calloused palms upward.

The young man approached two steps and duplicated the gesture. "I come on peace."

The accent was strange, but the words were understandable, and welcome. He replied, deeply, "In peace be it. You are welcome to the hospitality of the Group. Are you hungry? You shall eat. Are you thirsty? You shall drink."

Slowly, the reply came, "We thank you for your kindness,

195

and shall bear good report of your Group when we return to our world."

A queer answer, but good. Behind him, the men of the Group were smiling, and from the recesses of the surrounding structures, the women emerged.

In his own quarters, he removed the locked, mirror-walled box from its hidden place, and offered each of the guests the long, plump cigars that were reserved for great occasions. Before the woman, he hesitated. She had taken a seat among the men. The strangers evidently allowed, even expected, such effrontery. Stiffly, he offered the box.

She accepted one with a smile, and drew in its aromatic smoke, with all the relish one could expect. Lee Senter repressed a scandalized emotion.

The stiff conversation, in advance of the meal, touched politely upon the subject of farming on Trantor.

It was the old man who asked, "What about hydroponics? Surely, for such a world as Trantor, hydroponics would be the answer."

Senter shook his head slowly. He felt uncertain. His knowledge was the unfamiliar matter of the books he had read, "Artificial farming in chemicals, I think? No, not on Trantor. This hydroponics require a world of industry—for instance, a great chemical industry. And in war or disaster, when industry breaks down, the people starve. Nor can all foods be grown artificially. Some lose their food value. The soil is still cheaper, still better—always more dependable."

"And your food supply is sufficient?"

"Sufficient; perhaps monotonous. We have fowl that supply eggs, and milk-yielders for our dairy products—but our meat supply rests upon our foreign trade."

"Trade." The young man seemed roused to sudden interest. "You trade then. But what do you export?"

"Metal," was the curt answer. "Look for yourself. We have an infinite supply, ready processed. They come from Neotrantor with ships, demolish an indicated area—increasing our growing space—and leave us in exchange meat, canned fruit, food concentrates, farm machinery and so on. They carry off the metal and both sides profit."

They feasted on bread and cheese, and a vegetable stew that was unreservedly delicious. It was over the dessert of frosted fruit, the only imported item on the menu, that, for the first time, the Outlanders became other than mere guests. The young man produced a map of Trantor.

Calmly, Lee Senter studied it. He listened—and said gravely, "The University Grounds are a static area. We farmers do not grow crops on it. We do not, by preference, even enter it. It is one of our few relics of another time we would keep undisturbed."

"We are seekers after knowledge. We would disturb nothing. Our ship would be our hostage." The old man offered this—eagerly, feverishly.

"I can take you there then," said Senter.

That night the strangers slept, and that night Lee Senter sent a message to Neotrantor.

24. Convert

THE THIN LIFE of Trantor trickled to nothing when they entered among the wide-spaced buildings of the University grounds. There was a solemn and lonely silence over it.

The strangers of the Foundation knew nothing of the swirling days and nights of the bloody Sack that had left the Uinversity untouched. They knew nothing of the time after the collapse of the Imperial power, when the students, with their borrowed weapons, and their pale-faced inexperienced bravery, formed a protective volunteer army to protect the central shrine of the science of the Galaxy. They knew nothing of the Seven Days Fight, and the armistice that kept the University free, when even the Imperial palace clanged with the boots of Gilmer and his soldiers, during the short interval of their rule.

Those of the Foundation, approaching for the first time, realized only that in a world of transition from a gutted old to a strenuous new this area was a quiet, graceful museum-piece of ancient greatness.

They were intruders in a sense. The brooding emptiness rejected them. The academic atmosphere seemed still to live and to stir angrily at the disturbance.

The library was a deceptively small building which broadened out vastly underground into a mammoth volume of silence and reverie. Ebling Mis paused before the elaborate murals of the reception room.

He whispered—one had to whisper here: "I think we passed the catalog rooms back a way. I'll stop there."

His forehead was flushed, his hand trembling, "I mustn't be disturbed, Toran. Will you bring my meals down to me?"

"Anything you say. We'll do all we can to help. Do you want us to work under you—"

"No. I must be alone—"

"You think you will get what you want."

And Ebling Mis replied with a soft certainty, "I know I will!"

Toran and Bayta came closer to "setting up housekeeping" in normal fashion than at any time in their year of married life. It was a strange sort of "housekeeping." They lived in the middle of grandeur with an inappropriate simplicity. Their food was drawn largely from Lee Senter's farm and was paid for in the little atomic gadgets that may be found on any Trader's ship.

Magnifico taught himself how to use the projectors in the library reading room, and sat over adventure novels and romances to the point where he was almost as forgetful of meals and sleep as was Ebling Mis.

Ebling himself was completely buried. He had insisted on a hammock being slung up for him in the Psychology Reference Room. His face grew thin and white. His vigor of speech was lost and his favorite curses had died a mild death. There were times when the recognition of either Toran or Bayta seemed a struggle.

He was more himself with Magnifico who brought him his meals and often sat watching him for hours at a time, with a queer, fascinated absorption, as the aging psychologist transcribed endless equations, cross-referred to endless book-films, scurried endlessly about in a wild mental effort towards an end he alone saw.

Toran came upon her in the darkened room, and said sharply, "Bayta!"

Bayta started guiltily. "Yes? You want me, Torie?"

"Sure I want you. What in space are you sitting there for? You've been acting all wrong since we got to Trantor. What's the matter with you?"

"Oh, Torie, stop," she said wearily.

And "Oh, Torie, stop!" he mimicked impatiently. Then with sudden softness, "Won't you tell me what's wrong, Bay? something's bothering you."

"No! Nothing is, Torie. If you keep on just nagging and nagging, you'll have me mad. I'm just—thinking."

"Thinking about what?"

"About nothing. Well, about the Mule, and Haven, and the Foundation, and everything. About Ebling Mis and whether he'll find anything about the Second Foundation, and whether it will help us when he does find it—and a million other things. Are you satisfied?" Her voice was agitated.

"If you're just brooding, do you mind stopping? It isn't pleasant and it doesn't help the situation."

199

Bayta got to her feet and smiled weakly. "All right. I'm happy. See, I'm smiling and jolly."

Magnifico's voice was an agitated cry outside. "My lady—"

"What is it? Come—"

Bayta's voice choked off sharply when the opening door framed the large, hard-faced—

"Pritcher," cried Toran.

Bayta gasped, "Captain! How did you find us?"

Han Pritcher stepped inside. His voice was clear and level, and utterly dead of feeling, "My rank is colonel now—under the Mule."

"Under the . . . Mule!" Toran's voice trailed off. They formed a tableau there, the three.

Magnifico stared wildly and shrank behind Toran. Nobody stopped to notice him.

Bayta said, her hands trembling in each other's tight grasp, "You are arresting us? You have really gone over to them?"

The colonel replied quickly, "I have not come to arrest you. My instructions make no mention of you. With regard to you, I am free, and I choose to exercise our old friendship, if you will let me."

Toran's face was a twisted suppression of fury, "How did you find us? You were in the Filian ship, then? You followed us?"

The wooden lack of expression on Pritcher's face might have flickered in embarrassment. "I *was* on the Filian ship! I met you in the first place . . . well . . . by chance."

"It is a chance that is mathematically impossible."

"No. Simply rather improbable, so my statement will have to stand. In any case, you admitted to the Filians—there is, of course, no such nation as Filia actually—that you were heading for the Trantor sector, and since the Mule already has his contacts upon Neotrantor, it was easy to have you detained there. Unfortunately, you got away before I arrived, but not long before. I had time to have the farms on Trantor ordered to report your arrival. It was done and I am here. May I sit down? I come in friendliness, believe me."

He sat. Toran bent his head and thought futilely. With a numbed lack of emotion, Bayta prepared tea.

Toran looked up harshly. "Well, what are you waiting for —*colonel*? What's your friendship? If it's not arrest, what is

200

it then? Protective custody? Call in your men and give your orders."

Patiently, Pritcher shook his head. "No, Toran. I come of my own will to speak to you, to persuade you of the uselessness of what you are doing. If I fail I shall leave. That is all."

"That is all? Well, then peddle your propaganda, give us your speech, and leave. I don't want any tea, Bayta."

Pritcher accepted a cup, with a grave word of thanks. He looked at Toran with a clear strength as he sipped lightly. Then he said. "The Mule *is* a mutant. He can not be beaten in the very nature of the mutation—"

"Why? What is the mutation?" asked Toran, with sour humor. "I suppose you'll tell us now, eh?"

"Yes, I will. Your knowledge won't hurt him. You see— he is capable of adjusting the emotional balance of human beings. It sounds like a little trick, but it's quite unbeatable."

Bayta broke in, "The emotional balance?" She frowned, "Won't you explain that? I don't quite understand."

"I mean that it is an easy matter for him to instill into a capable general, say the emotion of utter loyalty to the Mule and complete belief in the Mule's victory. His generals are emotionally controlled. They can not betray him; they can not weaken—and the control is permanent. His most capable enemies become his most faithful subordinates. The warlord of Kalgan surrenders his planet and becomes his viceroy for the Foundation."

"And you," added Bayta, bitterly, "betray your cause and become Mule's envoy to Trantor. I see!"

"I haven't finished. The Mule's gift works in reverse even more effectively. Despair is an emotion! At the crucial moment, keymen on the Foundation—keymen on Haven— despaired. Their worlds fell without too much struggle."

"Do you mean to say," demanded Bayta, tensely, "that the feeling I had in the Time Vault was the Mule juggling my emotional control."

"Mine, too. Everyone's. How was it on Haven towards the end?"

Bayta turned away.

Colonel Pritcher continued earnestly, "As it works for worlds, so it works for individuals. Can you light a force which can make you surrender willingly when it so desires; can make you a faithful servant when it so desires?"

Toran said slowly, "How do I know this is the truth?"

"Can you explain the fall of the Foundation and of Haven otherwise? Can you explain—my conversion otherwise? Think, man! What have you—or I—or the whole Galaxy accomplished against the Mule in all this time? What one little thing?"

Toran felt the challenge, "By the Galaxy, I can!" With a sudden touch of fierce satisfaction, he shouted, "Your wonderful Mule had contacts with Neotrantor you say that were to have detained us, eh? Those contacts are dead or worse. We killed the crown prince and left the other a whimpering idiot. The Mule did not stop us there, and so much has been undone."

"Why, no, not at all. Those weren't our men. The crown prince was a wine-soaked mediocrity. The other man, Commason, is phenomenally stupid. He was a power on his world but that didn't prevent him from being vicious, evil, and completely incompetent. We had nothing really to do with them. They were, in a sense, merely feints—"

"It was they who detained us, or tried."

"Again, no. Commason had a personal slave—a man called Inchney. Detention was *his* policy. He is old, but will serve our temporary purpose. You would not have killed him, you see."

Bayta whirled on him. She had not touched her own tea. "But, by your very statement, your own emotions have been tampered with. You've got faith and belief in the Mule, an unnatural, a *diseased* faith in the Mule. Of what value are your opinions? You've lost all power of objective thought."

"You are wrong." Slowly, the colonel shook his head. "Only my emotions are fixed. My reason is as it always was. It may be influenced in a certain direction by my conditioned emotions, but it is not *forced*. And there are some things I can see more clearly now that I am freed of my earlier emotional trend.

"I can see that the Mule's program is an intelligent and worthy one. In the time since I have been—converted, I have followed his career from its start seven years ago. With his mutant mental power, he began by winning over a condottiere and his band. With that—and his power—he won a planet. With that—and his power—he extended his grip until he could tackle the warlord of Kalgan. Each step followed the other logically. With Kalgan in his pocket, he had a first-class fleet, and with that—and his power—he could attack the Foundation.

"The Foundation is the key. It is the greatest area of industrial concentration in the Galaxy, and now that the atomic techniques of the Foundation are in his hands, he is the actual master of the Galaxy. With those techniques—and his power —he can force the remnants of the Empire to acknowledge his rule, and eventually—with the death of the old emperor, who is mad and not long for this world—to crown him emperor. He will then have the name as well as the fact. With that—and his power—where is the world in the Galaxy that can oppose him?

"In these last seven years, he has established a new Empire. In seven years, in other words, he will have accomplished what all Seldon's psycho-history could not have done in less than an additional seven hundred. The Galaxy will have peace and order at last.

"And you could not stop it—any more than you could stop a planet's rush with your shoulders."

A long silence followed Pritcher's speech. What remained of his tea had grown cold. He emptied his cup, filled it again, and drained it slowly. Toran bit viciously at a thumbnail. Bayta's face was cold, and distant, and white.

Then Bayta said in a thin voice, "We are not con . If the Mule wishes us to be, let him come here and con us himself. You fought him until the last moment of y conversion, I imagine, didn't you?"

"I did," said Colonel Pritcher, solemnly.

"Then allow us the same privilege."

Colonel Pritcher arose. With a crisp air of finality, he said, "Then I leave. As I said earlier, my mission at present concerns you in no way. Therefore, I don't think it will be necessary to report your presence here. That is not too great a kindness. If the Mule wishes you stopped, he no doubt has other men assigned to the job, and you will be stopped. But, for what it is worth, I shall not contribute more than my requirement."

"Thank you," said Bayta faintly.

"As for Magnifico. Where is he? Come out, Magnifico, I won't hurt you—"

"What about him?" demanded Bayta, with sudden animation.

"Nothing. My instructions make no mention of him, either.

I have heard that he is searched for, but the Mule will find him when the time suits him. I shall say nothing. Will you shake hands?"

Bayta shook her head. Toran glared his frustrated contempt.

There was the slightest lowering of the colonel's iron shoulders. He strode to the door, turned and said:

"One last thing. Don't think I am not aware of the source of your stubbornness. It is known that you search for the Second Foundation. The Mule, in his time, will take his measures. Nothing will help you— But I knew you in other times; perhaps there is something in my conscience that urged me to this; at any rate, I tried to help you and remove you from the final danger before it was too late. Good-by."

He saluted sharply—and was gone.

Bayta turned to a silent Toran, and whispered, "They even know about the Second Foundation."

In the recesses of the library, Ebling Mis, unaware of all, crouched under the one spark of light amid the murky spaces and mumbled triumphantly to himself.

25. Death of a Psychologist

AFTER THAT there were only two weeks left to the life of Ebling Mis.

And in those two weeks, Bayta was with him three times. The first time was on the night after the evening upon which they saw Colonel Pritcher. The second was one week later. And the third was again a week later—on the last day—the day Mis died.

First, there was the night of Colonel Pritcher's evening, the first hour of which was spent by a stricken pair in a brooding, unmerry merry-go-round.

Bayta said "Torie, let's tell Ebling."

Toran said dully, "Think he can help?"

"We're only two. We've got to take some of the weight off. Maybe he *can* help."

Toran said, "He's changed. He's lost weight. He's a little feathery; a little woolly." His fingers groped in air, metaphorically. "Sometimes, I don't think he'll help us much—ever. Sometimes, I don't think anything will help."

"Don't!" Bayta's voice caught and escaped a break, "Torie, don't! When you say that, I think the Mule's getting us. Let's tell Ebling, Torie—now!"

Ebling Mis raised his head from the long desk, and bleared at them as they approached. His thinning hair was scuffed up, his lips made sleepy, smacking sounds.

"Eh?" he said. "Someone want me?"

Bayta bent to her knees, "Did we wake you? Shall we leave?"

"Leave? Who is it? Bayta? No, no, stay! Aren't there chairs? I saw them—" His finger pointed vaguely.

Toran pushed two ahead of him. Bayta sat down and took one of the psychologist's flaccid hands in hers. "May we talk to you, doctor?" She rarely used the title.

"Is something wrong?" A little sparkle returned to his abstracted eyes. His sagging cheeks regained a touch of color. "Is something wrong?"

Bayta said, "Captain Pritcher has been here. Let *me* talk, Torie. You remember Captain Pritcher, doctor?"

"Yes— Yes—" His fingers pinched his lips and released them. "Tall man. Democrat."

"Yes, he. He's discovered the Mule's mutation. He was here, doctor, and told us."

"But that is nothing new. The Mule's mutation is straightened out." In honest astonishment, "Haven't I told you? Have I forgotten to tell you?"

"Forgotten to tell us what?" put in Toran, quickly.

"About the Mule's mutation, of course. He tampers with emotions. Emotional control! I haven't told you? Now what made me forget?" Slowly, he sucked in his under lip and considered.

Then, slowly, life crept into his voice and his eyelids lifted wide, as though his sluggish brain had slid onto a well-greased single track. He spoke in a dream, looking between the two listeners rather than at them. "It is really so simple. It requires no specialized knowledge. In the mathematics of psycho-history, of course, it works out promptly, in a third-level equation involving no more— Never mind that. It can be put into ordinary words—roughly—and have it make sense, which isn't usual with psycho-historical phenomena.

"Ask yourselves— What can upset Hari Seldon's careful scheme of history, eh?" He peered from one to the other with a mild, questioning anxiety. "What were Seldon's original assumptions? First, that there would be no fundamental change in human society over the next thousand years.

"For instance, suppose there were a major change in the Galaxy's technology, such as finding a new principle for the utilization of energy, or perfecting the study of electronic neurobiology. Social changes would render Seldon's original equations obsolete. But that hasn't happened, has it now?

"Or suppose that a new weapon were to be invented by forces outside the Foundation, capable of withstanding all the Foundation's armaments. *That* might cause a ruinous deviation, though less certainly. But even that hasn't happened. The Mule's Atomic Field-Depressor was a clumsy weapon and could be countered. And that was the only novelty he presented, poor as it was.

"But there was a second assumption, a more subtle one! Seldon assumed that human reaction to stimuli would remain constant. Granted that the first assumption held true, *then the second must have broken down*! Some factor must be twisting and distorting the emotional responses of human beings or Seldon couldn't have failed and the Foundation couldn't have fallen. And what factor but the Mule?

"Am I right? Is there a flaw in the reasoning?"

Bayta's plump hand patted his gently. "No flaw, Ebling."

Mis was joyful, like a child. "This and more comes so easily. I tell you I wonder sometimes what is going on inside me. I seem to recall the time when so much was a mystery to me and now things are so clear. Problems are absent. I come across what might be one, and somehow, inside me, I see and understand. And my guesses, my theories seem always to be borne out. There's a drive in me . . . always onward . . . so that I can't stop . . . and I don't want to eat or sleep . . . but always go on . . . and on . . . and on—"

His voice was a whisper; his wasted, blue-veined hand rested tremblingly upon his forehead. There was a frenzy in his eyes that faded and went out.

He said more quietly, "Then I never told you about the Mule's mutant powers, did I? But then . . . did you say you knew about it?"

"It was Captain Pritcher, Ebling," said Bayta. "Remember?"

"He told you?" There was a tinge of outrage in his tone. "But how did he find out?"

"He's been conditioned by the Mule. He's a colonel now, a Mule's man. He came to advise us to surrender to the Mule, and he told us—what you told us."

"Then the Mule knows we're here? I must hurry— Where's Magnifico? Isn't he with you?"

"Magnifico's sleeping," said Toran, impatiently. "It's past midnight, you know."

"It is? Then— Was I sleeping when you came in?"

"You were," said Bayta decisively, "and you're not going back to work, either. You're getting into bed. Come on, Torie, help me. And you stop pushing at me, Ebling, because it's just your luck I don't shove you under a shower first. Pull off his shoes, Torie, and tomorrow you come down here and drag him out into the open air before he fades completely away. Look at you, Ebling, you'll be growing cobwebs. Are you hungry?"

Ebling Mis shook his head and looked up from his cot in

a peevish confusion. "I want you to send Magnifico down to-morrow," he muttered.

Bayta tucked the sheet around his neck. "You'll have *me* down tomorrow, with washed clothes. You're going to take a good bath, and then get out and visit the farm and feel a little sun on you."

"I won't do it," said Mis weakly. "You hear me? I'm too busy."

His sparse hair spread out on the pillow like a silver fringe about his head. His voice was a confidential whisper. "You want that Second Foundation, don't you?"

Toran turned quickly and squatted down on the cot beside him. "What about the Second Foundation, Ebling?"

The psychologist freed an arm from beneath the sheet and his tired fingers clutched at Toran's sleeve. "The Foundations were established at a great Psychological Convention presided over by Hari Seldon. Toran, I have located the published minutes of that Convention. Twenty-five fat films. I have already looked through various summaries."

"Well?"

"Well, do you know that it is very easy to find from them the exact location of the First Foundation, if you know anything at all about psycho-history. It is frequently referred to when you understand the equations. But Toran, nobody mentions the Second Foundation. There has been no reference to it anywhere."

Toran's eyebrows pulled into a frown. "It doesn't exist?"

"Of course it exists," cried Mis, angrily, "who said it didn't? But there's less talk of it. Its significance—and all about it—are better hidden, better obscured. Don't you see? It's the more important of the two. It's the critical one; *the one that counts!* And I've got the minutes of the Seldon Convention. The Mule hasn't won yet—"

Quietly, Bayta turned the lights down. "Go to sleep!"

Without speaking, Toran and Bayta made their way up to their own quarters.

The next day, Ebling Mis bathed and dressed himself, saw the sun of Trantor and felt the wind of Trantor for the last time. At the end of the day he was once again submerged in the gigantic recesses of the library, and never emerged thereafter.

In the week that followed, life settled again into its groove. The sun of Neotrantor was a calm, bright star in Trantor's

208

night sky. The farm was busy with its spring planting. The University grounds were silent in their desertion. The Galaxy seemed empty. The Mule might never have existed.

Bayta was thinking that as she watched Toran light his cigar carefully and look up at the sections of blue sky visible between the swarming metal spires that encircled the horizon.

"It's a nice day," he said.

"Yes, it is. Have you everything mentioned on the list, Torie?"

"Sure. Half pound butter, dozen eggs, string beans— Got it all down here, Bay. I'll have it right."

"Good. And make sure the vegetables are of the last harvest and not museum relics. Did you see Magnifico anywhere, by the way?"

"Not since breakfast. Guess he's down with Ebling, watching a book film."

"All right. Don't waste any time, because I'll need the eggs for dinner."

Toran left with a backward smile and a wave of the hand.

Bayta turned away as Toran slid out of sight among the maze of metal. She hesitated before the kitchen door, about-faced slowly, and entered the colonnade leading to the elevator that burrowed down into the recesses.

Ebling Mis was there, head bent down over the eyepieces of the projector, motionless, a frozen, questing body. Near him sat Magnifico, screwed up into a chair, eyes sharp and watching—a bundle of slatty limbs with a nose emphasizing his scrawny face.

Bayta said softly, "Magnifico—"

Magnifico scrambled to his feet. His voice was an eager whisper. "My lady!"

"Magnifico," said Bayta, "Toran has left for the farm and won't be back for a while. Would you be a good boy and go out after him with a message that I'll write for you?"

"Gladly, my lady. My small services are but too eagerly yours, for the tiny uses you can put them to."

She was alone with Ebling Mis, who had not moved. Firmly, she placed her hand upon his shoulder. "Ebling—"

The psychologist started, with a peevish cry, "What is it?" He wrinkled his eyes. "Is it you, Bayta? Where's Magnifico?"

"I sent him away. I want to be alone with you for a while." She enunciated her words with exaggerated distinctness. "I want to talk to you, Ebling."

The psychologist made a move to return to his projector, but her hand on his shoulder was firm. She felt the bone under the sleeve clearly. The flesh seemed to have fairly melted away since their arrival on Trantor. His face was thin, yellowish, and bore a half-week stubble. His shoulders were visibly stooped, even in a sitting position.

Bayta said, "Magnifico isn't bothering you, is he, Ebling? He seems to be down here night and day."

"No, no, no! Not at all. Why, I don't mind him. He is silent and never disturbs me. Sometimes he carries the films back and forth for me; seems to know what I want without my speaking. Just let him be."

"Very well—but, Ebling, doesn't he make you wonder? Do you hear me, Ebling? Doesn't he make you wonder?"

She jerked a chair close to his and stared at him as though to pull the answer out of his eyes.

Ebling Mis shook his head. "No. What do you mean?"

"I mean that Colonel Pritcher and you both say the Mule can condition the emotions of human beings. But are you sure of it? Isn't Magnifico himself a flaw in the theory?"

There was silence.

Bayta repressed a strong desire to shake the psychologist. "What's *wrong* with you, Ebling? Magnifico was the Mule's clown. Why wasn't he conditioned to love and faith? Why should he, of all those in contact with the Mule, hate him so."

"But . . . but he *was* conditioned. Certainly, Bay!" He seemed to gather certainty as he spoke. "Do you suppose that the Mule treats his clown the way he treats his generals? He needs faith and loyalty in the latter, but in his clown he needs only fear. Didn't you ever notice that Magnifico's continual state of panic is pathological in nature? Do you suppose it is natural for a human being to be as frightened as that all the time? Fear to such an extent becomes comic. It was probably comic to the Mule—and helpful, too, since it obscured what help we might have gotten earlier from Magnifico."

Bayta said, "You mean Magnifico's information about the Mule was false?"

"It was misleading. It was colored by pathological fear. The Mule is not the physical giant Magnifico thinks. He is more probably an ordinary man outside his mental powers. But if it amused him to appear a superman to poor Magnifico—" The psychologist shrugged. "In any case, Magnifico's information is no longer of importance."

"What is, then?"

But Mis shook himself loose and returned to his projector.

"What is, then?" she repeated. "The Second Foundation?"

The psychologist's eyes jerked towards her. "Have I told you anything about that? I don't remember telling you anything. I'm not ready yet. What have I told you?"

"Nothing," said Bayta, intensely. "Oh, Galaxy, you've told me nothing, but I wish you would because I'm deathly tired. When will it be over?"

Ebling Mis peered at her, vaguely rueful, "Well, now, my . . . my dear, I did not mean to hurt you. I forget sometimes . . . who my friends are. Sometimes it seems to be that I must not talk of all this. There's a need for secrecy—but from the Mule, not from you, my dear." He patted her shoulder with a weak amiability.

She said, "What about the Second Foundation?"

His voice was automatically a whisper, thin and sibilant. "Do you know the thoroughness with which Seldon covered his traces? The proceedings of the Seldon Convention would have been of no use to me at all as little as a month ago, before this strange insight came. Even now, it seems—tenuous. The papers put out by the Convention are often apparently unrelated; always obscure. More than once I wondered if the members of the Convention, themselves, knew all that was in Seldon's mind. Sometime I think he used the Convention only as a gigantic front, and single-handed erected the structure—"

"Of the Foundations?" urged Bayta.

"Of the Second Foundation! Our Foundation was simple. But the Second Foundation was only a name. It was mentioned, but if there was any elaboration, it was hidden deep in the mathematics. There is still much I don't even begin to understand, but for seven days, the bits have been clumping together into a vague picture.

"Foundation Number One was a world of physical scientists. It represented a concentration of the dying science of the Galaxy under the conditions necessary to make it live again. No psychologists were included. It was a peculiar distortion, and must have had a purpose. The usual explanation was that Seldon's psycho-history worked best where the individual working units—human beings—had no knowledge

211

of what was coming, and could therefore react naturally to all situations. Do you follow me, my dear—"

"Yes, doctor."

"Then listen carefully. Foundation Number Two was a world of mental scientists. It was the mirror image of our world. Psychology, not physics, was king." Triumphantly. "You see?"

"I don't."

"But think, Bayta, use your head. Hari Seldon knew that his psycho-history could predict only probabilities, and not certainties. There was always a margin of error, and as time passed that margin increases in geometric progression. Seldon would naturally guard as well as he could against it. Our Foundation was scientifically vigorous. It could conquer armies and weapons. It could pit force against force. But what of the mental attack of a mutant such as the Mule?"

"That would be for the psychologists of the Second Foundation!" Bayta felt excitement rising within her.

"Yes, yes, yes! Certainly!"

"But they have done nothing so far."

"How do you know they haven't?"

Bayta considered that, "I don't. Do you have evidence that they are?"

"No. There are many factors I know nothing of. The Second Foundation could not have been established full-grown, any more than we were. We developed slowly and grew in strength; they must have also. The stars know at what stage their strength is now. Are they strong enough to fight the Mule? Are they aware of the danger in the first place? Have they capable leaders?"

"But if they follow Seldon's plan, then the Mule *must* be beaten by the Second Foundation."

"Ah," and Ebling Mis' thin face wrinkled thoughtfully, "is it that again? But the Second Foundation was a more difficult job than the First. Its complexity is hugely greater; and consequently so is its possibility of error. And if the Second Foundation should not beat the Mule, it is bad—ultimately bad. It is the end, may be, of the human race as we know it."

"No."

"Yes. If the Mule's descendants inherit his mental powers — You see? Homo sapiens could not compete. There would be a new dominant race—a new aristocracy—with homo sapiens demoted to slave labor as an inferior race. Isn't that so?"

"Yes, that is so."

"And even if by some chance the Mule did not establish a dynasty, he would still establish a distorted new Empire upheld by his personal power only. It would die with his death; the Galaxy would be left where it was before he came, except that there would no longer be Foundations around which a real and healthy Second Empire could coalesce. It would mean thousands of years of barbarism. It would mean no end in sight."

"What can we do? Can we warn the Second Foundation?"

"We must, or they may go under through ignorance, which we can not risk. But there is no way of warning them."

"No way?"

"I don't know where they are located. They are 'at the other end of the Galaxy' but that is all, and there are millions of worlds to choose from."

"But, Ebling, don't they say?" She pointed vaguely at the films that covered the table.

"No, they don't. Not where I can find it—yet. The secrecy must mean something. There must be a reason—" A puzzled expression returned to his eyes. "But I wish you'd leave. I have wasted enough time, and it's growing short—it's growing short."

He tore away, petulant and frowning.

Magnifico's soft step approached. "Your husband is home, my lady."

Ebling Mis did not greet the clown. He was back at his projector.

That evening Toran, having listened, spoke, "And you think he's really right, Bay? You think he isn't—" He hesitated.

"He is right, Torie. He's sick, I know that. The change that's come over him, the loss of weight, the way he speaks—he's sick. But as soon as the subject of the Mule or the Second Foundation, or anything he is working on, comes up, listen to him. He is lucid and clear as the sky of outer space. He knows what he's talking about. I believe him."

"Then there's hope." It was half a question.

"I . . . I haven't worked it out. Maybe! Maybe not! I'm carrying a blaster from now on." The shiny-barreled weapon was in her hand as she spoke. "Just in case, Torie, just in case."

"In case what?"

Bayta laughed with a touch of hysteria, "Never mind. Maybe I'm a little crazy, too—like Ebling Mis."

Ebling Mis at that time had seven days to live, and the seven days slipped by, one after the other, quietly.

To Toran, there was a quality of stupor about them. The warming days and the dull silence covered him with lethargy. All life seemed to have lost its quality of action, and changed into an infinite sea of hibernation.

Mis was a hidden entity whose burrowing work produced nothing and did not make itself known. He had barricaded himself. Neither Toran nor Bayta could see him. Only Magnifico's go-between characteristics were evidence of his existence. Magnifico, grown silent and thoughtful, with his tiptoed trays of food and his still, watchful witness in the gloom.

Bayta was more and more a creature of herself. The vivacity died, the self-assured competence wavered. She, too, sought her own worried, absorbed company, and once Toran had come upon her, fingering her blaster. She had put it away quickly, forced a smile.

"What are you doing with it, Bay?"

"Holding it. Is that a crime?"

"You'll blow your fool head off."

"Then I'll blow it off. Small loss!"

Married life had taught Toran the futility of arguing with a female in a dark-brown mood. He shrugged, and left her.

On the last day, Magnifico scampered breathless into their presence. He clutched at them, frightened. "The learned doctor calls for you. He is not well."

And he wasn't well. He was in bed, his eyes unnaturally large, unnaturally bright. He was dirty, unrecognizable.

"Ebling!" cried Bayta.

"Let me speak," croaked the psychologist, lifting his weight to a thin elbow with an effort. "Let me speak. I am finished; the work I pass on to you. I have kept no notes; the scrap-figures I have destroyed. No other must know. All must remain in your minds."

"Magnifico," said Bayta, with rough directness. "Go upstairs!"

Reluctantly, the clown rose and took a backward step. His sad eyes were on Mis.

Mis gestured weakly, "He won't matter; let him stay, Stay, Magnifico."

The clown sat down quickly. Bayta gazed at the floor. Slowly, slowly, her lower lip caught in her teeth.

Mis said, in a hoarse whisper, "I am convinced the Second Foundation can win, if it is not caught prematurely by the Mule. It has kept itself secret; the secrecy must be upheld; it has a purpose. You must go there; your information is vital . . . may make all the difference. Do you hear me?"

Toran cried in near-agony, "Yes, yes! Tell us how to get there, Ebling? Where is it?"

"I can tell you," said the faint voice.

He never did.

Bayta, face frozen white, lifted her blaster and shot, with an echoing clap of noise. From the waist upward, Mis was not, and a ragged hole was in the wall behind. From numb fingers, Bayta's blaster dropped to the floor.

26. End of the Search

THERE WAS not a word to be said. The echoes of the blast rolled away into the outer rooms and rumbled downward into a hoarse, dying whisper. Before its death, it had muffled the sharp clamor of Bayta's falling blaster, smothered Magnifico's high-pitched cry, drowned out Toran's inarticulate roar.

There was a silence of agony.

Bayta's head was bent into obscurity. A droplet caught the light as it fell. Bayta had never wept before.

Toran's muscles almost cracked in their spasm, but he did not relax—he felt as if he would never unclench his teeth again. Magnifico's face was a faded, lifeless mask.

Finally, from between teeth still tight, Toran choked out in an unrecognizable voice, "You're a Mule's woman, then. He got to you!"

Bayta looked up, and her mouth twisted with a painful merriment, "I, a Mule's woman? That's ironic.

She smiled—a brittle effort—and tossed her hair back. Slowly, her voice verged back to the normal, or something near it. "It's over, Toran; I can talk now. How much I will survive, I don't know. But I can start talking—"

Toran's tension had broken of its own weight and faded into a flaccid dullness, "Talk about what, Bay? What's there to talk about?"

"About the calamity that's followed us. We've remarked about it before, Torie. Don't you remember? How defeat has always bitten at our heels and never actually managed to nip us? We were on the Foundation, and it collapsed while the Independent Traders still fought—but *we* got out in time to go to Haven. We were on Haven, and it collapsed while the others still fought—and again we go out in time. We went to Neotrantor, and by now it's undoubtedly joined the Mule."

Toran listened and shook his head, "I don't understand."

"Torie, such things don't happen in real life. You and I

216

are insignificant people; we don't fall from one vortex of politics into another continuously for the space of a year—unless we carry the vortex with us. *Unless we carry the source of infection with us!* Now do you see?"

Toran's lips tightened. His glance fixed horribly upon the bloody remnants of what had once been a human, and his eyes sickened.

"Let's get out of here, Bay. Let's get out into the open."

It was cloudy outside. The wind scudded about them in drab spurts and disordered Bayta's hair. Magnifico had crept after them and now he hovered at the edge of their conversation.

Toran said tightly, "You killed Ebling Mis because you believed *him* to be the focus of infection?" Something in her eyes struck him. He whispered, "He was the Mule?" He did not—could not—believe the implications of his own words.

Bayta laughed sharply, "Poor Ebling the Mule? Galaxy, no! I couldn't have killed him if he were the Mule. He would have detected the emotion accompanying the move and changed it for me to love, devotion, adoration, terror, whatever he pleased. No, I killed Ebling because he was *not* the Mule. I killed him because he knew where the Second Foundation was, and in two seconds would have told the Mule the secret."

"Would have told the Mule the secret," Toran repeated stupidly. "Told the Mule—"

And then he emitted a sharp cry, and turned to stare in horror at the clown, who might have been crouching unconscious there for the apparent understanding he had of what he heard.

"Not Magnifico?" Toran whispered the question.

"Listen" said Bayta. "Do you remember what happened on Neotrantor? Oh, think for yourself, Torie—"

But he shook his head and mumbled at her.

She went on, wearily, "A man died on Neotrantor. A man died with no one touching him. Isn't that true? Magnifico played on his Visi-Sonor and when he was finished, the crown prince was dead. Now isn't that strange? Isn't it queer that a creature afraid of everything, apparently helpless with terror, has the capacity to kill at will."

"The music and the light-effects," said Toran, "have a profound emotional effect—"

"Yes, an *emotional* effect. A pretty big one. Emotional

217

effects happen to be the Mule's specialty. That, I suppose, can be considered a coincidence. And a creature who can kill by suggestion is so full of fright. Well, the Mule tampered with his mind, supposedly, so that can be explained. But, Toran, I caught a little of that Visi-Sonor selection that killed the crown prince. Just a little—but it was enough to give me that same feeling of despair I had in the Time Vault and on Haven. Toran, I can't mistake that particular feeling."

Toran's face was darkening, "I . . . felt it too. I forgot. I never thought—"

"It was then that it first occurred to me. It was just a vague feeling—intuition, if you like. I had nothing to go on. And then Pritcher told us of the Mule and his mutation, and it was clear in a moment. It was the Mule who had created the despair in the Time Vault; it was Magnifico who had created the despair on Neotrantor. It was the same emotion. Therefore, the Mule and Magnifico were the same person. Doesn't it work out nicely, Torie? Isn't it just like an axiom in geometry—things equal to the same thing are equal to each other?"

She was at the edge of hysteria, but dragged herself back to sobriety by main force. She continued, "The discovery scared me to death. If Magnifico were the Mule, he could know my emotions—and cure them for his own purposes. I dared not let him know. I avoided him. Luckily, he avoided me also; he was too interested in Ebling Mis. I planned killing Mis before he could talk. I planned it secretly—as secretly as I could—so secretly I didn't dare tell it to myself. If I could have killed the Mule himself—But I couldn't take the chance. He would have noticed, and I would have lost everything."

She seemed drained of emotion.

Toran said harshly and with finality, "It's impossible. Look at the miserable creature. *He* the Mule? He doesn't even hear what we're saying."

But when his eyes followed his pointing finger, Magnifico was erect and alert, his eyes sharp and darkly bright. His voice was without a trace of an accent, "I hear her, my friend. It is merely that I have been sitting here and brooding on the fact that with all my cleverness and forethought I could make a mistake, and lose so much."

Toran stumbled backward as if afraid the clown might touch him or that his breath might contaminate him.

Magnifico nodded, and answered the unspoken question. "I am the Mule."

He seemed no longer a grotesque; his pipestem limbs, his beak of a nose lost their humor-compelling qualities. His fear was gone; his bearing was firm.

He was in command of the situation with an ease born of usage.

He said, tolerantly, "Seat yourselves. Go ahead; you might as well sprawl out and make yourselves comfortable. The game's over, and I'd like to tell you a story. It's a weakness of mine—I want people to understand me."

And his eyes as he looked at Bayta were still the old, soft sad brown ones of Magnifico, the clown.

"There is nothing really to my childhood," he began, plunging bodily into quick, impatient speech, "that I care to remember. Perhaps you can understand that. My meagerness is glandular; my nose I was born with. It was not possible for me to lead a normal childhood. My mother died before she saw me. I do not know my father. I grew up haphazard; wounded and tortured in mind, full of self-pity and hatred of others. I was known then as a queer child. All avoided me; most out of dislike; some out of fear. Queer incidents occurred—Well, never mind! Enough happened to enable Captain Pritcher, in his investigation of my childhood to realize that I was a mutant, which was more than *I* ever realized until I was in my twenties."

Toran and Bayta listened distantly. The wash of his voice broke over them, seated on the ground as they were, unheeded almost. The clown—or the Mule—paced before them with little steps, speaking downward to his own folded arms.

"The whole notion of my unusual power seems to have broken on me so slowly, in such sluggish steps. Even toward the end, I couldn't believe it. To me, men's minds are dials, with pointers that indicate the prevailing emotion. It is a poor picture, but how else can I explain it? Slowly, I learned that I could reach into those minds and turn the pointer to the spot I wished, that I could nail it there forever. And then it took even longer to realize that others couldn't.

"But the consciousness of power came, and with it, the desire to make up for the miserable position of my earlier life. Maybe you can understand it. Maybe you can try to understand it. It isn't easy to be a freak—to have a mind and

219

an understanding and be a freak. Laughter and cruelty! To be different! To be an outsider!

"You've never been through it!"

Magnifico looked up to the sky and teetered on the balls of his feet and reminisced stonily, "But I eventually did learn, and I decided that the Galaxy and I could take turns. Come, they had had their innings, and I had been patient about it—for twenty-two years. My turn! It would be up to the rest of you to take it! And the odds would be fair enough for the Galaxy. One of me! Trillions of them!"

He paused to glance at Bayta swiftly. "But I had a weakness. I was nothing in myself. If I could gain power, it could only be by means of others. Success came to me through middlemen. Always! It was as Pritcher said. Through a pirate, I obtained my first asteroidal base of operations. Through an industrialist I got my first foothold on a planet. Through a variety of others ending with the warlord of Kalgan, I won Kalgan itself and got a navy. After that, it was the Foundation—and you two come into the story.

"The Foundation," he said, softly, "was the most difficult task I had met. To beat it, I would have to win over, break down, or render useless an extraordinary proportion of its ruling class. I could have done it from scratch—but a short cut was possible, and I looked for it. After all, if a strong man can lift five hundred pounds, it does not mean that he is eager to do so continuously. My emotional control is not an easy task. I prefer not to use it, where not fully necessary. So I accepted allies in my first attack upon the Foundation.

"As my clown, I looked for the agent, or agents, of the Foundation that must inevitably have been sent to Kalgan to investigate my humble self. I know now it was Han Pritcher I was looking for. By a stroke of fortune, I found you instead. I *am* a telepath, but not a complete one, and, my lady, you were from the Foundation. I was led astray by that. It was not fatal for Pritcher joined us afterward, but it was the starting point of an error which *was* fatal."

Toran stirred for the first time. He spoke in an outraged tone, "Hold on, now. You mean that when I outfaced that lieutenant on Kalgan with only a stun pistol, and rescued you —that you had emotionally-controlled me into it." He was spluttering. "You mean I've been tampered with all along."

A thin smile played on Magnifico's face. "Why not? You

220

don't think it's likely? Ask yourself then—Would you have risked death for a strange grotesque you had never seen before, if you had been in your right mind? I imagine you were surprised at events in cold after-blood."

"Yes," said Bayta, distantly, "he was. It's quite plain."

"As it was," continued the Mule, "Toran was in no danger. The lieutenant had his own strict instructions to let us go. So the three of us and Pritcher went to the Foundation—and see how my campaign shaped itself instantly. When Pritcher was court-martialed and we were present, I was busy. The military judges of that trial later commanded their squadrons in the war. They surrendered rather easily, and my Navy won the battle of Horleggor, and other lesser affairs.

"Through Pritcher, I met Dr. Mis, who brought me a Visi-Sonor, entirely of his own accord, and simplified my task immensely. Only it wasn't *entirely* on his own accord."

Bayta interrupted, "Those concerts! I've been trying to fit them in. Now I see."

"Yes," said Magnifico, "the Visi-Sonor acts as a focusing device. In a way, it is a primitive device for emotional-control in itself. With it, I can handle people in quantity and single people more intensively. The concerts I gave on Terminus before it fell and Haven before *it* fell contributed to the general defeatism. I might have made the crown prince of Neotrantor very sick without the Visi-Sonor, but I could not have killed him. You see?

"But it was Ebling Mis who was my most important find. He might have been—" Magnifico said it with chargin, then hurried on, "There is a special facet to emotional control you do not know about. Intuition or insight or hunch-tendency, whatever you wish to call it, can be treated as an emotion. At least, I can treat it so. You don't understand it, do you?"

He waited for no negative, "The human mind works at low efficiency. Twenty per cent is the figure usually given. When, momentarily, there is a flash of greater power it is termed a hunch, or insight, or intuition. I found early that I could induce a continual use of high brain-efficiency. It is a killing process for the person affected, but it is useful—The atomic-field-depressor which I used in the war against the Foundation was the result of high-pressuring a Kalgan technician. Again I work through others.

"Ebling Mis was the bull's-eye. His potentialities were high,

221

and I needed him. Even before my war with the Foundation had opened, I had already sent delegates to negotiate with the Empire. It was at that time I began my search for the Second Foundation. Naturally, I didn't find it. Naturally, I knew that I must find it—and Ebling Mis was the answer. With his mind at high efficiency, he might possibly have duplicated the work of Hari Seldon.

"Partly, he did. I drove him to the utter limit. The process was ruthless but had to be completed. He was dying at the end, but he lived—" Again, his chagrin interrupted him. "He *would* have lived long enough. Together, we three could have gone onward to the Second Foundation. It would have been the last battle—but for my mistake."

Toran stirred his voice to hardness, "Why do you stretch it out so, What was your mistake, and . . . and have done with your speech."

"Why, your wife was the mistake. Your wife was an unusual person. I had never met her like before in my life. I . . . I—" Quite suddenly, Magnifico's voice broke. He recovered with difficulty. There was a grimness about him as he continued. "She liked me without my having to juggle her emotions. She was neither repelled by me nor amused by me. She pitied me. She *liked* me!

"Don't you understand? Can't you see what that would mean to me? Never before had anyone— Well, I . . . cherished that. My own emotions played me false, though I was master of all others. I stayed out of her mind, you see; I did not tamper with it. I cherished the *natural* feeling too greatly. It was my mistake—the first.

"You, Toran, were under control. You never suspected me; never questioned me; never saw anything peculiar or strange about me. As for instance, when the 'Filian' ship stopped us. They knew our location, by the way, because I was in communication with them, as I've remained in communication with my generals at all times. When they stopped us, I was taken aboard to adjust Han Pritcher, who was on it as a prisoner. When I left, he was a colonel, a Mule's man, and in command. The whole procedure was too open even for you, Toran. Yet you accepted my explanation of the matter, which was full of fallacies. See what I mean?"

Toran grimaced, and challenged him, "How did you retain communications with your generals?"

"There was no difficulty to it. Ultra-wave senders are easy

222

to handle and eminently portable. Nor could I be detected in a real sense! Anyone who did catch me in the act would leave me with a slice gapped out of his memory. It happened, on occasion.

"On Neotrantor, my own foolish emotions betrayed me again. Bayta was not under my control, but even so might never have suspected me if I had kept my head about the crown prince. His intentions towards Bayta—annoyed me. I killed him. It was a foolish gesture. An unobtrusive fight would have served as well.

"And still your suspicions would not have been certainties, if I had stopped Pritcher in his well-intentioned babbling, or paid less attention to Mis and more to you—" He shrugged.

"That's the end of it?" asked Bayta.

"That's the end."

"What now, then?"

"I'll continue with my program. That I'll find another as adequately brained and trained as Ebling Mis in these degenerate days, I doubt. I shall have to search for the Second Foundation otherwise. In a sense you have defeated me."

And now Bayta was upon her feet, triumphant. "In a sense? Only in a sense? We have defeated you *entirely!* All your victories outside the Foundation count for nothing, since the Galaxy is a barbarian vacuum now. The Foundation itself is only a minor victory, since it wasn't meant to stop *your* variety of crisis. It's the Second Foundation you must beat— *the Second Foundation*—and it's the Second Foundation that will defeat you. Your only chance was to locate it and strike it before it was prepared. You won't do that now. Every minute from now on, they will be readier for you. At this moment, *at this moment,* the machinery may have started. You'll know—when it strikes you, and your short term of power will be over, and you'll be just another strutting conqueror, flashing quickly and meanly across the bloody face of history."

She was breathing hard, nearly gasping in her vehemence, "And we've defeated you, Toran and I. I am satisfied to die."

But the Mule's sad, brown eyes were the sad, brown, loving eyes of Magnifico. "I won't kill you or your husband. It is, after all, impossible for you two to hurt me further; and killing you won't bring back Ebling Mis. My mistakes were my own, and I take responsibility for them. Your husband

and yourself may leave! Go in peace, for the sake of what I call—friendship."

Then, with a sudden touch of pride, "And meanwhile I am still the Mule, the most powerful man in the Galaxy. I shall *still* defeat the Second Foundation."

And Bayta shot her last arrow with a firm, calm certitude, "You won't! I have faith in the wisdom of Seldon yet. You shall be the last ruler of your dynasty, as well as the first."

Something caught Magnifico. "Of my dynasty? Yes, I had thought of that, often. That I might establish a dynasty. That I might have a suitable consort."

Bayta suddenly caught the meaning of the look in his eyes and froze horribly.

Magnifico shook his head. "I sense your revulsion, but that's silly. It would be an artificial ecstasy, but there would be no difference between it and the genuine emotion. But things are not otherwise. I call myself the Mule—but not because of my strength—obviously—"

He left them, never looking back.